HOME AT LAST

THE LONG ROAD HOME
BOOK FIFTEEN

CAITLYN O'LEARY

To my father, thanks for saying the apple doesn't fall far from the tree.

SYNOPSIS

Who raised this guy? Wolves?
Is she for real!?
Better buckle up.
It's going to be a wild ride.

ROAN
I'd had a plan.
Serve my eight years in the Marines.
Go to college, come home and join the family business.
Then it all changed and I became a Marine Raider.
Raw from my last year-long assignment in hell, I was
grateful to retire after twenty years.
Coming back to Jasper Creek and working with my dad
and brothers in our classic automotive restoration shop
had always been my dream.
Now here I am, damn near forty, retired, no degree, back
in Tennessee only to find my family's flown the coop.
What's more, they've put some upstart in charge of the
family business.
A female upstart.

A gorgeous, smart and funny, female upstart.
I'm in trouble.
Big trouble!

LISA
Who's the new guy?
Scratch that, who's the new *man*?
And who does he think he is?
Roan Thatcher.
What kind of name is that anyway?
How dare he come into *my* town and think he can take over?
Fine, the business hasn't been running perfectly, but considering I've got orders coming out my ears, and not enough staff, I'm doing pretty damn good!
And that's even with some asshat vandal/stalker trying to put me out of business!
Roan better stay out of my way or there's going to be trouble.
Big trouble!

This is an action, adventure, romantic, stand-alone novel.

PROLOGUE

"Sorry about that."

"Yeah," I muttered.

The Lyft driver stood by the trunk holding his hand out for a tip, not even bothering to try to take my duffle out of the trunk. First, he didn't drop me off at departures, he dropped me off at arrivals, and managed to drive past my airline stop by one hundred meters, even though there were plenty of spots available to pull into and I had pointed that out to him. It wasn't as though there was a language barrier—nope, he'd been too busy looking at his texts. God save me from dumbass, lazy civilians.

I grabbed my duffle from the trunk of the Lyft and slammed his trunk shut. I turned to start hoofing it to my airline and I heard him shout after me.

"Hey, mister, what about my tip?"

I turned. "Here's your tip. When someone has luggage and wants to catch a plane, take them to departures. That's my tip to you."

I heard him yell something foul, which I ignored as I

followed travelers who looked tired from having been on a plane for a while, or happy because they were finally home.

I took a couple of deep breaths to dismiss the whole Lyft experience so I could concentrate on what was important. Going home.

I was a couple of hours early for my flight, just like I planned. I always liked to be early, but this was one of the most important plane rides I'd taken in years, so it was doubly important that I didn't miss it.

Damn. It's going to be great to surprise the old man. I wonder what he'll say when I tell him. This time I'm coming home, for good. I hadn't seen him in two years, what with the last three back-to-back missions. The idea of sitting at the kitchen table and shooting the shit over coffee sounded fantastic.

The way I had it figured, I would hit Jasper Creek at nineteen hundred hours. Dad had been telling me he eats soup and sandwiches for dinner most days. Well, not on my watch. I'm definitely picking up something from Pearl's. *Hell, I think I'll pick up something from Pearl's for the next three weeks.*

Breathing deep again, I could almost smell the chicken and dumplings. Then there would be fried okra, hash brown casserole, and Pearl would always hook me up with extra cornbread. Dad told me they had him on cholesterol medicine, so I should probably get him the trout, but for my first night home, I thought I'd get him the country fried steak with all the trimmings. It was only right.

By the time I got to the front of the ticket counter, my mouth was watering, so I wasn't paying as close attention as I should have been.

"Huh? Can you repeat that?" I asked the twelve-year-old girl at the ticket counter. I'd been so busy trying to decide between pecan pie, cherry pie, or apple pie I didn't hear what she was saying.

"Your flight has been delayed."

Fuck!

"Really? How long?"

"We don't know. Do you have our app?"

Yes, I have your damned app. God forbid your company employ enough people so someone could call me.

"Yep, I sure do have the app," I smile wide. "Is there any other flight you might be able to get me on? I'm trying to surprise my dad."

She lets out a long sigh. "Everybody has a reason they need to make their flight. We're doing the best we can."

"I'm sure you are. What are my options?" I ask, still smiling.

"At this point there are none."

One of the things I knew from my twenty years in the military and my seventeen years as a Marine raider was that there were always options.

"I know your job must be tough right now. I promise, I'm not trying to make it tougher. Can you explain to me why my flight has been delayed?"

"Haven't you been watching the news? There's a big snowstorm that's screwing up everything. We can't predict when flights will be available. Like I said, there's nothing we can do. Most people are booking hotels. But you're probably too late to find one near here."

"Well, thank you for your time."

She didn't acknowledge my 'thank you.' She was already looking over my shoulder and shouting 'next.' I picked up my duffle, hitched up my backpack on my

3

shoulder, and walked away from the counter. I took a deep breath, trying to imagine hot apple pie with ice cream.

"Jerry, she hasn't even graduated high school," I heard a woman say. I looked over my shoulder to see the speaker. This lady was well past middle age. She had to be a great-grandmother. Great, I was now thinking like an eighty-year-old. I needed to spend some time with Griff. My baby brother would knock the fuddy-duddy out of me.

The idea of killing time in one of the seats near the ticketing area sounded God-awful. But seeing one family with a stroller with two kids, I realized I had it easy. But I sure as hell wasn't going to waste my money on a hotel. Shitty sleeping arrangements were not a problem as far as I was concerned. At least the heat was on and I'd be dry.

I went back to the main area in the Atlanta airport and looked around for a restaurant that would serve me a couple of beers. Hopefully not IPAs. I spotted a kiosk with a map, and when I found a decent restaurant, I also saw the USO was over on another concourse.

Going to have to take advantage of that.

When I got to the restaurant, it looked perfect. I saw that there were two tables near the back, both with a lovely view of the tarmac. Perfect for zoning out.

"I'll be right with you," the middle-aged hostess said as she left her podium. She went back behind to the kitchen. I was the only person in line. She came back out after five minutes, I clocked it, and she smiled at me.

Okay, this had possibilities; maybe I would get my beers.

"It'll be a little longer before I can seat you."

Okay, maybe I wouldn't get my beers.

I looked over at the dining area. Besides the two tables I'd scoped out near the window, the restaurant was half

4

full. By my estimation, they had three servers for nine occupied tables. Was she kidding me?

"That's okay, I'll sit at the bar."

She looked over her shoulder. "The bar is at capacity,"

"Ma'am, are you still on Covid restrictions? Because that's been lifted."

"Oh no. The bartender just doesn't like to have too many people at the bar when he just has one helper."

I closed my eyes and shook my head. Thank God the military wasn't run like this place.

I picked up my duffle and turned around.

"Wait a minute, didn't you want a table?" she called after me.

I didn't bother responding. Instead, I headed to the other concourse where the USO was. I prayed to the sweet baby Jesus that they had someone competent, and that *they* actually had a policy where they could let me in.

When I walked through the glass door into the USO I immediately felt my stress level come down a couple of notches. It could've been how it blocked the sound from outside. I needed it. Just a quiet place to hide and get my thoughts together. A place to think of pecan pie and what I wanted to say to Dad.

"Ah, here he is now. Welcome. If you'll follow me, I'll get the two of you signed in and show you to your seats."

Hmmm. Odd. But all considered a really a *nice odd*. And, she was welcoming. That was a huge plus in my book. She was one of those women where you couldn't figure out their age, but she had it going on with her black hair

5

framing her face, showing off big eyes and that sweetheart of a smile.

"Here's the book to sign," she prodded me with a genuine grin.

"Oh yeah, right."

"Good, you're both signed in. Now I'll be able to take you to your seats. I know between the four of you, you'll all have a lot to talk about."

"Huh?" I turned to the other guy. "Did I miss something?"

"Easier to just smile and go with it, man."

"Gotcha." I held out my hand. "Roan Thatcher."

"Quin Baldwin." The man gave a half smile. Well, any smile would seem less after the woman running the place.

I turned to her. "By the way, I didn't get your name."

"Blessing. My name is Blessing. Almost as uncommon as yours, Roan."

"Did you get teased too?" I asked.

"Not often. I've been blessed to find many friends in my life."

I laughed. I liked her sense of humor.

"I bet that's the truth."

"Here we are." She smiled that big smile. "Hello, gentlemen, I'd like to introduce all of you. This is Roan Thatcher," she said as she tipped her head towards me. "This next gentleman is Quinn Baldwin. Sitting on the right is Alex Thompson and on the left is Ian Ridgeway. Please don't hesitate to come up front if you need anything."

With easy confidence and a swing in her shapely backside, she walked back down the hall. *Finally, somebody competent. Cheerful too.*

"Flirting with Blessing are you?" A man with an amiable

smile stood up to shake my hand. "My name is Ian Ridgeway."

"Just being nice to someone competent," I replied. "There aren't enough people in this world who know how to do their job, you know?"

"Don't I know it," Ian agreed.

I watched as the other three men nodded their heads.

"But she tends to give out a lot of hocus pocus advice. I guess that's the price we have to pay," Alex said as I sat down.

"Huh?"

"They're just talking about her little tendency to predict our future and give us a little advice. Some of the older folks in my family would call it 'having a wee bit of the fae.'"

Oh yeah, Donovan. Irish.

I chuckled as I smiled at him. He winked at me.

"Well, I'm not as special as all of you. I wasn't worthy of a reading."

"Be happy," Alex muttered.

I grinned at the other men who were seated around me. It felt good to be surrounded by my tribe one last time before I headed home. As much as I loved my dad and brothers, they'd never understand me like others who'd served.

I fished my phone out of my backpack and started where I'd left off in my Carl Hiaasen book. Damned if that man couldn't make me laugh out loud. As the hours drifted on by, I said goodbye to Alex, then Ian, Danny and finally Quinn.

The timing couldn't have been better when my alternate flight was ready, since I was on the last chapter of

Tourist Season. That meant I could dive into the next book as I flew home.

"I guess this is it, Quinn," I said as I stuffed my book into my backpack. I stretched as I got out of the comfortable chair. I'd been sitting far too long.

Quinn stood up.

"I guess it is," he smiled. "Have fun surprising your dad." He grinned.

"Hope you can salvage your time while you're home, even though you won't be seeing your parents," I said.

He sighed. "Something tells me there'll be something to keep me occupied."

I laughed at his resigned expression.

"Take care," I said as I held out my hand.

He shook it and I headed out toward the door. I was surprised to find Blessing still manning the front desk.

"What? They force you to work here twenty-four/seven?"

Blessing gave a soft laugh. "No, normally we're not open all night, but with the snowstorm and all the delays, they let me keep it open."

Yep, competent and thoughtful.

"Well, thank you for that. This way, I'll be rested up when I see my dad."

"Oh," she frowned. "Well, yes. I guess when you eventually see him, things will be good."

"Eventually?"

"It's just that things don't always go the way you plan, now do they?"

There was her smile again. And a twinkle in her eye.

"No, they don't." I chuckled. "That was one of the first things I had to learn in the Marines, when plans changed, come up with a new plan. It wasn't easy, but I learned."

"They train you well. I bet not judging a book by its cover must be another edict you live by."

"I don't know, Blessing. Your cover tells me that you're all sweetness with a little bit of spice, am I right about that?"

I watched as a blush tinged her cheeks.

This is fun.

"You're quite the flirt. What are you going to do with all that skill?"

That stopped me short. "The ability to flirt?"

"All of it. You might like to flirt, but you're a protector at heart. Have you really given thought to what your life's work should be?"

I grinned. "I heard about the wisdom you've been shelling out, but you don't have to worry about me. I've got it all figured out. I'm going into business with my dad and my brother."

"It sounds like you do. But do me a favor, will you?"

I grinned. "You name it."

"Just remember that surprises often turn out to be beyond special."

Well, there it was. I just got hit with the Woo-Woo.

"I'll try to remember that." I gave her a wink before I turned to leave.

Damn, she had a pretty laugh. I saw a family of four heading our way from down the hall. She followed my glance.

"It was nice meeting you, Roan. Savor that pecan pie when you get home."

I was still staring at her when she turned to talk to the bedraggled family. How did she know I was thinking about pie, let alone had settled on the pecan pie?

Yep, the guys were right. She was definitely a little *Woo Woo*.

As she was passing out suckers to the two children, she looked up at me and winked.

"*Good-bye, Sweetness,*" I mouthed.

I was still smiling as I went out the door.

1

Why did Tennessee air always smell sweeter than anyplace else on Earth? I stretched when I got out of the car. It felt great to be standing. When I saw the sign off the highway that had Pearl's Diner on it, I knew I was home. Now, here in Pearl's parking lot, life couldn't get much better. The restaurant's sign hadn't changed in at least fifty years. It had the pin-up waitress bent over in her red-and-white-striped dress holding a tray with a milkshake, burger and fries. Yep, I could almost smell the grease.

Dad had kept me up to date with daily calls when the fire had ripped through Jasper Creek a few years back. A lot of people had to rebuild and Pearl was one of them. But like most of the town she kept on keeping on. And miraculously, her sign had survived. I couldn't wait to see Pearl. She was one of my touchstones in this town.

The cowbell rang as I opened the door to the diner. I laughed as damn near every head in the place turned to see who had come in. As soon as they realized it wasn't anybody they recognized, they went back to their grub.

The young hostess gave me a welcoming smile.

"How many in your party?" she asked.

"Just me."

"Would you like to sit up at the counter, a booth, or a table?"

After the man beside me on the plane damn near managed to talk my ear off, I needed a little bit of privacy. "How about that booth back there, next to the window?"

"Sure. Let's go."

She led me to the table I requested.

"Your server will be right with you."

Within a minute, somebody delivered water and warm cornbread muffins. I said thanks to the guy's back. He was already hustling to the next table. I slathered on some warm honey butter and took a huge bite.

A waitress showed up just as I finished my muffin. I hadn't had time to look at the menu, but I took a shot.

"Are chicken and dumplings on the menu?"

"Of course." I got another smile. "Did you have a chance to read our menu?"

"Nope, was enjoying the cornbread too much," I admitted.

"That happens a lot. You get two sides that go with the main course. I'd definitely recommend the fried apples as one of them."

"Is there anything else you'd recommend?" I really didn't want to have to read through the menu.

"Turnip greens or the sweet baby carrots. We just got those in, and they're delish."

"Sold. I'll take the fried apples and the baby carrots."

"Do you want a coke with that or sweet tea?"

"I'll take sweet tea."

She put her pencil behind her ear. "Coming right up. Your dinner should be out in about ten minutes."

"I want to put in a to-go order. Should I do that now?"

"Depends. Are you going to eat dessert here?"

"Nah, I'm going to eat that with my dad."

"I'll get your order when you get your supper. Then everything will be piping hot when you're ready to go."

Lord love an efficient operation!

"That sounds great, Jenny." I said as I quickly read her nametag. "Thanks."

"No problem."

Dad would understand that I couldn't wait to eat supper at Pearl's. He would have done the same thing, since his place was a half hour from here. Sitting back in the booth, I soaked in the feeling of home. I even loved the duct tape that covered my red vinyl seat. It was just as it should be.

I hoped that Thatcher's Automotive and Restoration was as it should be. For the last year when I'd asked dad about it, he'd been pretty evasive. So had Griff. I understood why Forrest didn't know much. He had a wife and a baby to contend with up in Nashville. A nephew that I was dying to meet. I'd only met his wife Sharon twice and once was at their wedding. I really wanted a chance to get to know her. The fact that Griff and Dad liked her so much told me that Forrest had chosen well.

But the shop? Well, that was something else again. I'd asked Dad on multiple occasions if he needed cash for the place. Sometimes when a business was floundering, an influx of money would help put it back on track. Each and every time, Dad had said he didn't need money, things were running smooth. But when I asked who was working there, and what jobs they were working on, that's when he would change the subject. Yep, something was wrong. Very wrong. I was going to find out what it was and help him out. I just had to figure out how to do it without hurting his pride.

"Here's your supper," Jenny said as she placed a plate of heaven in front of me. "Mind the plate, it's still really hot. But while it cools, you can give me your to-go order for your dad."

My sheepish laugh must have told the story, because she laughed as well. "I take it you still haven't read the menu."

"Nope."

"Tell me what he likes, and I bet we have it."

"He likes a steak smothered in gravy."

Jenny smiled. "You're in luck. We serve a country fried steak with our signature Pearl down-home gravy."

"Sounds great."

"And the two sides?"

"Surprise me."

"Two desserts?"

"Make it three. I want three slices of pie. Pecan, cherry and apple."

She gave me a great big grin. "How far are you driving after this?"

"'Bout a half hour."

"I'll pack the ice cream and the whip creams in separate containers with ice. Keep 'em cool for you."

"Much appreciated."

Did I just hear my Southern accent coming back?

"Dig in. Your to-go order will be ready by the time you're done."

I was still smiling when I pulled up the driveway to Dad's place. I knew he'd be happy to see me, but I figured he'd be happier to see the food.

Wait, a minute. Was the front door red?

What in the hell?

There was no way on earth that my dad would have painted the door red. Come to think of it, there were cut back rose bushes and non-blooming hydrangeas out in front of the house. They were definitely not here the last time I visited. Neither were the ferns on either side of the front door.

The porch light wasn't on. It was always on.

Dad would have told me if he'd sold the house. That would definitely be something he would have mentioned. Granted, the last mission I'd been on had lasted nine months, with no communication stateside. It'd been a royal bitch. Still, Dad selling the house wouldn't have just happened in nine months, would it?

Nah.

I parked under the empty portico at the side of the house, which was easy enough since Dad's car wasn't there. I guess I'd surprise him when he got home. I grabbed the takeout bag and walked up to the front door with my house key in my hand.

I stopped dead in my tracks.

Holy hell, the regular lock wasn't there. Instead it had a keyless entry pad. I pocketed my keys.

I whipped out my phone. As soon as Dad said hello, I started talking.

"What the fuck Dad? I came home to give you a surprise visit. What's with the keyless entry? Hell, what's with the red door?"

"You're at the house in Jasper Creek?"

15

"That's what I just said. Can you give me the code? I brought you dinner from Pearl's. It's getting cold."

"Sure. The code is your mom's birthday. Eight-seven-six-nine."

"Got it."

I opened the door. It looked a bit like the house I grew up in, but the entry had actual, live flowers on the side table, with an orange decorative bowl with pinecones in it. I walked straight back to the kitchen and just stared.

"What the fuck?"

"Son. Roan."

I put the phone back up to my ear. "What in the hell is this? Did you sell the house?"

"It's an Airbnb."

What is he talking about?

"You rent out a room?"

"No, I rent the entire house. I don't have guests coming until Christmas, so you can stay there. Just make yourself at home. I'll fly out and see you. How long are you on leave?"

"I retired. I came home to surprise you."

"Well, this *is* a surprise. Damn, Roan," my dad practically yelled. "This is the best news I've heard all year. When did you get out?"

"I finished all the paperwork three days ago. I landed here. We've always talked about me joining the family business, and I'm ready."

I set down the plastic bags on the kitchen table. A table that now had a tablecloth. "Dad, where are you? What's going on? Are you all right? I told you I had plenty of money I could shove your way. You didn't have to rent out your house."

"Son, I'm doing fantastic. I'd fly out tonight if I could.

But I promised the boys that I'd go fishing with them. Wes finally got his boat seaworthy, and he swears we can catch a marlin."

"Where are you?"

"Florida."

"Do you live there?" I asked slowly.

"Yeah, I got me a place out here thirteen months ago. The Avery girls manage the house, so I don't have to think about it. I just watch the money roll in, and pay them some. It's a sweet deal. More than covers my mortgage here in the Keys."

Avery girls. Yeah, Drake Avery.

He was younger than me, but I remembered him and his younger sisters. I especially remembered what went down with him with his daddy and the sheriff. When Dad had told me the story, I had been enraged.

"Dad, I can grab a motel, I don't want to infringe on your livelihood. Maybe I should fly down to Florida. See your new place."

"Nah. I'm going to be out on the water. If this wasn't such a big deal to Wes, I'd cancel, but this is the first time he can take his boat out since he was in the hospital, so I gotta go. I'll be there next Friday. You sit back and enjoy yourself. The beds are made, and I'll give Trenda a call and she'll make sure that groceries get there. I know you must have had a rough deployment the last little while."

I didn't even try to deny it. He knew that when I went dark, it was usually bad. "Yeah," was all I said.

"So take this time to just relax. Downtime will be good for you."

I gave a weak chuckle. "I'll give it my best shot. But there's fresh flowers in the hallway, not sure I can really relax."

17

Dad laughed. "Those girls. There's no stopping them, but I am an Airbnb superhost because of them. You can't beat that."

"That's great." I had no idea what in the hell he was talking about, but he seemed excited so *that's great*, seemed like the appropriate answer.

"Hey, what about the shop?" I asked.

"Oh, everything's under control. No worries there. You say you brought dinner for me from Pearl's?" he asked.

"Yep."

"Well don't let it get cold. Eat up, son, then go get some sleep. Can't wait to see you."

I put his dinner in the fridge and pulled out the pecan pie and the whipped cream. "Have fun fishing. I'll see you next Friday."

"I will, Roan. I can't tell you just how tickled I am that you're home. I love you, son."

"Love you too, Dad."

It was after I hung up that I realized he hadn't answered my question about the family business.

2

"For fuck's sake. Are you kidding me? Why can't you just have slashed my tires like a normal whack job so I could report your ass?"

I tried not to hate anyone. But this person was on my last damned nerve. He was definitely testing my limits. I looked over at my baby—my pretty baby-blue Dodge Charger. She looked sad with the air let out of her tires.

I pulled my cell out of my back pocket and called Hollister.

"What now?" he answered. He sounded irritated. It wasn't great when your guys were irritated with you. It made it hard for a person to tell them what to do.

"Good morning, Gene. I need the portable air compressor."

"Why don't you have one with you?" There it was, that damned condescending attitude. It had been like that since the day Warren Thatcher had hired me to run his business.

"Because I don't," I snapped.

Dammit, I swore I wasn't going to get into it with him this week.

"I'll send Lucky."

I plastered a smile on my face, hoping that it would come through in my tone. "Great. Could you make sure he leaves soon?"

"I'll do what I can."

Of course, he hung up before I could say anything else, like have Lucky make it a priority. Which meant I'd be *lucky* if he showed up in the next two hours.

Fuck! Most days I wanted to fire Hollister, but he was the best damn restoration guy I'd ever met, and he knew it too.

I looked around my little neighborhood. It was quiet. No drama; hell I was the youngest person who lived here, and I was pushing thirty. My charger had been parked under the portico beside the house, which meant somebody had been close to my side door. Most likely in the middle of the night.

I shivered.

"To hell with it."

I called Hollister back.

"What now? With you calling all the time, I'm never going to get this T-Bird stripped, and you know this is a rush job."

"I do know. Which is why I want to be there. When will Lucky be available to come fill my tires?"

"On his lunch break."

"What the hell, Hollister? Last I saw, he was working with Shep. All he was doing was detailing the Buick Riviera."

"Yeah, well, I switched him out after you called. Now he's doing the powder coating on the new job."

"Are we talking the Trans-Am? Last I heard, you were bitching you couldn't start the powder coating because there was too much rust. Did elves come and grind that all down last night?"

"Missy, you're in charge of the office. I take care of the restoration."

"Gene, I'm in charge of everything. Including your paycheck, that has been pretty healthy with all the over-time you've been pulling lately. Normally I don't butt my nose into your side of the shop, because you run the restoration area like clockwork. Same as Jimmy runs the service center. But you keep trying to put your size thir-teen boot on my neck, and I'm damn sick of it. You're not going to get me to leave, no matter what you do. You've tried for over fourteen months and I'm still here. So send Lucky now."

I hung up on him this time. My hands were shaking. This was it. I hated that our showdown was over the phone. It had been escalating the last three months. Ever since he asked for that last raise and I hadn't given it to him. I told him the shop couldn't afford to give him a raise, what with all the OT he was working. It just wouldn't work. I'd already slipped him part of a bonus when we got one from one of our clients.

Well, the time it took Lucky to get here would tell me if Gene Hollister was with me, or still against me. I gave one more look at my poor little baby. I hated seeing her with her tires flat, and her basically sitting on her wheel rims.

This time, I took a good look at the lock on my side door. It didn't look like anyone had done anything funny to it. I didn't see any signs of someone trying to jimmy it open.

But still.

I rubbed my hands up and down my arms. It didn't help to warm me up, because I was shivering for a whole other reason than the cold. This was the fourth time something hinky had happened. I let myself back into the house, thinking about the first three incidents.

One, all the flowers I'd planted in the front yard had died over a week's time. That was back in August. It was now November. I figured I'd used the wrong mulch or something. Let's face it, I was new to this whole home ownership thing. Trying to beautify my house and plant things was above my level of competence. But when I'd looked around the rest of the neighborhood, none of their flowers looked like shriveled up weeds.

Then there was the time I had my groceries delivered because of the late nights I was working. When I got home, they weren't there. I called Roger's Supermarket to ask where my order was. Somebody told me it should be there, that Dennis had delivered it that afternoon. I groaned, because Dennis was as sharp as a bowling ball.

I asked her to get Dennis on the line so I could find out what had happened to my order, but she explained he'd gone home after delivering my order. I figured there was a damn good chance that my order was still in the kid's car.

I'd asked to talk to the manager, and that was when Roger Clemmons, the store owner, got on the line. I always figured that Dennis had to be related to Roger, because why else would he hire someone who couldn't tie his own shoes? Not that the kid wasn't sweet, because he was. But still…

Roger was very solicitous and assured me that the delivery had been made. I explained it wasn't on my front porch or at my side door. At that point I was walking around to the sliding glass door at my patio.

Nothing.

It had been a hundred-dollar order, and it was heavy on

my wallet, and it was going to be hard on Roger's bottom line too.

Roger said he'd call Dennis and get back to me. When he did, he assured me that Dennis made the delivery. I had to assume someone had swiped a six-pack of beer, hot pockets, frozen pizzas and ice cream, then a bunch of fruits and veggies to make up for the aforementioned hot pockets and ice cream.

I told Roger to just charge me again and send another order tomorrow. Now the great thing about living in a small town? He personally delivered the order to me that night.

Gotta say that was pretty darned nice of him.

But come September, I started to think I was being targeted. That was when my water spigot in the backyard mysteriously turned on one morning while I was at work. It was a late night for me at the shop, and I didn't notice til the next morning when I looked out the kitchen window and saw I was now the proud owner of swampland.

That had cost me big time. Not only did someone have to come in and pump all the water out, it had fucked up my septic system. I had to throw thousands at the problem. Talk about a hit to my wallet. I called the sheriff's office, and they sent out a deputy. He was nice enough. But bottom line, he didn't think that somebody turned on my spigot; he was positive I had turned it on and forgot about it. It was frustrating as fuck. But I had no choice but to suck it up. What I did do was install a Ring doorbell, because I was beginning to wonder if the groceries and the water spigot might be related.

Now my tires? There was no question. Nobody could say this was something that I did. Somebody deliberately

23

and maliciously did this to my car. On my property. Close to my door while I was probably sleeping inside my home.

I went over to my desk and pulled out the deputy's card and called him. I got his voicemail and left a message. No point in explaining things all over again. I went to the fridge and looked to see what was appetizing. I'd skipped breakfast, like I normally did.

"Oh yeah, hot pockets. The breakfast of champions."

I threw one into the microwave and pulled it out when it was overdone. How I managed to fuck up a microwaveable meal was one of life's mysteries, but I did. Thank God I knew how to wield a wrench.

I scraped off the crispy bits and bit into the pocket.

"Fuck!"

I turned on the water in my sink and dipped my head down and started drinking straight from the tap. Anything to save my tongue from falling off.

Dammit, it just wasn't my day.

I wiped the water off of my chin and blew on the hot pocket for a minute then started eating. By the time I was done, I'd gone from really pissed off about my tires to scared that someone had done this when I was sleeping and vulnerable. Then, because I hate being scared, I decided to be pissed off again.

When my cell phone rang, I about jumped a foot.

Okay, apparently, I was still a little bit scared.

I picked it up, and it said the Jasper Creek Sheriff's Dept.

That was fast.

"Hello."

"Ms. Reynolds?"

"That's me. Is this Officer Wagoner?"

24

"Yes. You said you had some trouble this morning. Is there a reason you didn't call 9-1-1?"

"It wasn't an emergency. I would like you to come over. I have a situation. Somebody let the air out of all four of my tires. It was parked under the portico by the side of my house. It had to be done while I was sleeping. This time we know I couldn't have done it."

"I'll be there within the hour. In the meantime, don't disturb the area, okay?"

"You mean don't have someone inflate the tires?"

"Yes, that's what I mean."

Dammit.

"Okay. Thank you for coming out. Do you need my address?"

"I have it in our computer."

"Oh. Okay. I'll see you in an hour."

I hung up and went to the fridge. Might as well make this a full breakfast. After I pulled out the semi expired OJ, I poured a glass. When it didn't come out too thick, I knew I was in luck. I grabbed a banana and a peach, peeled and cut them both into a dish, then started eating. Fruit I liked.

I meandered into the dining room that I'd made into an office and started plowing through my personal stuff and some bills, receipts, and invoices from the shop.

How'd I miss this?

I put down the bowl and took another sip of my orange juice before I sat down to open the letter from my grandfather. He loved to write letters, whereas my dad and I could talk for hours on the phone.

I wasn't surprised when a check for twenty-five dollars floated to the floor. The old man still liked to spoil me. The first line of each letter always started the same. He'd tell me to buy myself something pretty. It was November. I was now up to three-hundred-and-fifty dollars' worth of checks from him. I was going to splurge on the leather duster I'd been eyeing and take a picture for him. I'd even wear it with a dress. It'd make his day. I'd probably have to borrow a dress, though.

Maddie Avery would take the picture. Plus, she would be fun to shop with and I could definitely borrow a dress from her. I continued to read Granddad's letter. The old man had me laughing out loud by the second paragraph. He and I were a lot alike. He had had a lot of adventures in his younger days, floating from state to state, job to job. He'd wanted to see and do everything.

This time he told me about his time working as a volunteer firefighter up in Ketchikan, Alaska. Okay, so I'd heard the story plenty of times, but this was the first time he'd written it down. Seeing it in his perfect script that he'd learned at the end of a ruler from the nuns was fascinating.

He explained again how they were getting the blaze contained until the newbie opens the door on the opposite side of the bowling alley, and the blaze whooshes across the lanes in seconds, damn near killing the men who'd been fighting the fire on the other side.

I could picture Granddad's sneer as he wrote that part. I didn't think he'd forgiven that kid to this day. But other than that, he loved his time up in Ketchikan. He worked as a longshoreman up there and he'd gone hunting and fishing with men who were still friends. I kept telling him he should come and visit me here in Tennessee. It would be his kind of place. But he likes it in Oregon. At eighty-seven, I could see where he wouldn't want to travel.

Then Granddad went on to tell me how he worried about how my dad doesn't take care of his cholesterol.

That is funnier than shit, considering that Granddad still eats a full farmer's breakfast. I didn't think a piece of fruit had passed his lips in forty years, but he has never needed a statin drug, so he hasn't changed a thing. Meanwhile, Dad had to have a stint put in because of a blockage and Granddad's been riding his ass ever since.

I loved those two men.

I put the check and letter aside as I started going through Thatcher Automotive's paperwork. Once again, I saw that the receipts easily covered all the outgoing expenses and that made me smile. I'd done the right thing increasing the restoration area and hiring more men.

But before I hurt myself patting myself on my back I looked at the two ninety-day past due invoices. I was not impressed when I saw that the invoices were for friends of Gene Hollister. And they weren't small amounts.

One was for an engine rebuild on a 2015 Ford Taurus. A friend of his had brought it in when his twenty-year-old son hadn't replaced the oil on the thing for two years and killed the engine. I think the guy was teaching the son a lesson by making the kid pay fifty bucks towards the bill. Fifty bucks that our shop still hadn't seen.

Next on the list was a job that I'd been pretty psyched about. It was a ground up restoration on a 1978 Dodge Midnight Express. Only two hundred of the trucks had been produced, and I would bet there were less than one hundred in working shape floating around the US today.

It took us nine months to pull that together. Everybody in the shop spent some time working on it, including me. It was a labor of love. But even a labor of love ended up costing a whole hell of a lot of money. Lou-Ray had paid a quarter up front, then continued to make payments as we sourced parts. He always paid on time. Gene convinced me that we should let Lou-Ray take the truck, even though he still owed nineteen grand on the thing. I worked out a monthly payment plan of two grand a month with Lou-Ray. Four months later, and I still hadn't seen a dime. Next week I intended to call a collection agency. Why in the hell had I trusted a friend of Hollister's? Hell, why in the hell had I trusted Hollister? Time and time again, he had stuck a knife in my back, either with bad advice on hires or suggesting I use bad suppliers. It took me five months to smarten up on that shit, but I lowered my guard with Lou-Ray. This shit was all on me.

I sighed.

I'm sure Hollister had already told Warren Thatcher about this. I knew they shot the shit on a regular basis. Luckily Warren was too smart to fall for it, so I wasn't worried.

As for the Taurus, at least the no payment had happened before we finished with the job. I had the guys stop midway through the first time Ed Rickers didn't pay for additional parts. I was holding it ransom until Ed Rickers paid up. He wouldn't. I heard he bought his kid a used Mustang convertible. I was half tempted to start docking Hollister's paycheck for both vehicles, but he'd lawyer up in a heartbeat.

Pissed, I decided to do something that I knew would put me in a better mood. I picked up the phone to call Dad. He picked it up on the third ring.

"Baby Girl. How are you?"

"I'm doing fine. Missing you and Granddad. How are you?"

"I'd be doing better if my daughter wasn't lying to me."

Damn my dad and his spidey senses. He could catch me

in a lie even though I lived five states away from him. Still, I was going to do the dance.

"Seriously, I'm doing fine. It's just the same little things going on at the shop. I'm annoyed."

"Hollister?"

"You got it in one," I grinned.

"You don't sound annoyed, like this is just a Hollister issue. You sound unsettled. The same way you used to sound when you'd come home from Becky's house after you two would watch scary movies. Now tell me the truth."

I sighed.

Seriously.

My dad.

"Somebody let the air out of all four of my tires. It was just some prank. I'm letting myself get upset about it, and I should just be blowing it off. I know I'm not because I didn't get much sleep after talking to Maddie half the night. She has man problems," I lied.

"Where was your car parked?"

Damn, he was sharp as a tack.

"By the side of the house," I admitted.

"Under the portico? Right by your side door?"

"Yep."

"Dammit, Baby Girl, if someone was malicious enough to do that, they could have just as easily jimmied your door open."

I should never have sent him pictures of my house.

"Dad, you taught me better than that. I installed good locks when I bought this place."

"You better be telling me the truth, Lisa. When I get down there, I'll be able to tell if the locks have been there awhile, or if you had them newly installed."

"Wait a minute, what are you talking about? Why would you come to visit?"

"I've been thinking about it for a while. I know how enmeshed you are in the shop, and your granddad isn't getting any younger. It's about damn time we came to visit, since it doesn't sound like you're coming this way."

"Dad. Now isn't a good time, I'm working long hours. And when I say long hours, I mean *long* hours. Fourteen-hour days during the week, and I'm working at least eight hours every weekend. I wouldn't be good company."

"Then I'll come to the shop. You and I both know I could come and turn a wrench. I taught you everything you know."

I dropped my forehead on my desk. The spread-out papers softened my landing, otherwise it would have really hurt.

"Dad, this is really a bad time. Can I talk you into next month?"

"No can do, Baby Girl. We want to spend Christmas with you. We'd been talking about it already. Now, hearing about somebody coming to your house and messing with your car will have us just coming out a little sooner."

"Yeah, a month sooner," I whined. I winced when I heard my voice.

"Lisa Jane, you listen to me. It is my job to take care of you. I don't care how old you are, it will always be my job to worry about you and do my best to take care of you. Until the time that you have a man that can replace me. And not some cowardly half-man artist like Darren."

I winced again. Not because Dad was putting down the man I almost married, but because his description was so on the money.

"Darren was sensitive."

"He cried at the Thanksgiving prayer. Said it touched his heart."

"It was a beautiful blessing," I defended my former fiancé.

"All we did was bless the food, Lisa."

I cringed, just like I had that night. Dad was right. Granddad had done his best not to sneer, but he failed. That, too, had hurt Darren's heart. As soon as we'd finished the pumpkin pie, I'd hustled the man out of Aunt Leslie's house.

"Dad, we're getting off track. How about you come the week before Christmas? The shop will be a lot less busy, because we'll be telling customers we won't be working the week of Christmas and New Year's."

"You won't?"

"No. We will. But if we tell people that, it'll give us a chance to catch up. Our backlog has gotten out of control. I'll still be able to give everybody Christmas Eve and Christmas off, as well as New Year's Eve and New Year's off."

"Sounds like a good plan, Baby Girl. I'm impressed."

I grinned.

"I'll talk to your granddad about postponing our trip to Tennessee. I'm not guaranteeing anything. But I'll try."

"It's the best I can ask for, Dad. Thanks."

"You're welcome. But if something else happens, I want your word you'll tell me."

"I'll be fine."

"Your word."

Shit, he just used the serious as fuck, 'dad voice'.

"You have my word."

"Well then. I love you. I'll talk to you later. Eat a vegetable. It won't kill you." Then he hung up.

I went over to my refrigerator and opened it. Then I pulled open the crisper. When I pulled out the baggie with the yellow squash that I had considered using for stir fry, the squash was squishy.

"Squishy-squash, squissy-squass. Yeah, can't say that three times fast."

I opened up the compost bin, dumped the squash, then pulled out the zucchini. Same problem, so I threw that out. Bell peppers? Out. Carrots? Still looked good. If I ignored them for another couple of weeks, I could probably throw those out, too.

Why did I keep buying vegetables when I knew they were going to rot in my fridge?

Dad's voice. I was such a daddy's girl.

I was going to have to figure out a way to wash his voice out of my head when I went grocery shopping.

I closed the refrigerator door when I heard the knock on my front door. I thought it must be the deputy, because Lucky would have knocked on the side door near my car.

When I saw Deputy Wagoner, I got pissed. Why in the hell was he giving me a dirty look?

When I pulled up to the shop, I felt good. This place and Pearl's were the first two welcoming sights I'd seen since arriving in Jasper Creek. Red door my ass.

Staying at the old house had given me the creeps. Pale green sheets? I shuddered just thinking about them. The whole room had felt wrong. There was even an abstract lilac pattern on the comforter. If I hadn't wanted to save Dad on his electric bill, I would have yanked it off the bed. But I wanted the window open so I could smell the Tennessee air, so I was stuck with the fancy comforter. However, I did set the bowl of potpourri in the hall. There was only so much a man could take.

I saw that all three car lifts were in use in the service center, which was a damn good sign. Only two of the trucks were being worked on, which wasn't so good. I parked my car and wandered around back to where the paint booth was located and the restoration work was done. Dad had finally done what Griff and Forrest had been suggesting for years. He'd expanded the restoration area. Hell, he'd owned the land so there was nothing stopping him, except for sheer stubbornness.

I looked around. I saw eight cars, all in different stages of prep. Two were on rotisseries, one of which was new. When I was here last, Dad only owned one. Seeing as how they were only two grand a piece, he should have invested in a second one years ago, but Dad had always been tight with a dollar.

Shrugging, I looked around some more. Another truck was prepped for paint. One car was in the middle of having the interior stripped. Another looked to be having the rust removed. Two were finished with the painting process and looked like they were ready for reassembly.

But there was one huge problem. There wasn't one single person working. It was a ghost-town.

I prowled through the cars and heard a woman talking. It was in the breakroom.

"Shep, I need you to start working on the Challenger up on the rotisserie. I want to know exactly what needs replacing, and what just needs repairing. I want that information by the end of the day. I need that so I can give the customer a good start on the cost of the job. We've had his car for a week; it's been too long."

"That's not how Hollister would do it. He would have someone from the service center look it over."

"Are you telling me you can't do what I asked?"

There was a bite to the woman's tone.

I knew Shep. Hell, he started in the service center. He could do that assessment with one eye closed.

"I'm not saying that, Lisa, I'm just saying that's not how Hollister does things. Gene always said that the grease monkey's time wasn't as valuable as our time."

"Oh really? At the end of the month, you want to know what area is more profitable?"

Yep, a definite bite. But who in the hell was she, and why was she giving Shep such a hard time? He'd been working for Dad for over ten years. What's more, where was Gene Hollister?

"You can't tell me that the service center makes more than we do," another voice chimed in. "Gene told us that the price tag on the Midnight Express was almost seventy grand."

I winced. Gene shouldn't have been talking pricing with the men. That was a hell of a price tag—was it actually one of the infamous old Dodge trucks? I'd sure as hell love to see that.

"Well isn't that wonderful that he was keeping all of you in the loop." This time when I heard the bite, I totally got it. Dad would have been perturbed; I would have been pissed. They were lucky she was just sounding annoyed.

"Did he tell you how much the parts cost? Did he explain how much your labor cost? And tell me, Rick, did he tell you that his good buddy Lou-Ray has shafted us on the last part of his payments?"

Now she just sounded pissed.

Shafted on the payment? I'd be enraged.

"Lou-Ray wouldn't do that. He's too good of a friend of Gene's."

I hated the idea of eavesdropping, so when I got to the breakroom, I leaned against the doorframe. Shep saw me, so did two of the new guys, but the woman with the long blond ponytail had her back to me.

"Oh really? Are you doing the books now, Shep?"

He crossed his arms over his chest. I thought he was going to call her a liar, then he let out a breath and shook

35

his head. "No, I'm not doing the books, Lisa. I believe you. Lou-Ray's in debt down at the feed store, too. Sounds like Gene fucked up."

I watched as her shoulders slumped.

"Nope, this is on me. I'm in charge of Thatcher's. Gene might have given me his opinion, but ultimately it was my decision to let Lou-Ray drive off with his truck before paying in full. But Shep, even if he had paid in full, restoration would still be less profitable than the service center."

"Why?"

It was a younger kid asking. There were about twelve men sitting and standing in the breakroom. Last time I was here, there were only seven. If she was in charge, she'd probably over-hired.

"Because we take too damn long turning the jobs. We do great work. The word of mouth is fantastic, and we have a long-assed waitlist. But we take too long."

"That's because we do a quality job. Are you wanting us to just shit out turds?"

I snorted.

I turned and saw it was Grady talking. Of course, it was Grady.

Lisa turned around and looked at me.

"Can I help you?" she asked.

"Nope, just listening," I answered.

"You must be lost. There's a customer lounge in front of the service center. Lucky, why don't you take this gentleman there. I should be able to meet with you in ten or fifteen minutes."

"Hell, that ain't no customer. That's Roan," Shep grinned.

"When the hell did the Marines finally decide to kick you out? Or are you just on leave again?" Grady asked.

Both men walked over to me, and we shook hands. Grady pulled me in for a man hug. He was my dad's age. He taught me how to replace my first engine.

Lisa came over and gave me a very professional smile. I recognized it. It was the same smile I got from every single newly minted lieutenant who didn't know what to do when confronted with a team of seasoned Marine Raiders under their command. She knew she was out of her element, but she was determined to catch up.

"Hello, Roan, I'm Lisa Reynolds. It's good to finally meet you," she said. "Warren's had a lot of good things to say about you."

"Damn right he has. He's a hero," Grady damn near shouted.

I winced. I hated it when someone said that. Hell, I hated it when someone said 'Thank you for your service.' It always made me uncomfortable. I always smiled politely and nodded, but inside I just winced. What did that mean, really? I didn't join the Marines for someone's thanks, I joined to get my college paid for. I stuck around because it allowed me to play with explosives, shoot guns, and when I became a Raider, I learned amazing shit. It was about then I thought about what I was doing to protect my country and the difference I was making, but I sure as hell didn't become a Raider for someone's thanks or to have old man Grady call me a hero.

"How are you connected to the shop?" I asked.

"She thinks she runs it," Shep answered.

Lisa sighed.

"I'm the general manager. Jimmy Manning runs the service center and Gene Hollister runs the restoration shop."

"Until you fired him," Shep put in.

"For the last time, I didn't fire him. Gene is taking a leave of absence."

"And who's running the shop in his absence?" Shep asked. God, he sounded like a snotty pre-teen.

"I am. I already explained that."

"What do you think, Roan? Is that a good idea?"

"Did Dad put her in charge of Thatcher's?" I asked.

"Yep," Grady answered. "It was when he moved to Florida. She's been running the place for the last year and a half."

"No she hasn't, it's only been a year," Shep corrected him.

"It's been fourteen months," Lisa interjected. She turned to me. "It would be fine for you to sit in on this meeting, but I'd really appreciate it if you could just listen while I hand out job assignments. Otherwise, you can wait in the customer lounge."

"Lady, I haven't done a damn thing to interrupt your meeting. It seems to me you have some disgruntled employees that you need to get a handle on."

"And I will. But having them looking to you for guidance is not helping me get a handle on things as you so eloquently put it."

"Shep, shut the hell up and listen to the lady," Grady said.

"And if she tells us to do stupid shit, are you going to just eat it?" Shep asked. "And how about you, Roan? Are you going to step in and make sure she's not doing anything stupid?"

"How would I know what's stupid or what isn't, since I haven't worked here since I was eighteen? Seems to me you should listen to her."

"Seems to me she shouldn't have run off Gene," Shep mumbled.

"Do you need to take some of your vacation now?" Lisa asked Shep.

"You know I'm not going to take vacation until fishing season rolls around," he said hotly.

"Then I suggest you pipe down and let me tell everyone else their assignments. You already have yours."

Quite the spitfire.

"That can't be done by the end of the day," he protested.

"You just said that someone from the service center could get it done. Are you saying they're better than you are?"

Shep shook his head.

She pulled a pencil from behind her ear and lined through something on her clipboard.

"Rick, didn't you say yesterday that you were going to need help stripping the Camaro? I need photos uploaded of everything so I can get them to the client. Especially of those headlights that we're going to have to replace. They're going to be a bitch to source. Wasn't Lucky helping you?"

"Yeah," Rick nodded. "He's labeling everything for me."

"I didn't see anything labeled." She turned to a kid who couldn't be more than twenty years old. "Lucky, what's the deal? I saw a mess of wires on the tarp near the Camaro, and not one single label. How long is it going to take for Henry to put that thing back together when he's forced to untangle that knot of Christmas tree lights, and try to figure out what goes where?"

"I had to go to your house and help you yesterday," he whined.

"Which took two hours max. I saw you put in for overtime. So, what in the hell were you busy doing for that overtime?"

"I was helping...I was...I was doing some detailing on the Trans Am."

"Bullshit," another man spoke up. "I did all the detailing on the Trans Am. You were texting on the phone most of the day."

"Lucky, you and I are going to be discussing your time-card after the meeting, you got me?" Lisa asked.

The kid nodded.

"Larry, are you done with the Trans Am?"

He nodded.

"Can you work on the Lincoln on the other rotisserie?"

He nodded.

She crossed something else off on her clipboard.

She continued to talk, and soon had everything crossed off. Everybody left the breakroom, with Shep shuffling off last. "I'm still not sure I can get the job done by the end of the day," he muttered.

"If I asked Grady to do it, could he?" Lisa asked.

Shep looked like she'd slapped him, which meant that a man twice his age could get the job done.

"I'll see what I can do," he said.

"And I want it done right. I'm going to be pissed if you underestimated what we needed to get done, and I'm going to be doubly upset if you padded the job. Am I clear?"

"Yes, sir."

She rolled her eyes.

I watched as Lucky tried to slink out behind Shep.

"Lucky, we're still not done talking."

"I need to go label those wires while I still remember some of them, or while I can still ask Rick and he might remember."

"No. That wasn't what I said. I said we needed to go over your timecard."

God, the kid looked like a mini-Shep. All red-faced and belligerent. "Tom lied, I was only on my phone when I was on my break."

She crossed her arms over her chest.

"Is that the story you're sticking to?"

He shuffled his feet and didn't respond. She just waited. It was a great tactic, and one I often used with new recruits.

"I guess I was on my phone a lot," he finally admitted.

"How many hours of actual work did you put in here at Thatcher's? You said eight regular and two hours of overtime. Is that correct?"

Now she was in teaching mode. Again, it was the tack I would have taken.

His Adam's apple bobbed up and down.

"Maybe six."

"Maybe?"

"Five."

"I'm putting you in for four, because you lied on your timecard. If you go out and hustle today, and I'll ask Rick and Henry if you actually did an honest day's work, I'll let you put in some overtime. From now on, your overtime will have to be approved by me, and it will be contingent on me getting a good report from the men in the yard."

"Contingent?"

"Depending on what Rick and Henry tell me."

"Oh. You use big words."

She sighed. "If I use a word you don't understand, ask me. It's good to have a large vocabulary. So, when you really want to get your point across you'll be able to do it precisely and effectively."

"That'd be good. Roberta keeps saying I need to tell her how I feel, but I don't know what to say."

Lisa sighed again. "That's above my pay grade, Lucky."

I snorted.

She looked over her shoulder at me. It was like she just remembered I was in the room with her.

"Okay, get out of here. I'll fix your timecard for yesterday. Go tell Rick and Henry that I said you're under their supervision for the day. They'll understand."

She and I both watched as Lucky walked out of the breakroom with just a little more pride in his step. I think she might have gotten through to the kid. She hadn't done half bad with the men.

"So, Roan, huh?"

"You're the GM, huh?"

She nodded. "Yep. Warren didn't mention you were coming home, but to tell the truth, we don't talk much anymore."

"You don't?"

What the hell?

"You run this place for him, don't you? Why the hell aren't you checking in with him? Giving him progress reports?"

"He must have been excited as all get-out to hear you were home. I'm surprised he wasn't here to meet you."

I let her sidestep the question...for now.

"Why don't I take you to lunch?" I suggested. That way I'd have her pinned down and get my questions answered.

"Let me talk to Jimmy and let him know I'm taking an early lunch."

"Jimmy? Jimmy Maddox? Why him?"

"He's in charge of the service center."

"When did that happen?"

"About ten months ago. Lester left and I promoted Jimmy. It's been kicking ass and taking names."

I nodded. "That sounds about right. Jimmy Manning and I went to school together. Played on the same football team."

"Of course you did. Seems to me that everybody played football with Jimmy. Before you do the old home thing with Jimmy, let me just tell him I'm going out and put him in charge, then you and I can go to lunch, and I'll give you the lay of the land."

"I'd appreciate it."

4

"I'll drive," he said as soon as I came out of the first garage bay. "We can go to Pearl's."

"I was thinking of going to Down Home on the town square," I told him.

"I was hoping for pie," he said.

"Down Home has pie," I offered.

"Can't be as good as Pearl's."

Let it go.

Just let it go.

Don't explain that Down Home has better pie than Pearl's.

"Okay," I mumbled. I was determined not to let this stupid little disagreement color my thinking of him. I wasn't.

Roan drove like a man who was comfortable behind the wheel. I liked that. Fifteen miles over the speed limit. Another thing I approved of.

"So why wasn't Hollister working today?"

"I told him he needed to take a few days off and reevaluate if working for Thatcher's was really the career he wanted."

His eyes cut over to me. Assessing.

"You did, did you? Did you discuss this with Dad?"

That question threw me for a loop. "Why would I?"

"Because Hollister has been working for Dad for over twelve years. Seems to me if you're that close to writing him up, you should be running that past my dad."

"Huh." I rolled down the window of his shitty rental so I could breathe in some fresh air and take a minute before I said something I couldn't take back.

"You don't have anything to say?" he asked after the silence stretched on for a good long while.

"Nothing that wouldn't cause indigestion."

"Huh." I knew he was just mirroring what I had said. Must have learned that in some fancy military communication training school.

He pulled into Pearl's parking lot. Even though it was only a little after eleven, the parking lot was three quarters full.

When we got inside, the hostess, who was probably fifty, simpered when she saw Roan. I'd forgotten, he was hot. And I mean *hawt*. But the way he was questioning me was really shaving points off his hotness rating.

"Hello." He smiled at the hostess. "We'd like a table for two. Also, is Pearl here today?"

"She's in her office. She'll be out during the lunch rush."

"Is there any way that you or someone else might could tell her that Roan Thatcher is out here, and he'd love to see her?"

Damn, I was jonesing on his slow Southern accent. And the way he said, 'might could'? Well, that just tickled me. I'd had my eye out for a muscled Southern man with manners and an accent, but please, *not him*.

"I'll let her know," the hostess assured him. "Let me get you seated. Would you like a booth?"

"That'd be great," he smiled at her.

She giggled. Yep, she actually giggled. I understood it, but come on, let's show some decorum for the sisterhood.

"What would you like to drink? Coke or iced tea?"

"I'll take a Coke," I said.

"What kind?" she asked.

"Sprite."

She nodded.

"Iced tea for me," Roan smiled.

"Jolene will be with you in a minute," she said as she dropped two menus on the table.

I didn't bother to pick up the menu. I knew it by heart. I wasn't much of a cook, so I had all the restaurants in town menus memorized. What had me pissed off is that they cut off breakfast at ten-thirty a.m., just like McDonald's. But Down Home didn't. They let you order breakfast all through lunch. Little Grandma said that's the way it should be, and nobody ever disagreed with Little Grandma.

"What are you going to have?" Roan asked me.

"A club sandwich."

"That's boring," he pronounced. "You're a Yankee, so you probably don't know, but having a club sandwich at a place like Pearl's is almost sacrilegious. You should order something fried. Something with gravy."

"You sure do have a lot of opinions."

He grinned at me. The same grin he'd given the hostess. Dammit, I wasn't immune, but I sure wasn't going to simper or giggle.

"Just about Pearl's cooking." He set the menu down, then looked at me. "Look, I can tell you're not liking what I have to say, but seriously, Lisa. This shop is my dad's life blood. He started it when he was twenty-two. You want to tell me why you're not asking my dad for direction on how to handle Hollister?"

I looked up at him and gritted my teeth.

"What makes you think I haven't?"

I smiled when I saw the surprise on his face.

Good.

"He agreed to put Gene on probation? I'm stunned."

"No, he didn't, because I didn't discuss it with him. I worked with Warren to write up a very clear job description before he moved to the Florida Keys. Trust me, handling all employee personnel issues falls under my purview. What's more, I didn't put Hollister on probation. I told him to take a couple of days' paid leave to sort his shit out. If he comes back with his head still lodged up his ass, *then* I'll put him on probation."

"You can't do that, Lisa. Obviously, Dad is in trouble. He moved someplace that is less expensive, and he's renting his house out to make ends meet. You even said that the restoration side of the business isn't making the money it should, and that you fucked up on bill collecting. Dad can't afford to lose Hollister. His expertise keeps Thatcher's reputation pristine."

For the love of God! Hollister isn't the only one who needed to pull his head out of his ass!

"Roan Thatcher!"

My head jerked up, and I saw Pearl Bannister barreling over to our table. She might have been little, but she was mighty. She was wearing black leggings and a long purple tunic that said 'The Boss Lady' in rhinestones. It was quite the color choice to go with her orange beehive hairdo and red lipstick, but somehow, she pulled it off.

Roan was on his feet faster than I could even acknowledge the woman. He had her wrapped up in a hug and she was squealing.

"Roan Thatcher! Aren't you a sight for sore eyes. Put me down so I can look at you."

Shit, he'd picked her up and she was loving every minute of it.

"Darlin', I think I'm going to take you home with me," he teased.

"Put me down and scootch over so I can hear every little thing that's been happening to you. Have you got a new woman yet? Your dad told me you got rid of that flighty mercenary thing. Thank the good Lord. She was as worthless as gum on a boot heel."

Roan groaned. "Pearl. I married her when I was twenty-two. That was eighteen years ago."

"Yeah, and you kept her around for six. Seems to me that was six years too long."

"You only met her once."

"Her name was Felicity, and she was from New York."

"New Jersey," Roan corrected.

"That's even worse. Please say you've found someone to make babies with. Your brother Forrest already has one, with one more on the way."

"Sharon's pregnant?"

I frowned. How could he not know that about his own brother?

"She's seven months along. Boy, where have you been? Hiding under a rock?"

"Something like that," he muttered.

"Well, you're in good hands. Lisa will give you the lay of the land. She's been keeping those boys and those two girls in line over at your daddy's shop." Pearl looked over at me.

"I hear tell Roan's daddy is looking at having you buy in. Is there any truth to that?" Pearl asked.

I wanted the red vinyl seat to swallow me whole, especially when Roan glared at me. I got the feeling he thought I was taking his dad for a ride.

Great.

"Yeah, we've talked about it," I admitted.

"It's been good to see some fresh faces who live here in town, that's for darn sure," Pearl said.

"What are you talking about?" I teased, desperate to change the topic. "There have been plenty of new faces with the new John Deere factory. That new apartment complex is almost full."

"Yeah, but they all work up in Knoxville. It's not the same as people who work here in town," Pearl disagreed. "You rented a house from Old Man Sebring. He told me you're thinking about buying it. So, you're practically town folk."

"How many more men have you hired since Dad left?" Roan asked.

"Isn't it seven?" Pearl answered before I had a chance. "And not all men. Lisa hired two women mechanics." Pearl cackled.

I nodded.

God, it really is a small town.

"I hear the deputy was over at your house the other day. Are you having some trouble?" Pearl asked.

"Nah, we agreed it was just some teenager playing a prank." At least, that was what the deputy decided.

Dipstick.

"It's because parents aren't giving their kids enough to do these days. It's not like it used to be." Pearl turned to Roan. "It's not like your mama and daddy. They raised you boys right. Y'all worked hard at school and were always in the Four-H club, playing sports or working with your daddy. Kept you out of trouble."

"Isn't that the truth," Roan said with a slow smile.

"I still miss your mama. She was one of my best friends. Good woman."

I saw a quick flash of pain cross Roan's face, which he quickly masked.

It reminded me of his father when he had talked about losing his wife. Even after ten years, I could tell it still hit him hard. I really hoped the move to Florida would be good for him.

"So, what are you going to have?" Pearl asked.

"Lisa was thinking about having the club sandwich. I told her nobody who moved to Tennessee could order a dry sandwich for lunch."

"Listen here, boy, my sandwiches aren't dry."

My lips twitched at the way Pearl took him to task. Then she turned to me. "But girl, you need a little more meat on those hips, to match what God gave you up top. If you're really in the mood for turkey, I can set you up with a lunch-sized turkey dinner. Or if you really want a sandwich, go with the brisket sandwich, with cornbread, macaroni salad and potato salad. That'll do you good."

"And pie," Roan put in.

"That goes without saying." Pearl chuckled as she kissed his cheek and jumped out of the booth. I hoped I still had that much gasoline in the tank at her age.

"You didn't take his order," I reminded her.

"I'll make sure he gets something he likes," she assured me.

Then she was gone, without having taken my order. *Figures*. And I was stuck talking to the man who thought I

50

was fleecing his dad and running the family business into the ground. I was vacillating between pissed and offended. But seeing how he teased and flirted with Pearl and making her day, I couldn't quite put him in the asshole category.

Yet.

"Lisa? Did you hear what I said?" Roan asked.

"Sorry. No, I didn't. Let me guess. You want to discuss me buying into your dad's business, right?" I asked wearily.

"Yeah. I do. But." He reached over with his right arm and massaged his left shoulder. I realized he was hurting.

"But what?" I asked in a softer tone. I didn't like to see anyone hurting.

"I'm not seeing the complete picture, am I?"

I made an obvious point of putting my phone on the table and looking at it. "Damn, that has to be the fastest about-face I've ever seen. What branch of the service were you in, and what did you do?"

It occurred to me he could have been in some kind of intelligence unit.

"Marines. I was a Marine Raider."

I had to go through my mental files. Then I leaned back. "Marine special operations. How long did you do that for?"

"Eighteen years. I hadn't intended to stay in twenty years. The plan was, do my four years, get out and get my free college education. Things changed."

"Are you happy about how it all came down?" I asked.

His head tilted to the side. "You know, only three other people have ever asked me that." He gave me a considering look. "Serving my country has been an honor. But it was those years that I spent side-by-side with my teammates that made it worth doing. I love Griff and Forrest, but the men I served with became my brothers. I still grieve for the brothers I lost, but yeah, I'm happy with how my life's played out so far."

He'd given me so much of an answer than I'd ever expected. I couldn't hold on to any irritation.

"Does that include Felicity?"

A corner of Roan's mouth tipped up. "Yep, even her. I learned some hard lessons, but I'd like to think I came out of it a better man."

Shit, now I like the guy.

5

_____

It was fun watching a woman who enjoyed her food. I'd been on too many dates where the woman I was with either ordered half an appetizer, or only finished a quarter of her meal and sat there looking deprived.

Not Lisa.

"This potato salad is to die for. I have not been ordering the right things off the to-go menu."

"Why not?" I asked.

"The only potato salad I ever had at home was the stuff dad bought at the deli section from our local supermarket. You know, the stuff at the counter with the little sheen of ick on top of it for having been on display all day?"

I chuckled. "I wouldn't know. I've never gone to a supermarket deli department."

"That's not true."

"Is too. Mom always cooked at home, and she taught the three of us boys. The last twenty years I've lived on different bases. When I wasn't deployed, I liked to cook. It was something I could be in control of, since I couldn't always be in control of the situations when I was on deployment."

"Well, I could see how you'd want to do something that you could be in control of when you came home from deployment. But cooking? That seems like an alien thing to do. Isn't it? I mean, there's always takeout."

"Yeah, and supermarket delis. Somebody recently told me how good they were."

She snickered. "But cooking?" she asked again.

"And baking."

Her eyes got huge. Pretty green eyes. At the moment she almost looked like one of those anime characters, with her parted lips and wide eyes.

Breathtaking.

"You bake?"

I nodded.

"A Marine Raider who bakes. Now I've heard everything."

I felt my lips twitch.

"What about you? I don't hear a Southern accent, and you were talking about the supermarket delis, so I know you're a Yankee. I'm pretty sure none of our markets have delis, so how do you survive?"

Her snicker turned into a chuckle.

"I manage."

"What brought you to Tennessee? A man?" Dammit, I shouldn't be liking her enough to check out her single status.

She took a sip of her Sprite. "I suppose that would make it more interesting, but no. I hauled up stakes when I was in Maine and followed the Appalachian Trail down south."

"Excuse me?"

"I take after my granddad; we both have itchy feet. I'd

been in Maine for nine months, working in a bookstore. You can only read so many books, even in winter. Actually, Jasper Creek is the longest I've stayed someplace since I was nineteen."

"So, you were living in Maine and decided to drive from there down to Georgia?"

"That was the plan. But I never made it that far. I stopped one hundred and fifty miles short of Georgia."

"Didn't that kill you? Not finishing til the end of the trail? How could you not go the last one-hundred and fifty miles? Isn't the trail two-thousand miles?"

She cracked a smile. "Two-thousand-one-hundred and ninety to be exact."

"And you bailed on the last one-hundred and fifty. Incredible."

"You're one of those OCD types, huh?"

"Even if I intended to stay in Jasper Creek, I would have gone the extra hundred and fifty miles, then come back to Tennessee."

She laughed. "Never had the compulsion. I knew I had found a place to sit and stay a while. When you feel that in your gut, you've got to plant yourself. You know?"

I thought back and realized I'd never experienced it. Never once. "I don't think that ever happened to me because I always knew Jasper Creek was waiting for me," I admitted. "So, what, you've been here fourteen months? That means you left Maine, what? A year and a half ago?"

"Try two and a half. I took my time," she grinned and started buttering her cornbread.

"A year? Did you bike, or hike?"

"Nah, I drove my Dodge Charger. She's a gem. 1969 baby-blue, two-door hardtop. Runs smooth as silk, with a 426 Hemi engine."

"Now that's a car." I grinned. "Can't wait to see her. But if you had a car, why take a year and a half?"

"There were a lot of spots I wanted to get to check out. If I was smitten, I stayed a little longer. I got a job in Vermont at a small gas station in the Green Mountains. The owner had a cabin nearby that came with the job. I use the term cabin loosely, but at least it had indoor plumbing." She laughed.

"Hot water?"

"Well, that was the rub. His set-up was for a hundred-gallon propane tank, and I'm a girl who likes hot baths, so that didn't last too long. I took off before I had to get the third one hauled in. But I hiked through the Green Mountains, so that made up for it."

"How long did it take you to go through two propane tanks?"

"Three months. It was cold that spring."

We'd both finished our meals, and she seemed fine just chatting with me, even if it wasn't about the business.

"Then where'd you go?"

"The northwestern tip of Connecticut."

"How long did you stay there?"

I watched as a soft smile hit her face. I thought she was pretty before, but now she was beautiful.

"What are you thinking about?" I asked.

"Fletcher and Jonas."

It took me by surprise how much I didn't like the sound of that.

Two men?

"Who are they?"

"I met them when I decided to camp at Gifford Woods. I'd set up a tent, and they were up in the cabin. I met them when I was hiking." She got a dreamy look on her face, and my gut clenched.

Two men?

"So, you stayed with them for how long?"

"Their mom and dad hired me as their nanny through the end of summer. Apparently, they were impressed by how I could bring their two boys back to the cabin happy but exhausted each night. I think that Roger and Ted were just grateful for the alone time."

She looked at me.

"You have a funny look on your face," she noted.

"It's nothing. So, you clerked at a gas station, and worked as a nanny. How else did you spend your time?"

"Twenty questions, huh? Is it going to be my turn soon?"

"Sure. Just remember, some of my stuff is classified."

She shrugged. "I'll remember to tiptoe," she promised.

"So?" I prodded.

"After the nanny gig, I continued south. I was kind of surprised at my next gig, but I really enjoyed it. I worked at a small farm picking apples in Pennsylvania. Dottie's husband had died the year before, so she was going through a tough time, and this was her first harvest. We agreed she would give me room and board for my labor."

"So that must have been just a month or two," I guessed.

"Nah, I really got along with Dottie. She was my age, and this was her first year alone, caring for her orchard during winter. If you ever have to care for fruit trees during the winter, I'm your gal," she grinned.

"Any other adventures?"

"I flew home to Oregon in January to spend a little time with Dad and Granddad, then I flew back, said goodbye to Dottie, and meandered south. I went off track seventy-five miles to hit our nation's capital. I definitely caught the political vibe. But I did do a couple of bus tours. The architecture was impressive, just not the childish bullshit going on inside the buildings."

I raised my eyebrow. "Tell me how you really feel." I smiled.

"Ah, you speak fluent sarcasm. I like it." Her grin got bigger. "Then there was Virginia. Absolutely beautiful. Loved all the green, and I fell in love with the Shenandoah Valley so I stayed there for a while. Needed a job, and there was a tattoo parlor in Elkton that was down two artists. I showed them my website. They were impressed, and they hired me."

"Your website?"

"It's basically an on-line portfolio of the work I've done. It also allows customers to leave reviews. Back when I was wet behind the ears, I apprenticed a year in a big shop in Idaho. Great guy named Beau taught me a lot. I got my license there."

"Let me get this right. Tattoo artist, farmer, nanny and you can run an auto repair and restoration business?"

"That's the stuff on the surface. I've had a few other odd jobs here and there."

I shook my head.

Lisa was wearing a long-sleeve Henley under her shirt and had put on a leather trenchcoat when we left the shop. If she had ink, I couldn't see it.

"How long did you stay in Elkton?"

"Five months."

"Why did you leave?"

She got a funny look on her face, then shrugged and finished off the last of her Sprite. "Itchy feet, I guess," she finally said. "Turned out to be the best move I could have made, though. It was as I left Virginia and traveled deeper and deeper into Tennessee that I found myself falling in love. There was just something about the air here in Tennessee. I can't really explain it."

I stopped rubbing my shoulder and examined her expression. Her head was tilted to the side and she was looking up, past my shoulder, lost in another world.

"Seriously, Roan. I can't explain it. Between the air, the beauty and the people, I was transfixed. I picked up a cheap month-to-month apartment in Gatlinburg and looked around for a while to get my bearings. I thought about getting a job in Gatlinburg."

"As what?"

"I damn sure didn't want to be a nanny again. I mean, I rocked it, but caring for someone else's kids? Putting in the work and then having to say goodbye wrecked me, so that was out. I was tired of the art gig. If I was going to draw pictures, it wasn't going to be skulls. Seriously, do you know how many people want to have skulls tattooed on their bodies?"

I laughed at her grimace.

"When I was growing up, I worked part time at Dale's automotive in town, and Granddad and I restored an old Corvette. Then he and I restored the Charger I'm driving now. While I was in Wyoming, I worked my way up to head mechanic before leaving. That was five years ago. So, I decided it was going to be either farming or wrenching."

"How'd you end up at Dad's place?"

"Roan? Is that you?"

I looked up and saw a middle-aged man with a full gray beard moving from the hostess stand over to our table. When he was standing over us, I could make out the wide grin that was buried beneath his beard. The slap on the

59

shoulder that he gave me radiated pain up my spine so that even my back molars hurt, but I ignored it. Instead, I tried to figure out who he was.

"It *is* you! My God, boy, you are a sight for sore eyes. Wait til I tell Missy that you're home. She's going to start planning a feast."

Missy. Missy.

I finally put it together. Missy Sandowski.

I stood up. "Mr. Sandowski, it's good to see you. How's Chip? How's Tina?"

"They're doing great. Between the two of them, I now have five grandchildren. You three boys need to do your part. I know your daddy would love to have more grandchildren to spoil. Forrest is married. What about you?"

"I think Forrest plans to make up for Griff and me, Mr. Sandowski. I think my nephew is two, and Sharon is due in a couple of months."

"Harvey. Call me Harvey. How long are you home for? Is Griff coming back to Jasper Creek to see you? What about your dad?"

"I left a voicemail for Griff. Haven't heard back from him yet. Dad said he'd be here next Friday. I think he plans to catch a marlin."

Harvey threw back his head and laughed.

"If he does, I'm going to take Missy and the family down there on vacation. They can do Disney World, and I'll go out fishing with your dad. Now, how long are you here for? Or have you retired? It's been about twenty years since you joined. I remember, my Tina had quite the crush on you. She's divorced now. Did you know that?"

Yep, I was definitely home. "You're right, I've retired. I'm sorry to hear about Tina."

"And are you married?" he persisted.

"Nope." I glanced over at Lisa, hoping against hope that she might rescue me. Her eyes were bright with mischief.

"Do you have plans this weekend? A hero like you in our midst. We want to welcome you home. Like I said, Missy will be cooking up a storm. And if I know my daughter, she'll want to wow you with her desserts. She bakes like a dream. Once you taste her cobbler and pies, you'll never want to come back to Pearl's for pies again. So how about this Sunday?"

"I still haven't talked to Forrest. I might be going up to Nashville." I hoped I wasn't lying, but even if I was, it was worth it. I remembered Tina, and she was a clinger back in high school, I couldn't imagine what she must be like if her dad was trying to foist her off on me.

"Hell, son, just bring Forrest and his family along. The more the merrier. Wait til you meet Tina's little boy. He's quite the little man, but his daddy moved to Texas and hardly sees him. Little Bubba needs a strong role model. Yep, you come along and meet Tina and Bubba. I think you'll like what you see."

He slapped me on the shoulder again, and I bit back a groan. Now my pain was twofold. The idea of running into Tina and the pain in my shoulder.

"I will definitely call you. Thank you for the invite, Harvey."

"And thank you for your service."

I smiled and nodded.

Harvey held out his hand and I shook it. Then he ambled back to the hostess station.

"I think if you go over to their house for dinner, he'd let you check out her teeth before you buy her." Lisa's eyes twinkled.

"Hell, I won't have to buy her. He'll provide a dowry," I muttered.

"You're right. So, did you and Tina go out in high school?"

"It was more like I hid in my locker to get away from her every time I saw her coming. She was a nice girl, don't get me wrong. Just a tad bit persistent."

I watched as Lisa bit her lower lip to hold back her laugh. "Just a tad," she agreed.

"What I don't get is why he's so hot and heavy to marry her off to me. He has no idea what I'm like now."

"Your dad bragged about you a lot."

I felt my neck and shoulders tightening. By magic, Jolene came up to our table at just that moment with refills on our drinks and another basket of warm cornbread muffins.

"You're a lifesaver, Jolene." She gave me a big smile, then headed over to Harvey to show him to a table. I picked up a muffin and turned my attention back to Lisa. "Where were we?" I asked Lisa.

"We were talking about how Tina is going to rope and brand you."

"No, we were talking about your life's adventure. I think you were going to show me your tattoos," I teased.

"You're going to need that sense of humor at dinner with the Sandowskis."

"Hopefully, I can get Griff to go with me. He's younger and better looking. I'm willing to offer him up as a sacrifice." I took my time buttering up another muffin. "I think you were explaining how you ended up working for my dad."

"I figured you'd want to know that story." She snatched a warm muffin from the basket and slathered on two pats of butter. "I was driving on the outskirts of Jasper Creek. I'd stopped off at Randolph Farms. I could see the orchard from the road, so I investigated. Nobody was at the main house, but I noticed someone in the fields out back. I hollered, but she didn't look up until I was almost on top of her."

I racked my brain to remember everything I knew about the Randolph family. I knew there had been a fire years ago that had burned down the entire house and killed Mr. and Mrs. Randolph. That was all I could remember.

"Her?"

Lisa smiled softly. "Yeah, Millie Randolph. She was listening to music. It was weird. She didn't freak out that I was there. She gave me this solemn look as she took out her ear buds and asked how she could help me.

"I asked her questions about her farm. Eventually, she invited me in for sweet tea. I gotta tell you she has one hell of a vision for the farm. The peach and pear orchards have been keeping the farm afloat for the last few years, but now she's planting lavender. I told her about my deal with Dottie, and she caught on right away that I was angling for the same thing with her. She gently declined my offer. But she said she could put in a good word with your dad."

"How is Millie doing?" I asked.

"Why do you ask? She's too young to be a contemporary of yours."

"Her family home burned down ten or fifteen years ago. Her parents died. I can't remember if she was in it or not. Dad told me about it. So, I was just wondering how she was doing."

"That's terrible. I thought it was bad when my mom just

63

up and left. To lose my dad in a fire, I don't know if I would ever recover."

"I feel the same way." I nodded. "So how was she?"

"She's quiet. Doesn't smile much, even though I tried to tease one out of her. I finally had to pull out my story about a drunken bachelor party coming into the tattoo parlor one night. That finally got a smile."

"That probably made her week."

"I doubt that. She's pretty self-contained. I think she's one of those people who's content with their own company."

I shrugged. "Maybe." I pushed the basket with the last muffin toward Lisa, but she shook her head, so I took it. "It sounds like you've been on the road for more time than just since Maine."

"When I left Oregon, I wanted to see the entire United States. In the end, I just went where the spirit moved me."

"Did you ever run into any trouble?"

Her eyes shifted left, then back to look at me. "Nothing that I couldn't handle."

"So, you did." I pounced.

"Shit, Roan, I'm damn near thirty. Every woman has some sort of story to tell. It's the way of the world. Dad was in the Army. He taught me how to shoot, and besides giving me some seed money when I left, he also gave me a pistol before I left home. He made sure I had a license to carry concealed. Most times it's locked in my glove box, but when I'm worried, I take it out."

"And when you really needed it, did you have it available?"

"No," she admitted. "But I took care of things," she said decisively. There was a hard glint in her eyes.

I didn't doubt that she did, but at what cost to her heart?

"Okay, enough about me. And I mean it, sincerely, forever, enough about me. I'm pretty sure that was more than twenty questions." She looked down at her phone. "It was definitely over twenty minutes. Do you trust me now? Or do you still think I'm out to fleece your dad?"

"Lisa, to tell you the truth, what I heard is you're a nomad, and maybe you're finally looking for a place to settle. I'm definitely liking you, but that doesn't mean I trust you."

She looked up at the ceiling and cracked her neck. Then looked back down at me.

"Fine. Have it your way. I've done what I can, Roan, take me back to the shop. Then call your dad, and while you're at it, call Forrest and Griff. I don't have time for this shit."

6

I shouldn't have let it, but for some reason, it hurt. The way Warren had talked about his oldest son, I'd really wanted to meet him. He sounded like an all-around good guy. And just like Grady said, a hero. Not someone who would be so quick to judge and deliberately hurtful.

I found it hard to believe that it was some woman fourteen years in his past who made him so damaged. What had done this, or had he always been like this?

God knew I had my scars and my triggers. But I generally gave people the benefit of the doubt. Especially if people I respected gave their approval. What in the hell was Roan Thatcher's damage?

The door to the restaurant opened behind me. I saw that Roan was holding two plastic bags. "I got you a dessert to go. Pearl said you liked chocolate cake."

"Thanks."

"Look, Lisa, did you want me to blow sunshine up your skirt, or tell you the truth?"

"I wanted you to listen with an open mind. That's what I wanted." I started walking toward his rental car.

"I did," he said as he caught up to me and pressed the key fob to open the doors.

I snorted. "If that's your idea of an open mind, I would hate to see you with your barriers up." I saw him coming my way to open the door, but I was too quick for him. I opened my door and slid into the passenger seat. Having him extend gentlemanly manners at this point just pissed me off. Or was that hurt feelings? I'd have to think about that when I got home.

We drove in silence back to the shop. I had my seatbelt unfastened before he stopped the car and was out the minute he stopped.

"Lisa, wait."

I turned around.

"Yeah?"

"You forgot your cake." He held out the plastic bag.

"You eat it. I think you need all the sweet you can get." I headed for the service center to let Jimmy know I was back.

By the time I got back to Dad's house, I was itching to call my brothers. I tried for Griff first, not surprised when I got his voicemail. Forrest was a crapshoot. He'd learned a lot from Dad about owning your own business, so he opened up a small store that sold high-end motorcycles in Nashville. When I'd last seen him, he was thinking about either moving to a larger space or opening a new shop across town. Forrest was smart. Damned smart.

He answered on the third ring. "Is this really you, Roan?"

I heard the excitement in his voice and it felt good. Damn good. Why hadn't I called him sooner?

"Sure is. I would have thought you would have been out on a ride with your wife or planning on opening a third shop by now. I feel privileged that you picked up the phone for me."

"Don't even," Forrest said. I heard the roughness in Forrest's voice. I should have called all of them the moment I'd gotten back to base. It was just that I had needed a bit of time to wind down and get my head straight before I could talk to my family. Hell, any civilian.

"Sorry, Forrest. Should have called yesterday. You in Nashville? Mind if I drive up to see you tomorrow?"

"What the fuck?" Forrest yelled. "Where are you? Jasper Creek?"

"Yep. Dad says he won't be able to make it here from Florida til next Friday. I thought I could take some time and visit you and your family."

"Abso-fucking-lutely. How long are you home for?"

"I'm out. Retired."

"Let me get this straight. You're home for good?"

"Yep."

"Where are you staying?"

"At the old house, the one with the potpourri and flowers. Dad says he doesn't have anyone renting it for a while, so I can stay. It kind of creeps me out."

"I haven't seen it, but I've looked it up on the Airbnb site. Yep, creepy is definitely one way to describe it. Pack a bag. We have plenty of room. Plan to stay for a while. Sharon doesn't believe in potpourri, so you're in luck. Get here early. You can make dinner while I wrangle Kade."

"I appreciate the pictures you sent. I hear Sharon is pregnant again. How is she doing?"

"They're watching her closely. Her blood pressure is elevated and they just put her on bedrest. Most of the time I'm working from home, but the last couple of days her mother's been with her."

"Shit. It's that serious?"

"They keep telling me everything is fine, but then they tell me preeclampsia is no joke. I've read up on it. It's no joke. I have a den downstairs where I normally do my shit, but Sharon kept getting out of bed. I had to carry her down to the couch in the den to keep an eye on her."

I heard the love and concern in my brother's voice.

"I'll be there tomorrow. Anything you need me to pick up at the store on the way to your house?"

"Anything you intend to cook for dinner." Forrest laughed.

I laughed with him. "How about Griff? Should we try to wrangle him in too?"

"Good luck with that," Forrest scoffed. "He's been in the wind since Dad turned the house into an Airbnb and put Lisa in charge of the shop."

"Did he want to be left in charge?"

"Hell no. Between you and me, he'd been sticking around to keep an eye on Dad. You know our father changed after Mom died. It got worse after you left. I didn't put two and two together, because I was too busy with high school sports and getting laid, but Griff was tuned into it. When I finally made the move to Nashville, Dad started to spiral."

"Why didn't you tell me?"

"Man, I didn't know. Griff gave me the lowdown after Dad moved to the Keys. Griff said that Dad getting in touch with his cousin was one of the best things he'd ever done."

"And this Lisa chick?"

"I know. She's great, isn't she?"

"She's something, that's for sure." I knew my tone did not match my brother's admiring one.

"What? You don't like her?" Forrest asked.

"Only met her today. Too soon to know if I like her or not."

"Hmmm."

I knew that hmmm. There might be five years between us, but even at thirteen, Forrest definitely let it be known when he had his teeth sunk into something just by the way he said 'hmmm'.

"Just drop it, okay? What time do you want me at your place?"

"The sooner the better. It's been too long, brother. The sooner the better."

"Same," I smiled. "I'll head out early.

When I drove up to my house, I saw Hollister leaning against my front door. All the good mood I'd had from visiting with Trenda and Maddie Avery trickled away. What's more, the asshole had his bike parked under my portico.

Asshole.

I parked my car at the curb and practically stomped up my walk to the door.

"Come to talk," Hollister said, before I could say anything.

"Shouldn't have started out by parking in my spot. Might have made a better impression."

He shot a look over to my Charger. "Yeah, you're right.

Well, at least that was something.

I unlocked my front door and ushered him in.

"Want some sweet tea?"

He shoved his fingers through his long gray hair. I'd taken him by surprise.

"Uh, sure."

I motioned for him to follow me, then pointed to the kitchen table. I puttered around, pulling down glasses, getting ice and pouring tea. I was silent, waiting for him to say something. My strategy worked. Hollister started talking.

"Hear you docked Lucky's pay."

"Yep."

"I wouldn't have."

"How would you have handled it?"

"Would have yelled and told him to get his ass out for the day and not to come back until he could give me an honest day's work."

"Would you have let me pay him for the ten hours he'd put down on the timecard?"

He shoved his fingers through his hair again. "Yes," he muttered. "What's more, it wouldn't have been the first time I yelled at the little shit, and apparently it hasn't gotten through."

"I'm not sure my way is going to get through either," I admitted as I put the tea in front of him and sat down kitty-corner from him.

"At least your way the company isn't out any money. He was my hire. Felt sorry for his mom."

I nodded. I totally got that.

"I don't like you," he said. Then took a big swallow of tea, his eyes never leaving my face. My lips twitched.

"That's not news to me, Hollister. You felt that Warren should have moved you up when he left, right?"

"Damn right." He slammed the glass down, and tea sloshed over the side and hit my tabletop. "Not only are you a woman, but you're also twenty years younger than me. It don't make no sense that you should be in charge. Everybody who comes into this shop who wants their car restored, they ask for me. Not you. Not Jimmy. Me."

I nodded. "You're right."

"Should be me running the place."

"What's more important to you, money or prestige?" I asked.

"Both." His answer was fast and unequivocal.

"Nope. You don't get to say both. It was an either-or question, Gene. Money or prestige. You've got two teenagers at home. Both of them are really bright and probably looking to go to college. So, what is it? Money or prestige?"

His face turned red. Pissed was too mild a word for what he was feeling, because he knew what his answer had to be.

"Money," he said reluctantly. "So what, you're going to give me that raise I was asking for and think I'm going to fart rainbows, while you try to boss my boys around?"

"Nope. No raise for you. But I'm willing to swap jobs with you. You've seen me work. I'm good. I could run the restoration side, and then you could run the overall shop. Is it a deal? Of course, you'd end up working more hours than I would, and you'd be on salary. No overtime."

He frowned.

"What do you mean, no overtime? How many hours do you put in a week?"

"At least sixty. When we have a good week, it's seventy hours."

"How much you making?"

"Less than you are with your hourly rate, and your overtime." I told him how much. "What's more, I passed the bonus we got from Rankin straight over to you."

I saw him doing math in his head. When it came to money, I knew Hollister was sharp.

"I'd be making only three quarters of what I'm making now, and working more hours."

I took a sip of my tea. "You would."

"You're not shitting me, are you?"

I walked over to my desk area. I pulled out my pay stubs. I gave him the last one. "There you go."

He frowned. "You even have more tax taken out than me, why?"

"You have dependents, I don't. I know I'm going to pay more taxes at the end of the year, because I have fewer deductions, so I have less take home. But look at the gross. It's less than yours, right?"

Glen looked down at my paystub again. "Shit, girl, why are you doing the management job? It doesn't make sense."

"I wanted to work here in Jasper Creek. It was the best job available for me and it sounded like a challenge."

Hollister picked up his tea and took a long sip. "I'm going to lay it on the line. Don't like working for a woman, especially one twenty years younger than me."

"Really? I couldn't tell."

"Nope, it's true."

Okay, discerning sarcasm wasn't a strong suit for the man. "Well, it's got to be your call, Gene. I know you're going to have your pick of jobs. Might not be a lead position, but I hear the shop in Knoxville is hiring."

He ran his fingers through his hair again.

"Yep, they made me an offer. I came here to quit."

"I'm not going to stop you. Come in on Monday and I'll have your last check ready for you."

"They're paying more than you."

Just go already. I have a book to read, and this back and forth is annoying the hell out of me.

"I can't stop you."

"But they cap my overtime."

"Gene, let me lay it on the line. If you decide to stay, I need an attitude adjustment. It's clear you don't respect me, and the way you treat me is trickling down to the other workers, especially Shep. It's got to stop. So if you decide to stay, you'd be on probation."

"Probation?"

"I don't yell when somebody is consistently doing wrong, like you do with your team. I give a warning and put them on probation. I'll say that for the next three months, if I see the same behavior again, I'll fire you. After three months, we'll start over."

"What kind of bullshit is that?"

"The way I figure it, I'm giving you an opportunity to keep your job, or fire yourself."

"That's a shitty deal."

"I wanted to let you know now, before you turn down a job in Knoxville."

"Fuck. You really like to bust a man's balls, don't you?" Hollister pushed back from the table hard enough that my tea sloshed out of my glass onto the table. I stood up too.

"Actually, I don't. To tell you the truth, I really admire the work that you do. I think we're lucky to have you. I've tried to give you the respect that your work deserves. I really hope that you'll stay and return the favor."

"Dream on," he said as he stomped through my living room and pushed through the front door. In minutes I heard the pipes of his Harley revving up in my driveway. When he was gone, I moved my car up under the portico.

It was the next day when I found a rat pinned to my house with a stiletto buried through its skull.

I dare Officer Wagoner to say this *was a teen prank!*

7

I looked out over the kitchen counter into the living room and saw my brother holding his son against his chest. The kid was passed out. We'd taken him to the park while Sharon slept and ran his little tushie from one end of that park to the other. The kid had shown no fear. He climbed the jungle gym like a pro, and when he was ready to get off, he turned his nose up at the slide. He wasn't having any of it.

"Gee-No-No!" he yelled.

Forrest was underneath him in a flash and caught the little stinker, then swung him up on his shoulders. Apparently, Gee-No-No, meant Geronimo.

My brother was living the good life. I couldn't imagine anything better than a chance to run around a park with my kid and get to stay close and watch over and protect my wife. Yep, Forrest had it going on.

Forrest saw me staring at him and gave me a quizzical look from the couch. I shook my head and went back to chopping up the veg for the salad. I wanted to give Sharon the most nutritious dinner possible. Forrest had groaned when I started unpacking all the vegetables. That part of my brother hadn't changed a bit, whereas my taste buds had grown up.

I caught movement out of the corner of my eye and saw that Forrest was getting up, presumably to take Kade to bed. The little stinker needed a nap. By the time Forrest got back to the kitchen, I had the salad made and put it into the refrigerator. Forrest opened the fridge again and pulled out two beers and handed me one. Modelo. Good choice.

"Please tell me there is going to be meat with the salad."

"You know a vegan diet would be good for Sharon—"

"You've got to be shitting me."

I snorted. "I am."

"Asshole."

"It's good to know you're still a gullible putz."

"Only with you. But because of you, I never take someone at their word, I always dig. I can't count the number of times that's saved me."

I lifted my beer and grinned. "Glad to have been of service."

Forrest grinned and shook his head.

"How about you? Did you meet anyone in the Marines who got shit over on you?"

"A couple."

"Are they still in, or did they retire too?"

I thought about Duke Samuels. Smartest man I ever knew. He was constantly yanking my chain. He ran circles around me.

"What?" Forrest asked.

"Hmm?"

"I don't like that look on your face."

I looked at my little brother and realized it was like

77

looking at myself in the mirror. Same jaw, same eyes, same hair color. Hell, we even had the same nose and eyebrows.

"What are you talking about? I look just like you," I teased. I was hoping to sidestep his question.

Forrest just kept staring at me.

I relented. "Just thinking of one of my team members who didn't make it. You would have liked him, Forrest. He could rub some people the wrong way, but you would have appreciated him. Whenever he had my back going into a shit situation, I knew I was covered."

"You're talking in the past tense. I take it he didn't make it?"

"No. He didn't." I took a long, slow swallow of my beer and leaned back against the counter. "The last time I was on leave, I flew out to Missouri and spent six days with Chantelle and their two kids."

"That must have been tough," Forrest whispered.

"A little. But I wasn't the only one who'd done it. Three other teammates had been there on their leaves before I showed up. The house was looking in good shape, and she told me that each of the men had done something. Rex was the last guy who'd been there. He'd repaired the roof. He'd told me that Chantelle was still struggling, and it was spilling over onto the kids. He was hoping I might be able to have a word with her."

"What'd you do?"

"The Cardinals were playing a couple of home games so I took the family. The kids loved it, and Chantelle loved seeing the kids loving it. The first three nights after she put the kids to bed we sat at her kitchen table, just talking. We'd talked for hours and hours. She had a lot of pain built up. She and Duke both grew up in foster care, so no actual family except each other. She didn't have a support system to draw on. They weren't churchgoers, so that was out. It was just his military brothers.

"She worked during the day as a flagger for a construction company. It coincided with her kids' school. That way they only needed to be in after-school daycare for three hours a day. But it wasn't really a job where you made friends. Both of her kids played sports and I asked her why she wasn't making friends with the other sports moms. She didn't have a good excuse. That's when I realized a little tough love was needed.

"I told her Duke wouldn't be happy with her. Not only would he want her to have friends, but he would also want her giving Sarah and Christopher good examples of a healthy parent, and that included going out and socializing. She fought what I was saying. She had every excuse in the book, until I said that at the rate she was going, she was going to have to put the kids into counseling, because they were getting depressed just watching her. That woke her ass up."

"Ouch," Forrest winced.

"Yeah. That night she hustled me out of her house. If I hadn't promised to watch Christopher's soccer game and take them out for pizza the next night, I think she would have ignored me until my leave was over."

"Foster care must have taught her strong barriers."

"That's for damn sure," I agreed. "Little did she know I would have shown back up at her house anyway."

Forrest chuckled. "Good to know the Marines didn't beat the stubborn out of you. Shit, Roan, I remember when Mom grilled the Brussels sprouts that one time. They were burnt and crispy. You refused to eat them, but Dad never wanted one of us to hurt Mom's feelings. So, he insisted we eat them, and I did. You refused. You were still sitting at the dining room table the next morning, with those burnt Brussels sprouts in front of you. If you didn't have to go to school, I bet you Dad would have made you sit there for days."

I laughed out loud. I hadn't thought of that in twenty years.

"My drill sergeant did a pretty good job at beating the stubborn out of me, but my time with the Raiders brought it back. Trust me, it got us out of a lot of tight spots."

"Anything you can talk about?" Forrest asked.

"Nothing you would like to hear. Besides that, there's nothing I could tell."

My brother just nodded. "So how did things end up with Chantelle?"

"I stayed in town the entire six days. By the time I'd left she'd made an appointment with a psychologist. She'd also volunteered to be team mother during basketball season for Sarah's team. She knew that would allow her to interact with the other moms more. She's still calling me. Not as much as she did in the beginning, but still... She's definitely doing a hell of a lot better."

"That's good to hear. Now, what do you mean that your stubbornness has gotten you out of tight spots? Are you okay with all of that? The tight spots I mean," he asked softly.

"You mean my brain? Yep, no PTSD. I've got a psych eval to prove it." I grinned. "My shoulder hurts. Got a flesh wound on my last mission. It's still healing," I admitted.

"How bad?" Forrest asked as he tipped his beer toward my right shoulder. He'd noticed the one I was favoring.

"I needed surgery, but it didn't hit bone. Just some muscle, tendons, and my bursa that they wanted to operate on. That happened just as we were getting done with the last mission."

"How long ago was that?"

"Four weeks ago."

"Shouldn't you be wearing a brace or something?"

"Nah. I stopped wearing it after three weeks. I just make sure I carry everything with my right hand, and I don't put my backpack over both arms like I normally do. Trust me, I'm doing what the doc said. I'm not going to hurt it again. See, I'm even stubborn about my recovery."

"That's good. I gotta tell you, I'm happy you're back in the States. I tried not to think about what you did for a living. Sometimes when I did, I would worry."

"I was always surrounded by good men."

"And Duke?"

"That's behind me now. I'm home." I winced.

"I meant, he was surrounded by good men, too."

"Forrest, that's all water under the bridge. I'm home now. I'm here with you and I got to run around a park and play with Kade. Life is good. Almost great."

"What do you mean, almost?"

"I always dreamed of working with Dad at Thatcher's then taking over one day when he felt like retiring. I knew you were out, but I thought maybe Griff would want to be part of that."

"Dad tried to get ahold of you, but he got the runaround, so we knew you were in deep somewhere. None of us had any idea that you would want to be part of Thatcher's. Shit, Roan, you never once talked about retirement. What the fuck, man?" He practically yelled. Then he looked around, afraid he might have disturbed Sharon or Kade. "Seriously, Roan? Why in the hell didn't you ever say something? The last time you mentioned something to

Dad about coming back to Jasper Creek was ten years ago. Since that time, you've never said word one, and I know Dad's asked you."

When I realized I was rubbing my injured shoulder, I stopped.

"Answer me, Roan. I mean, for fuck's sake, man. This is whacked."

I closed my eyes and thought about that firefight our team had been in. Only three of our team had made it out alive. That'd been eleven years ago, and I still sometimes woke up sweaty and not able to breathe, because I had just relived every single moment of that fucking fiasco in my dream.

"Talk to me, Roan." This time Forrest's tone was softer. Kinder. He must have seen something in my expression.

I shook my head, then relented. "A mission went bad. We had some faulty intel. There were eight of us, only three of us made it out alive. It was eleven years ago. Since then, I thought it was kinder not to talk about future dreams after I retired. Do you get me?"

Forrest looked grim. He got me.

"Still, as you got close to your twenty…"

"Hell, Forrest. My team had gone dark for the last year. No communication, them's the rules. Nobody outside of the military could contact me, and I couldn't contact non-military personnel. It was fucked-up timing." I sighed.

"It's not though. Even now, Dad would be more than happy to have you buy the house from him."

"Dude, he's put up paisley wallpaper."

Forrest laughed. "I saw that. Sharon helped pick it out."

I shuddered.

"And what would I do for a living?"

"It'd be a shame, cause I really like her, and according to

Dad, the business has never been as profitable, but you should fire Lisa. Take over Thatcher's."

My head jerked back. "You've got to be shitting me. She's made it more profitable? I went over there yesterday. She was talking about two big jobs she couldn't collect on. How in the hell could she have made it more profitable? She's probably cooking the books and showing Dad a rosy picture."

"You know that's not true. Dad always knew how much a new screwdriver cost. There is no way he wouldn't be looking at the accounting software and comparing it to the bank deposits and withdrawals."

"Dad has accounting software?"

"Of course he does. I installed it for him and trained him on it. The old man loved it."

"Holy shit. I really have been living under a rock."

"You got that right."

"I still think there's something going on with Lisa. But if what you say about her is true, and she really has made the place more profitable, there isn't a chance in hell I'd push her out of her job." But it sure would make me feel a lot less guilty about being so attracted to the woman.

Forrest grinned and went to slap me on the back, then stopped. I appreciated him remembering about my sore shoulder. "There's the honorable Roan Thatcher who's always been my hero."

"Well, your honorable brother could be in need of a job real quick. Let me know if you know of anything."

"You could always run the new store I'm opening up. It's the fourth one, and I'm opening it up in Knoxville."

"Retail?" I winced.

"What the hell, Roan? Thatcher's Auto Body and Restoration is retail."

83

"Thatcher's is service, and I get to wear oil-stained jeans and refuse service to anyone who annoys me."

Forrest laughed again. "Yeah, you might not be the best fit as GM for one of my stores."

"I'd be an awful fit, but thanks for throwing me a bone. Love you, Bro."

"Love you too. Now get back to cooking. Sharon's going to wake up hungry."

8

A rat. Yeah, there was a rat all right. I now slept with my gun on top of my nightstand, and that pissed me off too. I liked my sleep, and I did not appreciate someone making me wake up at the slightest little sound, because I was so jumpy. Besides the actual rat, there was also Roan Thatcher, a human rat. Albeit one hell of a good-looking rat. But a rat, nonetheless. I'd called Warren twice and he still hadn't called me back and I'd left him two messages and a text. I was beginning to feel nervous. So here I was, jumpy because of the actual rat and nervous about my job at eleven-thirty at night. Not the best feeling in the world.

I turned on the bedside lamp. Hit my pillows with my fist a couple of times before I could get them into the right consistency to sit up and read. I'd picked up some books from the library and I just needed to dive into one and get lost. Anything would be better than my jittery state of mind.

I started a book by Stephen King, and three pages into it I realized my mistake. The last thing I needed at this point was something that was going to scare me. I was nervous enough as was. I picked up *Anna Karenina*, but wrinkled my nose at the seven-hundred and forty pages. Yeah, I wanted to get lost, but I didn't want people to have to send out a search party for me.

The last book I had picked up was *Skin Tight* by Carl Hiaasen. Good. Not too long, and the blurb sounded promising. By the time chapter eleven rolled around I saw that it was now past one o'clock in the morning. I hit my pillows a couple more times to make sure they would be comfy for sleeping and finally fell into a nice, dreamless sleep.

When I got up the next morning I was in a good mood. I started the coffee, took a long luxurious shower with my cream-scented body wash, then shampooed with my strawberry-scented shampoo. By the time I jumped out of the shower, I had totally put yesterday out of my head and I was ready to grab the day by the throat. Hell, I might even eat a vegetable!

For breakfast, I found a banana that wasn't brown and there was still one blueberry muffin left from my trip to Down Home three days ago, so things were definitely going my way. I pulled the file I'd put together for work and shoved that into my backpack along with the food and my gun. Then I poured my coffee into a travel mug, doctored it up with cream and sugar, and went out to my baby. She was looking fine.

Since I knew today was a 'Lisa' day, I didn't check for anything that could have gone wrong. Not today. When I put my backpack into the passenger seat, I took out my pistol and locked it up in my glove compartment. Then I backed out and headed to Thatcher's.

I got there an hour before it was due to open. In the past, Hollister would have already had the restoration side of the shop open. It wasn't. My gut told me he wasn't going to be coming back, which was fine by me, but it did leave me with some problems. Number one, I wanted to change the locks, because even when I took Hollister's keys, there was no telling if he made copies.

Maybe I could just change over to remote controls, like a garage door opener. Then it wouldn't be so obvious that I didn't trust Hollister, and when someone left, all they'd have to do is return their remote, and they wouldn't have been able to copy that.

"Not a bad idea." I smiled.

I parked around back and took a deep breath of the early morning air. The sun was just beginning to rise. It was pretty cold today; I wondered how Millie was doing with her trees and newly planted lavender.

I let myself into the office, then I took a deep breath of motor oil. Yet another comforting scent that made me grin. Jimmy would be the next one to arrive, so he would unlock things. I grabbed breakfast and the file out of my pack and sat behind my desk. Damn, there was a lot that needed doing. I would've thought that things would have slowed down in winter, but it turned out that since people weren't driving as much, they figured now was the perfect time to get their vehicles worked on.

I was shelling out a lot on overtime, but I was making a mint in the service department. Restoration? Not so much. Restoration work seemed to be good early spring through late fall. I really needed to get the restoration guys more cross-trained into service. It was stupid as hell paying guys for twiddling their thumbs, while paying OT to guys who had work coming out of their ears.

Jimmy came in while I was looking over the personnel

roster. He was holding one of the large boxes of donuts from Down Home.

"Looking to see who you can put in place of restoration since Gene's quitting?" he asked.

I gave Jimmy a sharp look. "Is that a guess, or did you hear something definitive?"

"Definitive. He took a job over at Quality Restoration in Knoxville. Abe Harper is a friend of mine. He called me this morning and told me. The prick didn't even give a two-week notice."

Opening up the box and picking out a Bavarian cream donut, I smiled. "I wasn't expecting him to. He came over to my house on Saturday. He told me about the offer and how he didn't like working for a woman. I didn't have to be a mind reader to know he was going to jump ship and do it with no notice. It was too late to place help wanted ads in the newspapers, but I put ads online. Already have a couple of resumes. One looks a little promising. We'll see."

"Shep's going to think it should be him," Jimmy said as he sat down and helped himself to a cinnamon twist. I handed him a napkin.

"Well, Shep gets to think whatever he wants, but it's not. I just got rid of one misogynist manager, the last thing I need to do is promote a mini-Gene to replace him."

Jimmy was going to take another bite of his donut, but started laughing before he did. "I like that. Mini-Gene."

"Well soon, you're not going to like it. Your guys are working a hell of a lot of overtime. I know we need to do it. Your team is working fast, and we're more than making up the expense by what we're taking in, but...."

"But what?"

"Restoration is slow."

"It's always been like this. When we're slammed, they're slow. When we're slow, they're slammed."

"That's why we need to get some of the people cross-trained. I know not everybody can be, but those with potential, I want to see them cross-trained. Once they are, and they've proved they can work in either department without a problem, they get a raise. How does that sound?"

"Lisa, I like the idea. Some of my guys are getting burnt out on the overtime. Then there are the guys, and girls, who I want to give raises to, but they're either too new on the job, or they're already maxed out on our agreed upon pay scale. This would allow me to reward them for what they have done and challenge them as well."

I grinned. It hadn't occurred to me that Jimmy was thinking some of the people might need raises but felt like he shouldn't give them. I really liked his thinking.

"I heard about the rat," Jimmy said after he swallowed another bite of his donut.

"Dammit, this town doesn't have any secrets, does it?"

"You mean the fact that you and Roan had a nice conversation at Pearl's, but you walked away pissed? Nope, nobody knows about that either. Tell me about the rat, then tell me how you and Roan ended up fighting."

"Somebody actually buried a stiletto through a rat's skull into the siding of my house near my patio door. According to the deputy, the rat had to have been alive, otherwise there wouldn't have been so much blood."

"Aw man, Lisa. That's effed-up."

"Tell me about it. At least this time the deputy isn't saying it was a teenage prank."

"What do you mean?" Jimmy had finished his donut, and he wasn't going for a second one like he normally would have.

"Oh, there were a couple of other things. Nothing big. Just nuisances. But I reported them and Deputy Wagoner either thought I had done it on my own by accident or it was some kind prank pulled by kids."

Jimmy leaned forward, his elbows on his knees. "What things?"

"A month ago, somebody turned on the water spigot in my back yard. It went on for twenty-four hours. I ended up with a swamp that screwed up my septic."

"Shit."

I snorted. "Exactly."

Jimmy laughed. "Anything else?"

"My car was parked under the portico on the side of my house. One night while I was inside, probably sleeping, someone let the air out of all four tires."

"That's creepy. The rat is effed-up, but letting the air out of your tires is creepy. Have you upset somebody here in Jasper Creek?"

"Besides Gene and Shep?"

"They wouldn't have done that. They would just bad mouth you all over town."

"Have they been doing that?"

"I think Gene got out a few sentences when you first got here, but Warren shut that shit down mighty quick."

"And Shep?"

"Sure, he's still doing it, but not to anyone who matters."

I lifted my eyebrow.

"His best friend and his brother live out at Blue Ash Village. Shep's girlfriend works in Gatlinburg at Tootie's. So, there you go, you're being bad-mouthed at the trailer park and the strip club."

I barely held back a giggle. Jimmy saw it though, and

grinned. "Lisa, you have nothing to worry about, people think highly of you around these parts. Warren talked you up before he left, and the people who matter around here, well, they know what a bang-up job you've been doing."

I squirmed in my seat. Yeah, I wanted to make sure I wasn't being bad-mouthed, but I felt uncomfortable being praised. I knew enough about myself and my psyche that I craved validation because of how my mom just up and walked out that one day. But I refused to be led around by that need. Hence me trying to push away praise.

"Lisa, you get that, don't you? Just think about the seven new people you've hired. With you running the place, you've solidified our job security and you found us a better benefits package. You're doing good, girl."

"Don't you need to unlock the service door and pass out some donuts?" I asked.

Jimmy shook his head and laughed. "One day you'll take one of my compliments. I just know it."

He got up and hitched up the side of his pants, then picked up the box of donuts and let himself out the door to the service center. I called after him.

"Jimmy, can you open restoration, too?"

"I'm on it."

"Thanks."

He shut the door behind me, which was a good thing, since I needed a full minute to spew out every curse word I've ever heard and then to make up some phrases that didn't make sense but made me feel better.

That absolute asshole. I had been ninety-nine percent sure that Hollister wasn't going to come in today. But I was even more sure that the shop in Gatlinburg wasn't going to want to hire him if they knew he was going to leave

Thatcher's without giving notice. Obviously I was wrong. I hated being wrong.

I left my office and opened the customer door. My office had a window that allowed me to see any customer coming in through that door. The place was set up for a receptionist, as well as a supervisor in the office. When I'd arrived, there had been a receptionist named Darlene. Thank God she was gone now. For some reason known only to God, a quarter of the time she would answer the phone saying 'Snatcher's Auto Body'." Then there was the fact that one hundred percent of the time she failed to ask for a customer's number when she took a message. So now it was up to me to greet customers.

I peeked outside. No cars. All the employees parked in the back. I checked our service list for the day. We had six pick-ups before noon, and another seven drop-offs before seven. Another good payday for us.

I went back to my office and my hand hovered over my cell phone. I wanted to call Forrest Thatcher and whine to him that his big brother was a bully. In my mind, I considered exactly what I would say. When I got to the point where I explained that his brother was an egomaniac, I took my hand away from the phone. Apparently, I still wasn't in the right frame of mind to be making calls. I really needed to put Roan Thatcher out of my head and only deal with him when he showed back up. Other than that, he was a waste of my mental energy.

A gorgeous, distracting waste, darn it.

9

I raised my hand so Jimmy could see me through the crowd. When I was here last, probably twenty-one years ago, McClintock's wasn't nearly as popular. I'd had to really jump on this table when I saw three people leave.

"What can I get you?" the harried waitress asked as Jimmy sat down on the stool next to me.

"Modelo," I answered.

"Coors Light," Jimmy said.

She threw two coasters down on the dirty table. Jimmy and I waited until she was lost in the crowd before we started to laugh.

"Not sure the coasters are going to save this table," I said.

"Nah, wash it, call it vintage, and you'd be surprised how much money you could make."

I gave him a sideways look.

"The wife drags me to yard sales and antique malls on the weekends. I've learned stuff."

"Whatever floats your boat."

"My boat floats cause I go, if you get my drift."

"Lame, dude, that is a lame joke."

"I'm an old married guy with four kids, I only know lame jokes," Jimmy laughed. The waitress planted our drinks on the two coasters.

"Do you want to start a tab?"

"Yes," Jimmy said at the same time I said 'no'. I pulled out my wallet. If Jimmy wanted to stay for a while, then I was going to pay. I gave the waitress my credit card.

"I'll check back in on you," she said with a smile.

"You don't have to pay," Jimmy said.

"You can pay when I have four kids, how about that?" I asked.

"Seems reasonable. Issiah is starting college next year. He's going to Duke. Got himself a baseball scholarship. Even with that, and the student loans, it's still going to be a chunk of change each year for Beth and me to send him. But I'm really impressed with the kid. Turned out a lot smarter than his old man."

"I don't know, seems to me you always kicked my ass in trigonometry."

"That's because you were dating Darla and kept skipping fourth period so you could go make out with her during her free period."

I shrugged. "It seemed to me the better way to spend my time."

Jimmy gave me a slow grin. "Do you ever think about her?"

"Who? Darla? I haven't thought about her in years. Not until you just brought her up. Why?"

"Well, she's divorced now. She's looking pretty good. If you were planning on staying here in JC for a while, maybe you could look her up."

"Shit," I put down my beer. "What is up with people

around here trying to hook me up with divorcees? First there was Harvey Sandowski practically begging me to meet up with his daughter Tina, now you with Darla. What gives?"

"First, don't get near Tina. She hasn't changed. She's a one-date wonder. The guy she married was from up north. Rumor has it she told him she was pregnant and he bought it, so he married her. That was fifteen years ago. They only have one kid and he's five."

"If she's so bad, why did he stay with her?"

"He got a job with Harvey as Vice President of Harvey's construction company. He was incompetent, but Harvey kept him around for as long as he was married to Tina, and he kept Tina happy. Eventually Tina caught him with his dick in his secretary. She was no longer happy. For the last four years, she and her son have been living with mommy and daddy. To hear Harvey tell it, that is three years and fifty-one weeks too long. Run fast, my friend, run fast."

My shoulder began to throb. For my own sanity I needed to change the subject. "You have four kids. Is Issiah the oldest?"

"Yep. All boys. Issiah's eighteen, Brian is sixteen, Joe is fifteen and Damien is twelve. Issiah, Brian, and Joe are all girl-crazy. Beth and I will take it as a win if they don't become unwed fathers before their twentieth birthdays. As it stands, I've put condoms in their gym bags, in their rooms, and the two that have cars, I've put them in their glove boxes."

I laughed. "So, you've got them covered. Literally."

"That's definitely the hope. Don't get me wrong, I think the world of my boys. I think they're smart and caring kids. But I remember how I was. Hell, how *we* were when we were at that age. Our big head didn't always talk louder than our little head."

I was thankful that I hadn't taken a sip of beer, considering how hard Jimmy was making me laugh. By the time he was done filling me in on all of his sons' antics we were on our second round of beers.

"So, Roan, as much fun as it's been regaling you with the joys of fatherhood, this is not the reason I think you wanted to have this little get-together. Am I wrong?"

"No, you're not wrong."

"Lisa, right?"

I nodded my head.

"She's fantastic. I don't know what the two of you fought about over at Pearl's, but if anything, I would have thought the two of you would have really gotten along. She's good people."

"How was she with my dad? How was my dad doing when he decided to move to Florida and convert our old house to a bed and breakfast, or Airbnb, or whatever it is."

Jimmy stared at me for a few moments. "Are you asking me if your dad was in his right mind when he put Lisa in charge?"

"Not like that. I just wondered if he was maybe a little off in his thinking. You have to admit those were some pretty drastic changes."

"Not to put too fine a point on this, Roan. But how in the hell would you know what a drastic change for your dad would be? The last time I saw you here in Jasper Creek was three or four years ago, and you only stayed for two weeks. Yeah, I know you two talked on the phone, but Warren told me that for over a year he couldn't get in touch with you. So, I ask you again, how would you know if this was a drastic change, or the best move he ever made for himself?"

When I felt my hand moving toward my shoulder, I stopped it. "You're right, Jimmy. I wouldn't know. That's why I'd really value your opinion on this. I'm just trying to understand what in the hell is going on."

"Why in the hell are you asking me? Why not ask your daddy?"

"He'll be here in eight days. In the meantime, he said he wouldn't be available for calls, he's gone fishing for marlin." I shrugged my shoulders. "This is not my dad."

"Roan, your daddy getting ready to move to Florida was the happiest I saw him since your mama died. He was giddy as a little kid. Getting in touch with his cousin Marty was huge for him. Apparently, they were really tight growing up. Marty came out here for a visit. Stayed a month. He was a riot."

"I think I met him once."

"Big guy, red hair. If you'd met him, you'd have remembered him. He lost a leg in a boating accident. According to him, after that he wasn't the same. Took him years before he started traveling again. He moved from Arkansas down to the Florida Keys five years ago and loved it."

"That's why he contacted Dad?"

"I guess. You'd have to ask him. Damn good thing he did, though. Like I said, your dad was acting like a teenager. Even set Marty up with Florence Allen, and then your dad went out with Pearl so that they could double date.

"You're shitting me."

"Would I shit my favorite turd?"

I winced. But I saw his point. "And Lisa? How do you

feel about him putting Lisa in charge? Having Dad pass over you?"

"Hell, Roan. I wanted that job like I wanted a hole in my head. Do you know the number of headaches that job comes with? She has to be front facing with every customer, especially the ones that're upset. She handles them, smooth as silk. Better than your daddy ever did. He'd listen up to a point, then tell them to piss up a rope. Not Lisa, she lets them vent their entire spleen, then she asks a couple of pertinent questions. She's never confrontational. She usually turns them into our best customers. She pulls that same shit when it comes to her employees, and that includes me."

He hooted. "You should have seen the day I came in pissed at the world. Issiah had stayed out most of the night, Beth and the other boys had the flu and I nicked Beth's car as I was backing out of our driveway. I was twenty minutes late, which I hate, and by the time I showed up, I was ready to blow. Lisa read me before I hit the shop floor, she called me into the office and offered me a muffin and some coffee and got me talking. Before I knew it, she was off to take care of Beth and the kids, and I was smiling as I got to work."

Fuck me.

"So, you want to tell me how in the hell you pissed her off at Pearl's four days ago?"

"I'm thinking I might have jumped to some wrong conclusions. I tried calling Dad about her, but he was out fishing. I overheard her talking to Hollister and the rest of the restoration team, including Shep and this kid named Lucky. Seemed to me she was coming down hard. Then she admitted that she screwed up on two collections."

"On the Taurus and the Midnight Express?" Jimmy asked.

I nodded.

"Both of those were customers that Hollister vouched for. We got ripped off on Gene's word. I would have done the same thing that Lisa did in her shoes if Gene had told me what he had told her."

"How does she normally interact with the employees?"

"She's fair to a fault. She's fired two people since she's come to work here. One was the receptionist that your dad hired. Worthless as tits on a bull. Your dad felt sorry for her, so we suffered for three years, with her screwing up everything she got her hands on. Lisa let her go easy, now Darlene is working over at the daycare. Lisa never said, but if I had to guess, she had a hand in her getting that job. Working with three-year-olds was much more her speed."

Jimmy finished his second beer and was looking for the waitress to get him a third.

"How about the second firing?"

"It wasn't a firing exactly. The guy was selling drugs. Hollister had been turning a blind eye since the guy was a great detail man when it came to the final paint job. Larry had friends coming over to the shop all the time just to say 'Hey.' Gene was fucking out of line to let it continue. Lisa cottoned on real quick. The fifth time Darryl showed up to say 'Hey' she went back to where he was parked and started up a conversation about his ride. Stalled both of them long enough for the sheriff to arrive. Don't know what happened to Darryl, but the sheriff found out Larry and his brother were cooking meth out in a shack up on the mountain close near old Bertha. If the sheriff ever got his lazy ass up there, Bertha might could have told him about it."

"Anyway, Larry and Barry are still in lock-up awaiting trial. When Lisa confronted Hollister about turning a blind eye, he insisted he hadn't had any idea. Lying asshole."

Yep, I'd totally fucked up with Lisa. I finished my beer and waved the waitress over. I needed to get out of here and track her down. I wanted to apologize as soon as I could.

Jimmy smirked. "What's your hurry, Roan? Got some groveling you gotta do?"

"Maybe."

Jimmy grinned wide.

"Okay. Yeah. I definitely see groveling in my future," I admitted.

"Yeah, so do I, Buddy. So do I." He started laughing.

10

Oh great, just what I needed. Roan Thatcher.

He was smiling as he came into the shop and looked around. He smiled when he saw the stack of Thatcher calendars I'd had made up and displayed in a rack on the counter. He picked one up and started leafing through it. I wondered what he would find wrong with it.

When he was done, he looked up at the price list I had displayed on the wall above the counter. That was one of the things that always irked me whenever I went into an auto repair shop. I hated it when I didn't know what something cost up front. Now when people walked in, they clearly knew what the price of an oil change, multipoint inspection, brake pad replacement and on and on, was going to be. What's more, our policy was to never go above those prices for additional work without first talking to the customer.

Now Roan was just looking around at nothing in particular. I couldn't keep him waiting any longer. I wiped my sweaty palms on my jeans and winced.

Why should I be nervous? If anyone should be nervous, it should be him. He was the one who'd acted like an ass.

I forced myself out of my chair, plastered on a smile, and went out to greet him. I was surprised to see a sheepish smile on his face.

"Just the woman I was looking for."

"You've got me."

"I've come to apologize. Lisa, I was really out of line. All I can say is that it was my second day back in Jasper Creek and everything had changed. That's not an excuse for my behavior, but I wanted you to know where my head was at."

"Huh?"

I didn't know how to respond. What he said had come from left field.

"You're apologizing?" I clarified.

"Yeah. I am. I was totally out of line with you. I was an ass, and I feel like shit about it."

Looking at him, I could see he was really sincere.

"Can I ask why the turnaround?"

"I still haven't been able to reach Dad. But Forrest and Jimmy set me straight," he said slowly. "I'd like to think that if we'd had another conversation, I would have figured it out on my own. I really am a reasonably intelligent guy, despite evidence to the contrary."

He flashed a high-voltage smile.

Damn, that was powerful. I wondered how many women had their panties melt when he'd smiled at them like that.

"When was the last time you were in Jasper Creek?" I asked.

"Three years ago. Dad never once mentioned that he was thinking about moving. This came as a total surprise."

"Ouch. But surely he must have mentioned it when you talked on the phone."

"That's the thing. I was on an assignment where communication wasn't allowed. Sometimes that happens with my job. This went on for over a year and a half."

"And before that he never gave a hint on what he was considering?"

"Nope. I was totally blindsided."

"Damn, Roan. I can really see where that would have hit you hard. But I gotta ask. Why the turnaround on me? You were really convinced that I was a bad guy."

"Yeah, I was. Both Jimmy and Forrest knocked some sense into me. They told me how you've made the business thrive. That's another thing I need to apologize for. I assumed that you had messed up on those two jobs, therefore the business was losing money. Jimmy set me straight. He explained how Hollister recommended those two clients. Sounds like he's taken a turn to the dark side."

I smiled. "You could say that."

"I was hoping I could take you to lunch. Maybe you could get to know me when I'm not a dick."

I laughed. "I'd sure like to meet the Roan that Warren always bragged about. But this time can we eat at Down Home? Little Grandma serves breakfast until three o'clock. I want a waffle with bacon."

"Little Grandma?" I vaguely remembered something about Little Grandma, but our family ate exclusively at Pearl's. She and my mama were good friends.

"I'll introduce you. She's something else. I think she's turning one hundred and five this year, maybe one hundred and six. Let me tell Jimmy that I'm leaving."

"Are you going to give me a ride in your Charger?"

"You promise that you're going to be nice?"

His eyes gleamed. "If I promise that I'm going to grovel in order to get into your good graces, will you let me drive it?"

"Hell no, but I will give you a ride in it."

"Okay, then instead of grovel, I'll probably just tell you how impressive you are."

I shuddered at the thought. "If you do that, then we'll have to drive separately."

"So, ass-kissing doesn't work with you?"

"God, no. Does it work on you?"

"Hell no. How about flirting?"

I gave that serious consideration. "Are you any good at flirting?"

"You decide."

That drawl of his was getting to me. Yeah, something told me if the man put his mind to it, he would rock at flirting.

"Let me get my backpack, and we can hit the road."

"Sounds good."

I watched her stride back to Dad's office. Pearl was right, she could use a couple of extra pounds, but she was still all woman in those faded jeans. Especially with that ponytail swishing behind her as she walked. What would she look like with all that hair let loose?

She came back wearing the same sheepskin jacket that she had worn the last time we'd gone out.

"That coat must have come in handy when you worked in Wyoming."

"Absolutely. And don't forget the wool long johns," she laughed. "It never occurred to me that I would be buying long johns. There was a huge selection at the department store in Cheyenne. I found a pair in pink."

This time I laughed.

"I bet you looked cute."

"I wouldn't have said cute."

We got to Jasper Creek square and she parallel parked like a pro. It was a half-block walk to the restaurant. There was a line outside the restaurant. "Looks promising."

"It'll blow you away. Plus, they serve pie, but if I were you, I'd try the cobbler for dessert."

I lifted my eyebrow. "I'm a pie man."

"Your loss."

It didn't take too long for us to move to the head of the line.

The prettiest centenarian I've ever met was sitting on a stool handing out menus. Of course, she might be the only woman older than one hundred that I'd ever met. But she had a mischievous grin and a sparkle in her eye.

"Lettie, Lisa brought a beau. Get her a good table," she hollered out in a voice louder than I expected.

"He's not a beau, Little Grandma, he's Warren Thatcher's boy, Roan."

"Roan, huh? I never did hear of a man named Roan before. Warren named you that?" she asked.

I nodded.

"Hmm." She handed us menus. "You got that table ready, Lettie?"

"Grandma, I'm hurrying as fast as I can," the woman named Lettie said. I saw a middle-aged woman busing a table and picking up a tip. She looked up and waved us over. Before we started Little Grandma stopped us.

"My daughter is the cook, and all the recipes are mine.

Lisa can tell you what's good, but since I started this restaurant, I know what's best."

"Okay, hit me," I smiled at her.

"Definitely go with the cheesy grits and bacon casserole. Now my daughter did change it a bit—she added avocado slices. I didn't approve at first. Sounded too West Coast to me. But after I finally tried it, I gotta say, it tastes pretty dang good."

"Okay, that's what I'll have." I started to walk away, but she grabbed my wrist. She had quite the grip for such a little old woman.

"That's just the side dish. You'll need biscuits and sausage gravy or my brown sugar oatmeal pancakes, with a rasher of bacon." Then she stopped and looked down at my feet all the way up to my eyes. "Of course, a man your size should order both."

"I would have to run fifty miles to work off that much food," I protested.

"So?" she said. "It'd be worth it. Looking at you, fifty miles would be a walk in the park. Your daddy told me that you're a Marine. Suck it up, boy."

I threw back my head and laughed. I loved this woman.

"Okay, you convinced me. That's what I'll order."

"Good man." She let go of my wrist.

I was still chuckling when we sat down at our table. When I looked over, I saw that Lisa was laughing so hard that she was wiping away a tear.

"The big bad Marine was taken down by Little Grandma. I love it."

"Hell, I'm going to invite my old drill sergeant to town and invite him to breakfast. He won't stand a chance."

"Nobody ever does," Lisa said with a grin.

Lettie came over to our table with a pot of coffee.

"Would you like coffee or can I get you something else?" she asked.

We both turned over our coffee mugs, and she poured. "So, what did my grandmother talk you into?"

"The works," I replied.

"Cheesy casserole, biscuits and gravy, pancakes and a rasher of bacon? Do you want a cinnamon roll with that?"

"God, no."

Lettie grinned.

"He's saving room for cobbler," Lisa spoke up.

I gave Lisa the side-eye and she laughed.

"I'll bring out a bite size so he can sample, that'll change his mind. It always does," Lettie teased. "Can I bring you kids some orange juice?"

Lisa nodded and I shook my head. "What'll it be for you, Lisa? The French toast or the waffles?"

"What are you serving on top of the waffles?"

"Millie's pears. Mama's making them with cinnamon and a few other spices and melting them until they're syrupy. But she really got creative with the French toast. She stuffed it with chocolate chip cookie dough."

I watched Lisa's eyes light up. Apparently, my girl had a major sweet tooth.

"To hell with cobbler. I'm having waffles, with French toast to go." She rubbed her hands together like a super villain.

"Please tell me you're not putting maple syrup on that monstrosity," I begged.

Both women looked at me in horror. "Of course not," Lettie said.

"If anything, it's chocolate syrup or hot fudge," Lisa explained.

"Good God." My teeth ached just thinking about it.

"So how is your daughter doing?" Lisa asked Lettie.

"She's doing great. She's class president and has a three-point-eight grade average. Add in how well she plays volleyball, she has a good chance at a scholarship. Her daddy and I are real proud."

"You should be," Lisa beamed.

"Let me get your orders in. I know you don't have a lot of time for lunch. It was nice meeting you, Roan. Is your daddy going to come back to visit you?"

"Yep, he should be here on Friday."

"Tell him to stop by. We miss him."

"I will."

She left and I looked over at Lisa. "Please tell me that you go to the dentist on a regular basis."

"Do you need to check my teeth, like you do Tina's?" she jibed.

I shuddered. "Harvey caught me when I was getting gas after I came back from Nashville. I'm for sure going to his house on Wednesday for dinner. I don't suppose I could bring you along with me?"

"I don't know, how much is it worth to you?"

"What do you want? You're living over on Cypress, right? There are a lot of big trees over there. Do you need your trees trimmed? Gutters cleaned? How about I take you to a nice dinner over in Gatlinburg, or better yet, in Knoxville."

"I don't know, I already paid someone to trim my trees and clean my gutters. As for dinner in Knoxville, that would require dressing up. I haven't dressed up since I moved here. I don't know if anything would fit. Since discovering this restaurant I've put on more than a few pounds."

I suppressed a smile. "Then I'd say finding this restaurant agreed with you."

"Ah, the flirting has commenced."

"Just saying it the way I see it. Don't you like shopping for new clothes?" I thought about Felicity. You would have thought shopping was an Olympic event and she was going for the gold.

"Hardly. My friend Maddie has been trying to drag me out, and she's even sicced her sisters on me. I tell you, those Avery girls are hard to resist."

"Avery? Are they related to Drake Avery?"

"Yeah, he's their big brother. The way I hear it they got their stubborn from him."

"I wasn't around when he got railroaded by the sheriff, but even I knew the sheriff was crooked when I lived here."

"Yeah, I've heard the whole story from Trenda, Maddie's older sister. I especially like how Drake took him down. That was about five years ago. He and some of his SEAL buddies rocked this town. But…"

"But what?"

"It was just a shitty situation that even their mother was in on trying to have Drake killed. Can you imagine?"

"What the hell? Are you shitting me?"

"Nope. That's for real. She's doing time in prison. Trenda didn't tell me that part. I think that's something that hurt her too badly. But when Evie was in town with her husband, she told me everything. She's a bloodthirsty little thing."

"Evie?"

"Evie Avery O'Malley. Now she's the Drake sister most like Drake. If any woman could have made it as a SEAL, she's the one. Anyway, she told me all the gory details."

I shook my head. It was a lot to wrap my head around.

"So, let's get back to dress shopping and you going out with me. You know, you don't have to buy a dress, we could do casual. But I have to admit, seeing you all dolled up would be pretty damn sweet."

I watched as she blushed. "You're flirting again."

"Don't think I haven't noticed you deflecting."

She looked around. "Our food should be here by now."

Shaking my head, I smiled. "So, it's a date. You act as my wingman at the Sandowskis' on Wednesday, and I take you to a restaurant with the sweetest desserts I can find on Saturday."

"I haven't agreed to that."

"You haven't said no, either. Instead, you just ignored my invitations. I'm taking that as a yes."

"You're a persistent man," she observed with a slow smile.

"I wouldn't have survived if I wasn't tenacious."

"I guess not," Lisa said softly.

Lettie sidled up to our table. "Got your food. The plates are hot, so keep a mind to that."

Plate after plate was put in front of me. It was enough for two men. I then looked over at the plate Lettie put in front of Lisa. The pear sauce on the waffle looked great. I wondered if she would share just a bite. But when I saw the greed on her face, I realized that wasn't going to happen. A woman after my own heart.

"Dig in," Lettie said with a grin. "And Roan, if you don't finish every bite, I'll sic Little Grandma on you."

Lisa laughed.

This was the easiest groveling I'd ever had to do.

11

"You know this is a bad idea, right?" Trenda asked me for like the fifteenth time.

"Hush," Maddie said. "You've seen how Tina is on the hunt. Lisa is saving a life."

"Don't be so dramatic," Trenda admonished her younger sister.

"Whose life is Lisa saving, Mama?" Trenda's eight-and-a-half-year-old daughter asked.

"Nobody's. Your Aunt Maddie is being a drama queen."

Bella giggled. "She does that a lot."

"Come out of the dressing room already," Maddie hollered. "I know you've changed. I saw you step into the dress."

I sighed. The dress was perfect, and they were going to love it. How did Maddie know what to pick out?

I am so screwed.

Opening the dressing room door, Maddie screeched and Bella started clapping.

"You're like a princess, Lisa. Just like on T.V." Bella turned to Trenda. "Can I have a dress like that?"

I looked down at the high-necked, dark-purple scuba dress that followed the curves of my body, but not too tightly.

"We'll discuss it when you're Lisa's age," Trenda told her daughter.

"But that's forever. Lisa is really old."

Maddie and I giggled as Trenda hung her head. "Bella, you don't say that about people."

"But she is, Mama. She's not as old as you, but she's old."

Maddie and my giggles turned into laughs.

"Both of you behave," Trenda shushed us. "Bella, I'll explain things when we get home. But if you say that to the wrong person, it might hurt their feelings, and I know you don't want to do that, do you?"

Bella's little face crumpled. "Did I hurt your feelings, Lisa?" she asked me.

I crouched down in front of her. "No, darling, you didn't. But your mother's right. Let her explain things. She's really good at explaining things."

Bella smiled. "She's the bestest."

Maddie cleared her throat. "Now, back to the dress. It's perfect. Roan is going to want to jump you as soon as he sees you. There is no way you'll make it to Knoxville."

I gulped. "I'm not buying it." I turned to go back into the dressing room.

"Why would Mr. Roan want to jump on Lisa? That's not very nice," Bella said.

Oh shit, Maddie mouthed. I started giggling again.

"Now look what you've done." Trenda glared at her younger sister. "Aunt Maddie just means that Mr. Roan is going to want to kiss Lisa when he sees her."

"You mean like Daddy kisses you?"

"Yes, honey, that's exactly what Aunt Maddie meant."

Trenda turned to me. "You have to buy the dress."

I turned back. "Trenda, you can't be serious. Maddie I get, but you? This is just a one-off, it's not like we're starting a relationship or anything. Sleep… I mean getting tangled up with Warren's son would just make my life too complicated."

"Complicated can be a good thing. And Roan is a good thing," Trenda insisted.

"How do you know that?" I asked.

"Simon's checked him out," Trenda said, referring to her former-SEAL husband.

"How could he do that? They were in different branches of the military."

"They were both special operations. Simon was able to get the lowdown on Roan, and he's solid. What's more, people like Pearl and Doc Evans think the world of him. I think you should really consider not just dating him. But *dating* him."

"You're just saying that because you're all loved up and married to your special operations guy and you think everybody should be paired off."

"It's true. But there's also the far-off look in your eyes when you talk about him."

"I do not get a far-off look in my eyes," I protested.

"Trenda's right, you do. Your voice changes, too," Maddie broke in. "You're interested. Since you've been here in town, you haven't been interested in anyone."

"Like I was going to get involved with anyone I worked with," I scoffed.

"I'm not talking about the guys at Thatcher's," Maddie dismissed. "How many guys from the John Deere plant have asked you out?"

I squirmed. "Several."

"Chloe's been keeping count. Zarek is friends with one of the managers. You've turned down seven dates. They've now got a pool going to see who will manage to get a date with you."

"Ewww." Trenda shuddered.

"I second that ewww. Now all of them will be turned down."

"What's she mean a pool? She doesn't mean swimming pool, does she?"

"No, baby girl, she doesn't. She means a bet."

"Betting's bad."

"You're right, darling." I smiled down at the little girl. "Betting is bad. Especially when men are trying to date me. Men can be jerks, so you watch out, okay?"

"I'm only going to marry a man like my daddy," Bella said.

"There's my smart girl." Trenda smiled as she stroked her hand over her daughter's dark curls.

"What about Ed over at the garden center? He's really handsome and he owns the business. I know that he's asked you out. And he keeps running over nails on purpose so he has to come into Thatcher's so he can talk to you. Why do you shut him down?" Maddie asked.

"I'm not into men with blonde hair and blue eyes."

"Now you're just making things up," Maddie said. "If you don't buy this dress to go to dinner with Roan, I'm going to. If you don't go out with him, I'm not going to tell you the next time Evie's in town."

"That's just mean."

"But that means she has to go over to Missy and Harvey's house the day after tomorrow," Trenda pointed out.

"And she should. Again, that is the same as helping out at the food bank," Maddie said. "It's her civic duty."

"So, what do I wear there?"

"A skirt and a nice top," Trenda said.

"All the skirts I own don't fit."

"Then we'll find something. And we need shoes to go with that dress."

"Noooo. I don't want to shop anymore," I whined.

"Suck it up, girl."

"Can we go to the food court too, Mama?"

"If we have to shop more, absolutely. You and I are getting milkshakes, kid." I grinned at Bella.

"Yippee!" she launched her arms up in the air.

Roan picked me up, and this time it wasn't in the beige four-door rental. It was an extended cab, black F-250 truck that definitely seemed more his style.

"Is this new?"

"Yep, bought it yesterday. I needed something now that I was home."

"Nice pick," I complimented.

"Thanks." He opened the passenger door for me to get in.

I watched as he plugged in the address for the Sandowskis'. "This is new. I don't think two of these roads even existed the last time I was here."

"So you've never been here before? Not even to pick up Tina for prom?" I teased.

"Bite your tongue, woman."

"What's she like?"

"You're going to have to decide for yourself. My mom liked everybody, but when Tina would show up uninvited at our house, she would always grab either Forrest or Griff and send them off to warn me that Tina was at the house. As much as Mom might have liked the girl on her own, she didn't like her for me. What she told me was that the girl was far too forward. Especially seeing as how I already had a girlfriend."

"You had a girlfriend and she was pulling those kinds of stunts?"

"Yep."

"That's messed up."

"Yep."

I settled deeper into the leather seat.

"You know you can turn on the seat warmer."

I smiled and turned it on. Soon I felt languorous, surrounded by Roan's presence and cocooned in the warmth and safety of his truck.

"Is it too hot for you?" I asked.

"Nope."

"You're a man of few words."

"Oh, I'll talk when the situation warrants it." His voice was low and seductive.

Damn the man and that accent. Damn Trenda and Maddie for putting unwanted thoughts in my head.

"Do you think the whole family will be there? You know, Chip and his wife and kids?" I asked.

"I have no idea. A man can hope."

"Up ahead I think I see the private drive."

"Gotcha."

Even at five o'clock it was getting hard to see, but Roan didn't seem to have any problems maneuvering his truck along the narrow drive. When we moved past the trees, it was easy to spot the house; it was lit up like a

Christmas tree. The door swung open and I expected to see a woman about Roan's age. Instead, it was Harvey. He waved.

Roan parked the truck and got out.

"Hey, Harvey. Thanks again for letting me bring a guest."

"Not a problem," the big man bellowed. "Missy and I always say, the more the merrier."

Roan walked over to my side of the truck and opened the door, then put his hand in to help me out. It was kind of nice. I can count on one finger the number of men who had done that for me in the past. I liked it. And the accent. Have I mentioned his Southern accent?

He closed the truck door, then he grabbed my hand and we walked up the walkway and up the steps to meet Harvey.

"Well, aren't you gussied up? You're looking mighty fine, Lisa. Mighty fine."

I felt myself blush.

"Thanks, Harvey. Needed to look my best for you and your wife. I really appreciate you inviting me over for dinner. Or letting Roan do it," I qualified.

"Honey, you always have a standing invitation to come break bread with us. Neighbors are family."

"Harvey Sandowski, don't keep them on the porch," a woman called out from inside. "It's freezing. For goodness sakes, bring them inside and offer them something to drink."

I peeked up at Roan and saw him smothering a smile.

"Come in, come in," Harvey invited as he stepped aside.

"Lisa, I know you know Missy. You two have both volunteered at the library." Missy rushed over and gave me a hug.

"I love your apron," I said. I did. It totally had the nineteen-fifties vibe going on.

"I can make you one, if you'd like."

I laughed. "I don't think I need an apron to warm up a hot pocket."

"You don't know how to cook?" A younger version of Missy walked over to us. She was wearing the same apron only instead of covering a pretty sweater set like her mother, it covered a skintight caramel-colored Lycra dress. "It's one of my life's joys to feed those precious to me food that I have lovingly prepared."

Seriously, was this chick for real?

"Roan, it is so good to see you. I can't believe we have a real hero in our midst." She reached out to touch him and I grabbed her hand.

"It's so good to meet you," I said as I shook her hand. "You must be Tina."

For a moment I saw fire in her eyes as she looked at me, but she quickly masked it. "I am, and you're Laura. Welcome to our home. My mama says that you're a mechanic. How do you keep your hands so clean?"

I snorted. "When I'm wrenching, I use Goop, it works wonders. How did you keep your apron so clean if you did all the cooking, Tina? I see your mother has a couple of spills on hers."

"I'm just naturally tidy. Aren't I, Mama?"

I looked at Missy and watched her lips tighten.

"Her name is Lisa," Roan growled. "Can you remember that, Tina?"

"Of course I can, Roan. I can always remember something you tell me," she cooed. "Shall we retire to Daddy's study and partake in some libations?"

"Tina, since you want to lovingly prepare some food,

why don't you come into the kitchen with me as I finish up the gravy?" Missy said.

"But, Mama, I want to make sure Roan feels at home. After all, he did come to see me."

Missy shot me an apologetic glance.

"Tina, come into the kitchen now."

"Fine."

I looked up at Roan and saw him grin as Tina flounced her bony ass after her mother.

"You'll have to excuse Tina, she's naturally high strung." Harvey grinned. "Let's get you two set up with something to drink. Follow me."

That was the second time Lisa rolled her eyes at me. I was seriously trying to not laugh out loud. 'Feeding those precious to me'? Was she out of her mind?

Yes. Yes, she was.

"So what would you like to drink? I have a fully stocked bar. Lisa, I know that Tina usually likes a cosmo. Can I mix one up for you?"

"What kind of beers do you have?" she asked.

My lips twitched.

"Bud, Bud Light, Heineken and Coors."

"I'll take a Heineken," she said.

"Make that two," I said as I held up two fingers.

Harvey went over to the small refrigerator that he had tucked under the bar in his living study. This was definitely his room. There was a large deer mounted on the wall.

As he handed us our beers, he saw me looking.

"That's really something isn't it? Killed him over in

Montgomery County. Ten-pointer. Used a bow. We were eating deer steaks and deer sausage for over a year," Harvey grinned.

"Pretty impressive. Does Chip hunt with you?"

"Yep. Every year he goes out with me. I was really hoping Tina's husband would learn, but it was clear after the first year, he was a wash-out. Should have known right then and there, he was useless. Man who can't handle a bow or a gun? That ain't right. Now you? You I wouldn't have to worry about," he said, grinning.

I turned to Lisa. "Let's take a seat."

"Oh, where are my manners? Lisa, you're sure looking pretty tonight. I don't think I've ever seen you wearing something other than jeans. A skirt suits you."

She started to grimace, then she smiled. "Thank you. You look pretty good yourself. I've never seen you wear anything but work boots."

"Always like a chance to put on my cowboy boots," Harvey gave a wide smile.

"Hey y'all. I thought y'all might like something to tide you over. I wanted to make you my stuffed mushrooms, but Mama insisted on pigs in a blanket. Daddy, can you fix me a cosmo?"

Tina put the tray of mini hotdogs wrapped in dough and dipping mustard on the coffee table. She set down the little plates, then sat down on the couch, sitting far too close to me.

She leaned across me and looked at Lisa. "Are you drinking a beer? From the bottle?" She made it sound like it was the most uncouth thing she'd ever seen. I waited to see how Lisa would handle it.

"I couldn't handle a cosmo. Too much sweet sours my stomach."

I turned my laugh into a cough.

"Are you okay, Sug?" Tina started patting my back.

I looked over at Lisa. Her eyes were filled with mirth.

"Maybe you could get me a glass of water?" I choked out.

"Anything you need, Roan."

As soon as she got up I leaned over to Lisa. "You don't like sweets, huh? This must be something new."

"Yep, something about tonight just made me lose my taste for sweets. Or it might just be for saccharine," she whispered back.

Again, I had to hold back laughter. I didn't want Harvey looking over at us as he was mixing up Tina's cosmopolitan.

Tina swayed back into the room, her apron gone, and bent too far forward as she handed me my glass of water. I'm pretty sure I saw her bellybutton.

"Here you go. This should help you. I adore taking care of the people around me."

"Here you go, Darlin'," Harvey said as he walked over and brought Tina her pink drink. "I used a new vodka that one of my clients bought me. The name tickled me. It's called Woo-Woo vodka."

"Daddy, you know this is supposed to be made with lemon vodka," Tina huffed as she took a sip of her drink.

"Your mama had some lemon juice that I used. It'll be fine. Anyway, you just like this drink because it's pretty, alcoholic, and sweet. I added extra sugar, extra booze and made sure it came out looking pink. You'll love it." Harvey went and sat down in a worn leather chair and put his cowboy boots up on an ottoman as he took a sip out of a whiskey glass. I would bet anything he was drinking bourbon.

"Daddy, this is terrible. I need you to fix me something else. A Colorado Bulldog. That would be nice."

"I just sat down. You just sip that and like it," he said mildly. "So, Roan, tell me about your time away. What was it like being in the Marines for so long? Oh, wait a minute. You weren't just a Marine, were you? You were a Raider. What was that like?"

I took a sip of beer and thought about how I wanted to answer that question.

"Oh yes, do tell us. Did you have to kill very many people?" Tina asked.

Jesus. Is she for real?

Lisa leaned forward so that she could look at Tina. "Tina, if you had a job that required using deadly force, would you want to relive that?"

"Sure, I would."

"Well, I doubt that Roan does. I've met and worked with a few vets in my time, and I've never heard them rhapsodizing about killing people." Lisa's tone was scathing.

"But—"

"Enough, Little Girl. Lisa's right. Roan, I hope you didn't think that was what I was asking," Harvey said as he took another sip of his drink.

"No, I didn't. Still, a lot of the work I did overseas I can't talk about. What I can tell you is that I worked with some of the smartest and bravest men that have ever walked the earth. This job also allowed me to get to visit a lot of different countries, and really get to know the people who lived there. Most people assume that for the last twenty years I've been in the Middle East, but that's not true. I'd say, in total, I spent at least three years in Africa."

"Why?" Harvey asked as he leaned forward.

"The Boko Haram is a terrorist organization that has killed thousands. You probably heard about that girls' school where about two hundred and seventy-five girls were kidnapped, right?"

"What?" Tina gasped. "Where was that?"

"Nigeria. Fifty escaped. This happened in 2014. To this day, one hundred are still missing."

"How old were they?" Harvey asked.

"Sixteen to eighteen."

"So not girls, really," Tina said.

Lisa jerked her body in front of me. "They were too. And all of them were kidnapped against their will. By terrorists." She was fuming. I didn't blame her.

"Anyway, ISIS had the Boko Haram swear allegiance to them in West Africa in 2015," I explained further. "There were a swath of atrocities that swept through the region."

"Did you root them out?" Harvey asked.

"Not all of them," I said grimly.

"What are y'all talking about? You haven't even touched the little smokies," Missy said as she came into the room and sat down on the arm of Harvey's chair.

"I was just asking Roan, here, what he's spent the last twenty years doing."

"And he can't tell you, can he?" His wife said tartly.

"Well aren't you just full of knowledge Darlin'?" Harvey said admiringly. "How did you know that, Missy?"

"You laugh at me reading all of my stories. Well, I learn a lot from those books, Harvey Sandowski."

He laughed and put his arm around her waist. "I learn something new from you and about you every day, Missy Sandowski."

The smiles they gave one another were a thing of

beauty. How Tina fell so far from their trees was a mystery to me.

Missy pulled her gaze away from her husband.

"I came to tell y'all that dinner was just about ready. Tina, I'm going to need your help."

"But Mama, Roan was just telling me some interesting things about the Haram Bookoo."

"Boko Haram, Tina. It's the Boko Haram," her father corrected her. "Go help your mother."

Once again, I got to watch Tina flounce her bony ass away from me. It was even worse on the third viewing.

"I do hope you like beef stroganoff," Missy said as she stood up.

"Missy, I am thrilled to finally be tasting some of your cooking," Lisa said.

"I should have had you over months ago, Lisa. I feel terrible that I didn't think of it. Instead, we just go out to lunch."

"Maybe it's for the best," Lisa said with a smile. "If you had invited me over, I would have felt obligated to invite you over. Then I would have poisoned you, and I would have killed my friend. See how this worked out for the best?"

Harvey, Missy, and I all laughed. Tina…not so much, which made it all the funnier.

12

"So, you've lost your taste for sweets, huh?"

"Yeah, that was a stupid thing to say. I missed out on Missy's cobbler." Lisa pouted.

"That's okay, because I'm a growing boy, Missy gave me half of it to take home. I'm willing to share if you invite me in for coffee."

"You sure do know how to push your advantage. First you talked me into being your wingman, then you talked me into going out with you Saturday night, now you want me to make you coffee. What's next, I'm supposed to serve you a hot pocket?"

"I would never expect you to give up one of your morning meals," I assured her.

"Not just morning, they're good for dinner too. However, I do branch out for lunch."

"I'd ask you if you were kidding, but I'm pretty sure you're not."

"Now you're learning. So how much was on offer?"

I looked over at her for just a moment, then directed my gaze back to the road. "What offer?" I asked.

"How much of a dowry, or how high of a salary in his company was Harvey willing to give you if you took Tina off his hands?"

I gripped the steering wheel tighter.

"Holy shit, Roan. He didn't. And here I was, just kidding."

"He didn't come right out and say it. But after dinner, when he took me out back so he could smoke a cigar, he intimated that there was definitely an opening in his construction company. It was a real offer, don't get me wrong. But he went on to say that there was a better offer. He explained about a corner office available for family."

"I think I'm offended on Tina's behalf," Lisa said.

"Really? You met her, right?"

"Okay, I'm offended on behalf of womankind. We shouldn't be sold off like cattle. We should be making our own choices about who we date, who we love, and who we marry."

"There's a fly in that ointment," I pointed out.

She didn't say anything for a moment. "Oh, I get it. She might love, but that doesn't mean that marriage will be on the table. Hence the bribes from dear old dad."

"Yep." I squeezed the bridge of my nose. Tonight had been a lot to take on. "You do realize I think I would have lost my mind if you hadn't been there."

She giggled. "Even when you were totally pissed at me, and thought I was taking your daddy for a ride and running his company into the ground, you didn't raise your voice or berate me. You would have done fine tonight."

"It was iffy. Did you know that Tina was playing footsies with me under the table?"

"She was not." Lisa's voice was incredulous.

"She was too. She actually took her foot out of her shoe and tried to push it up my pant leg. Don't you remember the moment I jolted and my water glass sloshed?"

Lisa giggled again. "Can I tell you something, Roan?"

"Sure."

"I haven't had this much fun in ages. Seriously. I loved playing your wingman. Except for the point when Tina tried to say that those girls weren't girls, and somehow it wasn't a big deal that they were kidnapped. Except for that, it was all fun."

"It didn't bother you how she tried to put you down?"

"Hell no. I've been on the road since I was nineteen. I've got a shell like an armadillo, not an M&M. Rarely does something get to me."

She sounds a little like Chantelle.

"I suppose that's a good thing," I said as I pulled into her driveway behind her Dodge Charger. I turned off my truck and looked at her. "So, this is decision time. Just how much do you want some of Missy's peach cobbler?"

"You have to eat it with vanilla ice cream. I'm not sure it's worth having you come in if I can't have the dessert without the ice cream."

Damn, I'd been so sure she was going to invite me in.

"Luckily, I have vanilla ice cream in my freezer."

I grinned. "Well, isn't that lucky?"

I managed not to groan as Lisa took her time sucking the ice cream off her spoon. Once again, she was looking at me with mischief in her eyes. The same mischief that she'd had when she said she was going to change into something more comfortable and came back from her bedroom dressed in yoga pants and a silky red button-up shirt that looked like it might be a sleepshirt but was probably some kind of loungewear.

Yep. Lucky, lucky me.

But the best part was that her blonde hair was finally out of that damn ponytail. Instead, it was curled all around her shoulders and midway down her back. Yep, Lisa Reynolds definitely knew what she was doing. I was being tortured and loving every minute of it.

"So, when you're not working at Thatcher's, volunteering at the library, and trying to make men lose their minds, what else do you do, Lisa Reynolds?"

"Well, Roan Thatcher, let's be clear; you're the first man I've tried to make lose their mind since I've come to town."

"Then I'm honored."

"You should be. But I gotta tell you. I'm only trying to make you lose a little piece of your mind. Maybe enough to get to second base?" She winced at the last word.

"Baby, first base, no base, second base. Just the chance to see you indulge in your treat has been a pleasure." She started to open her mouth, and I held up a finger. "But... I wouldn't mind wandering over to your couch and finding out how peaches and ice cream taste from your lips."

The mischief melted away, and instead a dreamy expression crossed her face and she smiled at me.

"Why, sir, that sounds like a marvelous idea." She dropped her spoon into her empty bowl with a clang and got up at the same time I did. I held out my hand and she took it. I guided us over to her light-blue patterned sofa and sat down first, pulling her down against me.

"I'd been wondering how your hair would look when it wasn't in a ponytail," I whispered.

"And now you know." She smiled up at me.

"It's better than I imagined." I picked up a tendril and rubbed it between my thumb and forefinger. So silky. "It smells good, like strawberries."

"It's my shampoo," she whispered.

I wrapped my hand around the back of her head, sliding my fingers through her soft curls. Lisa's lips parted as her eyes drifted shut. I don't know why this seemed like such a big deal, but it did.

Our first kiss.

I pressed my lips against hers, and I immediately wanted—no, needed—more. I opened my mouth and she opened hers with me. I caressed her bottom lip with my tongue and tasted the sweet flavor of peaches, vanilla ice cream, and Lisa.

How could the start of one kiss be so powerful?

I wrapped my other arm around her waist and pulled her even closer and she whimpered.

Shuddered.

Moaned.

I thrust my tongue inside the warm cavern of her mouth, relishing the flavor that was Lisa. She was intoxicating.

I was *losing my mind.*

Her hands were now gripping my shirt. I felt her short nails through the fabric, clutching me closer. I obliged. I lowered us down onto the couch. It was narrow; there was no way we could lie side by side.

Perfect.

I positioned her under me, my elbows at her head, as I broke off our kiss and looked at her swollen mouth. Then I looked up into her dazed eyes.

"Don't stop." She twined her arms around my neck. Her intention was clear; she wanted more kisses, but I wanted to look at her. The lip gloss she'd started the night with was long gone, and she hadn't worn any other makeup. I traced her round cheeks that hid a dimple that showed when she smiled. The little frown lines between her eyes deepened when she was lost in thought or angry. I'd seen those frown lines a lot, but tonight I'd mostly seen the dimple.

"Roan, why did you stop?"

"I don't know that I've ever had a woman like you underneath me, and I want to savor this moment."

She frowned and those lines deepened.

I smiled.

"What do you mean by that?"

"I mean you're something special."

I watched the dreamy, wanton expression evaporate. "I'm not special. I'm just me. Trust me, I'm nothing."

Damn, really?

"Nothing?" I repeated.

"Nothing." She frowned again. "That's not what I mean. Not exactly. I just mean, I'm not special. I know my worth. I work hard and I'm good at my job."

She started wiggling. She wasn't quite trying to get away from me, but close. I wasn't having it. I wanted to finish this conversation.

"Honey, isn't it my opinion the one that counts on this? If I find you special, then you're special. At least to me, right?"

She pushed at my chest and I immediately pushed up off her. I pulled her up so we were once again sitting side by side.

"Sure, and then I start believing I'm special, and then one day that feeling is yanked away. Trust me, I know the drill. So, tell me I'm funny. Tell me I'm fun to be with. Tell me I'm a good kisser. But special? Nope, not going to buy it."

"You are funny. I haven't laughed so much in ages, and Honey, you're one hell of a good kisser. And if I think you're special, I'll keep that to myself. How's that?"

I got that frown again and the longest pause in the world as she mulled over what I'd said.

"If I say okay, does that mean I get more kisses?" she asked in a slow, husky voice.

"God, yes," I practically groaned.

"Then yes, I agree," she smiled.

I coaxed her back down on the sofa, this time even more gently, understanding better the vulnerable and oh-so-special woman who was offering herself to me. I'd been honest with her. Even if tonight just resulted in a few kisses, I would walk out of this house a very happy man.

———

When he looked at me, I melted. A sigh escaped as I looked into his eyes.

He's looking at me as no other man has before. It's not desire, not greed. It's almost with a look of reverence.

"Why are you looking at me like that?"

"I'm soaking in the moment." He dipped his head and licked my bottom lip, then lightly caught it between his teeth. His tongue continued to lick my lip and I started to pant. He let go, and I prayed he would kiss me. His hands cupped the back of my head, his elbows still holding his weight on the sofa.

When his thumbs swirled circles around my temples, my eyes closed. I felt him drifting down to kiss me again.

When our lips met it felt like lightning coursed through my body, lighting up every nerve, leaving them all tingling.

I opened my mouth and his tongue thrust in. Not far enough, so I wrapped my lips around him and sucked him deeper, pulling at his shoulders, trying to get him to lower all of his weight on top of me. I needed to be wrapped in his arms, surrounded by him, filled by him. I sucked his tongue even deeper and gloried at the deep, male groan that I swallowed.

I felt his fingers twining through my curls, sometimes gently, sometimes not. Both felt so good. None of this was enough. Not nearly enough. I moved my arms and guided them downwards so that I could get to the bottom of Roan's sweater. Every time I had seen the man, he had been wearing something that displayed shoulders and a chest that I'd been eager to touch.

Kiss after kiss, he distracted me from my task, but eventually I had my hands on the warm muscled skin of his back. Roan rumbled as I scraped my fingernails up and down his spine. The sound was wonderful and I wanted him to repeat it, so I traced the same path, and was rewarded with another groan.

"Lisa," he said huskily as he lifted his head. "Look at me, Baby."

I opened my eyes.

The power of his gaze shook me to my very foundation.

"Take off your sweater," I begged.

He rewarded me with a wicked smile right before he straddled me, then sat up and pulled it off. My hands immediately sifted through his chest hair so that I could feel the warm muscle underneath.

"And you? Can I unbutton your blouse?" His voice sounded like sin wrapped in silk.

"Yes please."

He didn't immediately go for the top button. Instead, he spanned my waist with his big hands, then meandered upward until he cupped my breasts. His thumbs swirled against my nipples in slow strokes and I arched up, wanting him to stroke harder.

Roan laughed, the bastard.

"I'll get there, Baby," he teased.

Finally, his fingers were at the top button of my shirt, and he released it. He bent and kissed the little bit of skin that he'd uncovered and I sighed. He continued to do this until he got to my bellybutton. There he took his time, swirling and twirling his tongue inside that little dent until I thought I would go crazy.

"Roan," I begged. But I didn't know what I was begging for.

He pulled my shirt open.

"Please tell me you weren't wearing this bra when you were sitting in front of Harvey Sandowski."

"I couldn't have worn it. It was red and I was wearing a beige blouse."

"How did you know red lace was my favorite color?" he asked.

"If it wasn't, I figured I could get you around to liking it."

He traced one finger along the lace on top of the bra and I shivered. He pulled down the barely there cup and bent his head and circled my nipple with his tongue, wetting it. Then he blew on it. My entire body lit up like a Roman candle.

"She likes that," he murmured. I heard the bone-deep satisfaction in his voice.

He pulled down the other cup and proceeded to do the

same thing. I stroked my hands down his back, remembering that his shoulder was injured, so my caresses were gentle. But his weren't. I let out a shriek of pleasure as he caught my nipple between his teeth.

Sublime.

I felt myself getting wet.

He is so going to get to slide into home plate.

13

She has to be able to feel me trembling. I can't ever remember feeling this turned on.

Well maybe.

But that was twenty-four years ago when I lost my virginity to Darla Cooper.

Lisa was kneading my chest hair like a kitten would. I left her pretty nipples, and kissed my way up her sternum, trailing kisses along the side of her neck until I could once again lick her behind the ear.

"Ahhh," she sighed. I blew on the spot I had just marked, and she bucked underneath me. Lisa was so damned responsive. I bit her earlobe, and she grabbed at my short hair, bringing my face in front of hers.

"Stop teasing me," she growled.

"But it's so much fun." I grinned.

"Do you have a condom?"

I had to think. I nodded.

"Thank God. Get off me."

I rested my forehead against hers. "But I like where I am." I teased.

"You'll like it better in my bedroom," she coaxed.

I was sure she was right, but I wanted to savor this moment. And the next one, then the next. I wanted to savor every damn one of them, and wasn't that just the strangest thing in the world?

I took a deep breath and smelled the peaches on her breath and the scent of strawberries in her hair. There was something about Lisa that drew me like a moth to a flame. She wasn't just a woman I wanted to have sex with, she was a woman I wanted to hold.

It was just days and already I wanted to know everything about her. After years of learning to trust my instincts to save my life and the lives of my teammates, I sure as hell wasn't about to stop listening to my gut now.

"Roan, are you listening to me?"

I didn't like that hint of insecurity in her tone.

"I am. I'm definitely listening to your every word and every move your body is making." I lifted her off the couch and pulled her up. Too bad I couldn't do the romance thing and sweep her up in my arms, but there was no way with my damned shoulder.

She cuddled up to my side and I put my arm around her shoulders.

This is good.

"Down the hall?"

"The door at the end of the hall," she confirmed.

As soon as we crossed the threshold, I could smell the heady mix of strawberries and lemons. Lisa turned toward me, pulling off her open shirt and bra. I adored the way she stood up straight, shoulders back. There was no maidenly modesty about her body, and there shouldn't be. She was gorgeous.

"This is going to be fun," she smiled.

I grinned. "Oh yes, it is." I grabbed her and slid her down onto her unmade bed. She started to work on my belt.

"I think you've forgotten a couple of steps, Baby. First my shoes, then we can go for my pants."

She frowned her delightful frown. "Oh, yeah." She sat up and waved her hand at me. "Take off your shoes," she commanded.

I laughed, and then I got to see her adorable dimple form. "Your wish is my command."

She started to giggle. I sat down on the side of the bed and proceeded to take off my shoes and socks. She immediately lunged for my belt.

"Not so fast," I admonished. "Your yoga pants have been driving me wild. I want you to go first, and I'll tell you what. I'll even help."

More giggles, and I got the dimple again. I pushed her down on the bed as she continued to giggle and I soon found myself confronted with a lacy red thong.

"This is a much better dessert than cobbler."

She lifted up on her elbows. "My turn now."

"Uh-uh," I said as I shook my head. I pushed aside the gusset of her panties and was rewarded with the glistening pink lips of her sex. Damn, she was pretty, and I needed a taste.

As my one hand held back her panties, I stroked my finger along the seam of her wet folds and brought my finger back to my lips. She watched me with wide eyes as I sucked her essence off the pad of my forefinger.

"You taste better than any pie I've ever eaten."

Her blush started at her collarbone and flashed up her neck to suffuse her face.

"No more teasing, Roan. Fish out that condom and fuck me already."

A laugh burst from my lips. "Lisa, are you feeling needy?"

"God yes," she moaned. "You're driving me out of my mind with all of this foreplay. But I need you inside of me. Now."

I shook my head. "I don't think so, Baby. You have to earn my cock. If you come all pretty-like on my tongue, then I'll give you my dick. How does that sound?"

I bit back a chuckle when I saw her frown.

"Well, be quick about it," she finally answered. "Do you know why?" Her voice changed to a sultry whisper.

"Why?"

"Because I want to feel you lying on top of me, my legs wrapped around you, our bodies writhing together, as you slowly enter me. I want to feel the heat of you, the strength of you, the length and the girth of you, pushing and pulsing inside my pussy. Driving me wild. So, Roan. Be quick with the foreplay, got me?"

"My God, Lisa. I almost came."

Her laugh was husky. "Hurry up, Cowboy."

I slid down the length of her body, and pulled her panties off, throwing them over my shoulder. I spread her legs wide. I was wrong; she wasn't pretty, she was as beautiful here as she was every place else.

I parted the lips of her sex with my thumbs and took one long lick. I was rewarded with a sigh. I played for long moments, just licking her up and down, loving the little sounds she made. But my body was demanding more, so I suckled her clit at the same time that I thrust two fingers inside her.

Lisa gasped.

She was tight.

Silky.

Warm.

And did I mention, tight.

Thank God I still had my jeans on, otherwise I would be skipping the foreplay. Gently, I pulled my fingers out, then thrust them back in until I found a rhythm that had Lisa moaning with pleasure. I carefully took her clit between my teeth and lashed it with my tongue.

"Roan," she cried out.

I thrust three fingers inside her.

"My God, Roan. Yes."

I continued with the rhythm I knew she liked, then I sucked on her clit hard. I couldn't make out what she was saying. It could've been because of the way she was holding my head in a viselike grip between her thighs.

I felt the first big shudder hit her. She bucked up. I thrust my fingers deeper. She lifted higher as another tremor rocked her body. For long moments I tenderly suckled her clit as I slid my fingers from her body.

When she released me from her grip I looked up and saw her staring down at me, a contented smile on her face.

"You're gorgeous, do you know that?" I asked.

She raked her fingers through my hair. "I think that's my line," she purred. "Now, can you find that condom?"

"Are you sure?"

"Oh yeah."

———

When my phone's alarm went off, I yawned. I considered throwing the damn thing across the room, I was so tired. I rolled over and grabbed the pillow where Roan had laid his head. It still smelled like him. Fresh and a hint of pine. I hated the fact that he'd left at two o'clock.

"Baby, it's a small town. If my truck is still here in the morning, everyone will know that I spent the night with you after only being home a week. You don't need that kind of gossip."

I'd tried to talk him into staying, but it hadn't done any good. But thinking about it in the morning light, I could see he was probably right.

"Dammit!" I yelled at my phone as it started beeping again. "I'll get up."

I rolled over and grabbed my phone and on my third attempt and finally shut off the alarm, yawning once more. I flopped back down onto my pillow and considered calling in sick. I just wanted to sleep and dream of last night.

Thinking about Roan made me shudder.

The way he touched me and the way I responded was out of this world. I'd never had a lover like him. Never. Not that I'd had a lot. Hell, I could count them on one hand. But still, even if I could count them on two, I would bet that Roan would still make the rest sad memories.

I looked up at the ceiling and took a deep breath. I adored sex with Roan.

Okay, okay. We didn't have sex, we made love. I adored making love with Roan. But it scared the hell out of me. I wasn't supposed to feel this way. Especially after only knowing the guy for a week.

But he got me. He seemed to really understand me, and wasn't that just kind of nice, weird and creepy?

"Up and at 'em." I jumped out of bed. *No more thinking anything about Roan as creepy, that's just wrong.*

I hit the bathroom and took care of business, brushed

my teeth, and went to the kitchen to start the coffee. Coffee was definitely going to be needed as soon as I got out of the shower.

When I went back to the bathroom I stopped just as I was getting ready to get under the hot water.

What the hell?

My hair looked like sex hair. I hadn't seen that look in over three years. I thought back to Roan's fingers tangling through my curls. The man seemed captivated by the scent of my strawberry shampoo. I stepped into the shower and looked over all of my different scented shampoos. It was definitely going to be strawberry from here on out.

When I got out of the shower I headed back to the kitchen and grabbed my coffee. I looked in my fridge to decide on breakfast. I'd gone shopping a couple of days ago, so I knew there was some yogurt. I grinned when I saw the leftover cobbler.

Score.

I took it out of the fridge, grabbed a spoon, and headed to my desk to see if the shop had any new emails. I took my phone out of the back pocket of my jeans before I sat down and saw that I had a text.

Ace Alarm Systems: *Miss Reynolds, we're going to have to delay the installation of your alarm system another week. We apologize for the inconvenience. Please don't hesitate to call us for further details of your installation. Again, we apologize for this delay. – Fred Silvers*

Fuck!

I pressed the number of Ace Alarm and when the

receptionist answered, I asked to be connected to Fred Silvers.

"Fred isn't in the office today. He's working from home. Can I take a message?"

"This is Lisa Reynolds," I started.

"Oh, wait a moment. He told me to give you his cell phone number if you called. Do you have a pen handy?"

"Yes."

She rattled off a number and I wrote it down, then called his number.

"This is Fred."

"Hi Fred, this is Lisa Reynolds. I got your message. What's with the delay? I told you about the dead rat that had been stabbed against my house. Whoever is harassing me has escalated. You assured me that my installation would be a priority."

"Miss Reynolds, trust me, you are a priority. My problem is I have two guys out with the creeping crud and one of them has passed it on to me. Our current job is running two weeks late."

He wheezed. He didn't sound so good. "Trust me I have not put any job ahead of yours. As soon as you told me what was going on, I put you to the top of our list."

I took a deep breath. Deputy Wagoner had told me that Ace was the best alarm company in all of Knoxville, and when I checked out their Yelp and Google reviews, they were heads and shoulders above their competitors.

"Okay, Fred. I understand. I appreciate you taking my situation seriously."

"Lisa, can I call you Lisa?"

"Absolutely."

"I'm concerned about what you've told me about the escalation of incidents. Do you have a gun?"

"Yes. And I know how to use it. I sleep with it on my nightstand."

"Good. I don't want to scare you, but I think that's wise."

"Deputy Wagoner isn't really investigating this," I admitted to Fred.

"Jasper Creek has a small sheriff's department. They don't have the resources. That's why he recommended the alarm system. I'll tell you what. When one of my guys comes back to work, I'll send him over and see what he can get started."

"I would really appreciate that, Fred. Thank you."

"You're welcome. Can I offer another suggestion?"

"I'll take anything at this point."

"I heard about a man in Jasper Creek. Former military. Word has it, he's put out a shingle. Well not exactly. But I think he's put out a few feelers that he might work a few jobs."

I was confused. "What does that even mean?"

"I've only met the guy once, Lisa. But he comes with thirty years of special operations training. He's retired in Jasper Creek, but none of those guys ever really retire. They're always on alert, you get my drift?"

I didn't, but I said yes.

"Let me see if I can get in contact with the man and see if he can poke around. He'll have more bandwidth than the sheriff's department, and he'll definitely take your situation seriously."

"What would a military guy know about a possible stalker?" I asked.

"They're trained to look over every detail and put together puzzles. If I had a problem, I'd want this guy helping me out."

Fred coughed again.

"I tell you what. When you feel a little better, you give this guy a call and see what he has to say. In the meantime, I appreciate you sending a guy over when they get back to work. You take care of yourself, okay?"

"You got it. I'm really sorry about the delay."

"Not a problem. It's out of your control."

I disconnected and looked down at the peach cobbler on my desk. For some reason it didn't seem nearly as appetizing.

14

Seeing Dad come off the escalator at the McGhee Tyson airport was one of the best moments of my life. I could tell the moment he saw me by the grin that came over his face.

"Roan," he bellowed.

If there weren't people in front of him, I knew he would have raced down the last few steps of the escalator. Hell, as it was, I thought he would shove people just to get to me.

I waved and waited.

As soon as I could, I pulled him into my arms and slapped his back.

"Aren't you a sight for sore eyes," he whispered into my neck. "Let me look at you, son."

"How about we move out of people's way first."

I grabbed his carry-on and maneuvered him toward baggage claim.

We used to be the exact same height, but he must have shrunk an inch since I last saw him. But despite that, he looked good.

Damn good.

"Son, you've lost some weight since I last saw you."

"And for every pound I lost, you gained it, old man. Looks good on you."

"Well, I can't say the same. There's my carousel," Dad said as he pointed. As soon as we picked a spot to wait for his bag to arrive, he turned to look at me. "Roan, seeing you here," he touched my arm. "Touching you? You'll never be able to imagine the relief and gratitude I'm feeling at this moment. You just won't. Not until you have a child of your own one day."

"I love you, Dad. I might not get it from your point of view. But from my point of view, I'm grateful too. I'm grateful to be home, and I'm so happy to be seeing you, and hearing you. I can't wait to sit down at the kitchen table and have a cup of coffee in the morning while I cook you breakfast."

"That sounds wonderful. You're really home for good now, right?"

"Well, that's what I intended. But we're going to need to talk about that. Home's not exactly how I left it. I finally got a text from Griff. He said he was heading back this way and he should be here next week. I spent a couple of days with Forrest and his family up in Nashville, and I've spent a little time with Lisa Reynolds, so I have a little bit of a handle on how Thatcher's is doing. But I'm not really seeing a place for me here in Jasper Creek."

"That's nonsense. Of course, there is. Jasper Creek is where you grew up."

I smiled. "I don't know about you, but I'm pretty hungry. How about we haul ass to Jasper Creek and either grab lunch at Pearl's or grab breakfast at Down Home?"

"Oh, you've branched out, huh? We were always a Pearl's family. But I gotta tell you, I've been stepping out on

Pearl for the last few years. Little Grandma's recipes are mighty fine."

I laughed. "Yes. Yes, they are."

By the time we got back to the house, Dad was ready for a quick nap, then he was itching to go see how things were going over at Thatcher's. I called Lisa and let her know that Dad and I would probably be over there at about four o'clock. Rather than sounding stressed, she sounded pretty excited.

"You know, you sound more excited to see my dad than about our date tomorrow night," I teased.

"Your dad is a better flirt."

"That's not true. I flirted enough to get you into bed, didn't I?"

"You flirted all right, I guess. But it was really the cobbler that helped you score."

I laughed. "I'll remember that for the future. So, is it going to be okay if we stop by at four o'clock?"

"Anytime is fine. Let me know if you're going to show up after five. I'll have the rest of the shop locked up, but I'll still be here in the office."

"Thanks, Lisa."

"Not a problem."

I hung up with a smile on my face. I went over to the Keurig coffee machine on the counter and put in a pod.

"This place is weird," I said for the umpteenth time.

I pulled out my phone while I waited for my cup of coffee to brew. I placed another call to Griff's number. Once again it went to voicemail.

"Bro, for the record, you're pissing me off. You can't

even leave a voicemail? Only a text? What the hell? Just so you know, Dad's here. He said he'll be here through Christmas. It'd be really nice to know what day you plan to be here, not just saying you're going to be here sometime next week. Some of us are planners, you know?"

I hung up. My message served no real purpose except it allowed me to vent my spleen. What the hell was his deal? Griff had always been the one who wanted to keep the family together. He acted like the middle child, not the youngest. He was always trying to get us together for holidays and shit. So, what was with his disappearing act?

I looked at my watch. It was a little past thirteen-hundred hours. Chances were good that Dad would be asleep for a couple of hours and wake up hungry. I needed to get my ass to the grocery store. I should have already had the refrigerator stocked up, but unfortunately my head was too busy doing things like buying a truck, getting a Tennessee driver's license, opening a bank account here in town, and thinking about Lisa Reynolds.

I poured my coffee into a travel mug, wrote a note for Dad in case he woke up before I was back, and left for the grocery store.

My cart was almost full by the time I got everything I wanted to feed Dad and me and hopefully Lisa for the next week. There was only one clerk working check-out and there was quite a line.

Right in front of me was a man, a woman, and a child. The guy looked to be ten years older than me, the woman was at least twenty years younger than him. But she couldn't be his daughter, not the way he had his arm around her.

"Mama, Amanda's working," the little girl said in a whisper loud enough for all of us to hear. "You don't like her cause she's really slow and doesn't know how to make change."

I watched as the girl's mother did a faceplant into her man's chest. He chuckled, same as me.

The woman straightened up then squatted down in front of her daughter.

"I like Amanda just fine, Bella. Sometimes she's a little slow for my taste, that's all. Everybody's different."

"And Dennis is putting things in bags. Daddy says that he's a few sandwiches shy of a picnic."

"Bella, honey, we've discussed two things, haven't we? First, there are some things that are private just for our house, right?"

The little girl nodded, her dark curls bobbing.

"Then we've talked about how if you want to say something privately to me in public, you're supposed to ask me to bend down and whisper in my ear, right?"

"Oh, I forgot that one. I'm sorry."

The kid really did look sorry. That was nice to see.

"But how do I know what things are just for inside our house?" she asked her mother.

The big silver-haired man turned and smiled down at his daughter. "Why don't you assume everything is private, and you just whisper about it, okay?"

She smiled brightly. "Okay, Daddy."

She turned to look at the magazines in the racks leading up to the check-up stands.

"Roger needs to get some new staff," the woman griped to her husband.

"Honey, I don't know why we don't just have our groceries delivered to our house," the big man whispered back to her.

"Lisa Reynolds had her groceries stolen right off her front porch."

Lisa had her groceries stolen?

He chuckled. "Trenda, I don't think anyone's going to be stealing anything off my front porch, and that's not just because we have an alarm system."

She looked up at him and giggled. "I think everyone in town knows not to mess with the retired Navy SEAL, huh?"

"Possibly," he agreed.

Interesting. Maybe I could find out what this guy was doing for a living here in Jasper Creek. It took another twenty minutes before it was my turn to check out. I could surely understand why the SEAL and his wife were frustrated with the checker and the bagger.

Dad still wasn't up when I got home, so that gave me some time to get together a potato casserole that I could put into the oven now, then I could start the pork chops when he came down.

I was just opening the oven door to put in the casserole when my phone dinged with an incoming text. I picked up my phone as I went to the fridge to pull out the fresh green beans I'd purchased. Looking down I saw that Griff had texted one word.

Friday.

I was tempted to text back something dickish, but I thought better of it. At least he had done what I'd asked. I tossed my phone back onto the counter and prepared the beans. By the time I heard Dad moving around upstairs, the casserole was almost done, and I had the pork chops all seasoned. I pulled the casserole out of the oven and threw the pork chops in.

"Something smells good," Dad said as he came into the kitchen. "Is that casserole your mother's recipe?"

"Only recipe I know."

"Can't wait. Can you figure out a way to get me a cup of coffee out of that machine?" Dad asked.

"You don't know how to use it?" I put a pod in for medium roast.

"Nah, I pull out the old percolator in the cabinet down below."

I grinned. "You had that when I was a kid."

"Roan, my mom and dad had that thing. Nothing wrong with it back then, nothing wrong with it now. It's just that the Airbnb people said I needed that Keurig coffee maker. Don't know why. Do you know how much those little pods cost? They're making a killing!"

I chuckled and handed my dad his cup of coffee.

"Griff's going to be here on Friday," I told him.

"That's good. I haven't seen him since last Fourth of July when he visited me in the Keys. He must be chomping at the bit to come see you."

"Must be," I muttered.

The kitchen timer rang and I took a look at the pork chops. They looked good so I took them out of the oven. "Do you want me to serve you up, Dad? Or do you want to do it yourself?"

"Why don't you do the honors, son."

I filled up both of our plates and put them on the table. "What can I get you to drink?"

"I'll take a beer. Did you buy Bud?"

"Of course." I grinned. I pulled out a bottle of Bud for Dad and a Heineken for me and we sat down to dinner. He started telling me about his fishing trip. They hadn't caught a marlin, but they had caught two cobia. Apparently, they were vicious bastards. One of the guys he was with had a line on a sailfish, but it got away.

"What about you, Roan? What have you been doing?"

"I've been getting settled. Bought a truck, got a driver's license, bank account. Things like that."

"Talked to Forrest when I got back home," Dad started. "He'd left a message. It sounds like you had some concerns about me leaving Jasper Creek."

"I do. But nothing I was going to hide from you. If you'd been here, I would have talked to you directly, Dad."

He gave me a steely eyed look. "Good to hear."

"Nothing's changed. We're always going to talk straight to one another. We might not talk for years, but we'll be straight with one another."

"Really?" Dad set his fork down on his plate. "It seems to me you haven't been straight with me for more than a few years."

Shit.

"You want to explain that?"

I rubbed at my injured shoulder.

"I figured it out after talking to Forrest. It's not a good excuse, but it's the truth. Eleven years ago, I was on a mission with eight guys. Only three of us survived."

Dad reached out and grabbed my hand. "I'm sorry, son."

"It was a long time ago."

"Don't matter. Still happened, and something like that will never leave a man."

I nodded. He was right.

"So, I take it after that you weren't real keen on making future plans? Am I right?"

"At least none I was willing to share. Felicity and I were

over. When I married her, I thought we were going to be married forever, just like you and Mom. So, my dream of a family and kids got blown to hell. But I knew that if things worked out with my job and I retired, I would always come back here to Jasper Creek and be a part of this family, and come work in the family business with you, Dad."

I hated the look of remorse on my dad's face.

"So, you didn't share this information because you didn't want me to be looking forward to something like that, in case you didn't make it home. Am I reading you right?"

I nodded.

"You were trying to spare my feelings, and instead we're in this mess. I'm living in Florida and not only do I have Lisa running the place, but she and I have been talking about her buying into the business."

"Yeah, I know. Pearl mentioned it."

"Ha! That woman never misses a trick!" He picked up his fork and started eating again. After he polished off both of his pork chops, he pointed his fork at me. "Do you think that working at Thatcher's was really going to satisfy you for the next twenty years? I know you had the good sense to turn down Forrest's offer, but are you sure Thatcher's is it for you?"

"Well, what else would I do here in JC?"

"That's a good question." He picked up his plate, rinsed it off, and put it into the dishwasher. Then he turned around and leaned back against the counter to look at me.

"You wouldn't have stayed in the Marines as a Marine Raider for damn near twenty years if you didn't like it. If it didn't fulfill you in some way. What did you like about that job?"

153

"Thatcher's would let me be part of a team, like I was overseas with my team."

Dad snorted. "Bullshit. You'd be supervising a bunch of guys who are working on cars. You'd be managing their timecards, their benefits, their vacation and overseeing their performance. That ain't teamwork, son."

I wanted to say that it would have been if he were still there, but that horse had already left the barn.

"So besides being part of a team, what else did you like about being a Raider?"

"We had each other's backs. I knew without a shadow of a doubt, these men would lay down their lives for me, and I would do the same for them."

"What else?"

"We were making a difference. We were fighting the good fight. We were protecting people who couldn't protect or help themselves."

"Did you feel fulfilled doing your job?"

"Absolutely."

"You're going to turn forty in two years, Roan. You still have at least twenty-five more years of work life in front of you. I can't imagine you doing a job that doesn't give you that same type of fulfillment, can you?"

I looked down at the half-eaten pork chop still sitting on my plate. I'd lost my appetite.

"No. You're right. But the problem is, I still want to stay in Jasper Creek. The last year and a half when I was on my last assignment, thinking about coming home was what kept me going. Seeing you, Forrest, and Griff... It meant the world to me. Then there's just something about this place. You know?"

"I know, Roan. I know."

"Then why'd you leave?"

"After your mother died, and all of you boys grew up and started your own lives, I was all alone. Yeah, I had the shop, but it wasn't enough."

"But all your friends," I protested.

"They were the friends that Darla and I had. As much as I hate to say it, I couldn't get past the fact that each time I saw them, there was still residual pain that I was seeing them without your mother by my side. Even after twenty-five years."

"So, your way of handling it was moving to the Florida Keys?"

"No. My way of handling it was moving next to my cousin Marty. He was my closest friend growing up. He and his family moved to Florida when we were both sixteen. As years went on, we lost touch. He lost his wife three years ago, and unlike me, he's been smart enough to rebuild a network of friends. He reached out to me two and a half years ago."

"How come I never heard of Cousin Marty before this?"

"You've met him. I think you were too young to remember him."

"Was he loud with red hair like a clown?"

Dad shouted out a laugh. "Yep, you called him Bozo, cause he was losing hair on top, but had red hair sticking out on both sides of his head. He hated it when you called him that. I'm going to have to remind him about that." Dad continued to chuckle. "He's a good man, Roan. He saw I was stuck here, getting more and more miserable each day, just putting in time at the shop. He had me come down and visit him for a couple of weeks and it was just what I needed. It opened my eyes. By the time I returned I was already working with a real estate agent in Florida. I tried to get ahold of you."

"I'm sorry, Dad. It was shit timing."

"I lucked out when Lisa showed up at the garage looking for work. Jimmy could have used her in the service department, but I was trying to figure out how I could sell the business, so I was trying to organize things in the office. I hired her to help me out. She understood how an Auto Service and Repair shop worked, so she took to it immediately. Plus, she could type with all ten fingers on the computer, instead of just with two like me."

I grinned. "I could see where that would be an asset."

"The more we got to working together, the more questions she asked. By the third week, she wasn't asking questions, she was making some damn fine suggestions. By week four it occurred to me that I could make more money if I didn't sell the business but put her in charge and taking the profits. We figured out the baseline profits over the last three years by month. I'd pay her a general manager's wage, but any profits she made above the baseline on any given month, we would split, fifty-fifty. I put her in charge fourteen months ago. We've been splitting profits for the last twelve months. The last four months, she's doubled the baseline."

I whistled. "Shit. That's pretty damned impressive."

"She had the guts to expand. I was complacent."

We stared at one another.

"So now I've explained why I've left and why it was the right move for me. You've explained why coming home was the right move for you, but now that you had more than a moment to think about it, is Thatcher's the right place for you? I mean, I'm sure Lisa would be more than happy to work with you. You two could be a team. But would that tick all your boxes?"

He was right. It wouldn't.

"It's quite the conundrum, isn't it?" I laughed glumly.

"Not really. I was talking to Bernie Faulks the last time I was here. He mentioned something about Trenda Avery's husband starting something up. I don't know if it's off the ground yet, but he's taken a couple of small cases. Just local things."

"What are you talking about?"

"Simon Clark. He was a Commander in the Navy, worked his way up. Started as a Navy SEAL. I think he might be starting something that just might could satisfy some of those things on your list."

15

As Roan drove us to the restaurant, I told him, "It was good seeing your Dad again. It's not the same as just talking to him. I've tried to get him to Skype, but he's just not into it."

Roan let out a laugh. "I know. I wanted him to upgrade his phone so he could Facetime me when I was overseas. No can do. Hell, do you know he didn't even get a cell phone until the year 2020?"

"You're kidding me. Even my granddad got one before that. As a matter of fact, he got one the year I left Oregon."

"When did you leave Oregon?"

"First you tell me about the restaurant we're going to."

Roan slowed to a stop at an intersection. "Forrest told me about it. He's been going to Knoxville a lot to scout out locations for his fourth store. My little brother is turning into quite the business mogul. Doesn't surprise me. He always won at Monopoly. Never cheated once."

I grinned at him. "He bought Park Place and Boardwalk, huh?"

"Nope, he always went for the utilities. Made money every time."

"Sounds like the two of you are close," I said.

"He's three years younger than me. Griff is five years younger. I feel for Griff. I was ten when Mom passed, he was only five. He doesn't have many memories of her, and I know it hurts him." The light changed and Roan started through the intersection. "Now, you start fessing up about leaving Oregon and your granddad."

"And Dad."

"Okay, and your dad."

"I was raised by my dad and my granddad." I grinned just thinking about them.

"You don't hear that very often. If ever."

"Yeah, it was pretty unconventional. Dad married late in life. At least that's what I always thought, but now that I passed thirty, I'm not thinking it is as late as I once did."

"How old was he?"

"Just turned forty. When he married my mom she was twenty-eight. He thought he was getting a good woman. That's how he tells it; Granddad says he was blinded by her looks."

He smiled. "You must have taken after her."

"Roan, I told you that flattery isn't going to get you anywhere."

He gave me a sideways look. "Yes, you did. But if you flatter *me*, it'll get you really far. Just saying."

"Such a flirt," I chuckled.

"You were telling me about your mom."

I didn't want to talk about it, but he was right. Because of Warren I knew a shit-ton about him and his family. It only seemed right that I tell Roan about mine.

"Unlike Griff, I have vivid memories of Mom. She laughed a lot. She would sing and dance with me in the living room to eighties hairband music. To this day, my stomach turns when I hear White Snake on the radio. But then there were the times that she was mean. Mean to me. Mean to Dad. She would scream at us about things that I didn't understand. Then she'd drive away in the car and not come back until the next day."

"Jesus. That sounds like a nightmare."

I shrugged. "It was what it was."

Roan glanced at me. "Your dad put up with it?"

"In hindsight I think there were some pretty big blow-ups between the two of them when she came home, but none that I saw or heard. Knowing my dad, and how protective he is of me, I'm sure he laid down the law. Or at least he tried to."

I fell silent.

Roan slowed to a stop again, his hands gripping the wheel tighter. "You said you were raised by your dad and granddad. Did he divorce her?"

"Eventually. To make a long story short. She left us when I was six. It was after I got home one day from school. I was in first grade. She didn't meet me at the bus, so I walked home with the neighbor girl's mom. When I got home, Mom was packing. I asked her where she was going. She told me she was taking a vacation from being a mom. When I asked her when she would be back, she told me she would be gone for a long time. She gave me a kiss on my forehead and told me to stop my crying. I needed to grow up."

The light changed but it took Roan a moment to start driving again. "Wait a minute. For real? She just walked out of the house?"

"Yep."

"Alone? She left you alone?"

That's why I hardly ever told this story. Everybody had

such a hard time grasping it. They asked all these types of questions.

"Yep," I answered succinctly.

"Baby, what did you do?" he asked softly.

"I didn't know dad's number at work, and I couldn't stop crying, so I just sat on the couch near the front room window so I could see if Mom would come back or wait for Dad to be done with work."

"And afterwards?" His tone was even softer. Achingly soft.

"And afterwards, it was just a new normal. Granddad would come and take care of me when Dad had to leave for work early. He'd cook me breakfast and pack my lunch for school. He'd walk me to the bus stop and he was always there to pick me up after the bus dropped me off. Sometimes he'd stay after dad came home and the three of us would eat dinner together, sometimes he wouldn't. By the way, it was always Granddad who won at Monopoly."

Roan reached across and put his big hand over my hands clutched together on my lap. His thumb stroked circles over them.

"And your mother?"

"Have no idea. Dad hired a private investigator, but they didn't find anything. The courts finally granted him a divorce. That was when I was fifteen or sixteen. I really hoped he would start dating or something, but he never did."

I could almost hear him trying to think of what to say next.

"She ruined him, Roan."

"No nothing? No cards or phone calls?"

"Nope." I moved my hands away from his. "Can we change the subject?"

He put his hand back on the steering wheel. "Sure, baby. Whatever you want. I vote for talking about the restaurant we're going to." His voice was full of mischief. It was just what I needed. I felt my shoulders loosen just a fraction.

"What's so great about this restaurant?"

"Besides my brother the tycoon suggesting it, it's a steakhouse. I figured you'd be good with that considering the way you dug into your bacon the other day. I even checked on-line to make sure you would approve of the dessert menu."

"I call bullshit."

His eyes shifted away from the road to look at me. "You'd be wrong. I definitely did. I like it when you get what you want, Lisa."

Ah hell. This man. What was I going to do with him?

After the conversation in the truck, I made it my mission to get Lisa to relax, feel good and hopefully laugh. If that meant I would try to coax her to drink just a little more than she was used to, then I was all in.

We were twenty minutes early for our reservation and the hostess told us they were running late. She said that we could wait in the bar and she offered us a complimentary cocktail.

"Beer?" Lisa asked as we sat down.

"Let's splurge, since it's on them." When the waiter came to us I asked if he had any suggestions for a tasty chocolate cocktail.

"It depends. Do you want something that is going to be

your dessert, or something that you might have two or three of with dinner, and still *have* dessert?"

"Option number two," I answered.

"Then I suggest a chocolate martini. It won't fill you up, you might need to skip the bread, but you can still eat your steak, potato, have three martinis, and still order dessert."

"Sold," I smiled.

"I'm not sure," Lisa frowned.

I loved her frown lines.

"Live a little," I coaxed.

"What are you going to have?"

"I'll have single malt scotch on the rocks for right now. I might have a beer with dinner. But remember, I'm driving," I reminded her.

"Oh yeah. Okay, I'll try the chocolate martini."

"You won't regret it," the waiter assured her.

It wasn't until dessert that I saw the dimple. The story about her mom had made some things clear for me. No wonder Lisa reminded me of Chantelle. Lisa might not have grown up in foster care, but she'd grown a tough outer shell just like Chantelle had. I wondered how things had worked out in her other relationships.

Fuck. Did I just think the word relationship?

"So, what about it? Did you ever do that when you were young?"

"Huh?"

"Not paying attention, huh? Thought so. I asked if you had ever raced for pink slips when you were young."

"God no. Dad would have sent me into next year if he

163

ever found out I did something that foolish. Why? Did you?"

"No. But I thought about it. That Corvette that Granddad and I built up was the shit. It went from zero to sixty in less than three and a half seconds. It wasn't great for endurance, but off the line, I was pretty sure nothing could beat it. I was up in Seattle with some friends of mine and this guy kept after me to race for pink slips. He had a Ford GT, and I should have been able to beat him, no problem. He didn't have a nitrous pipe showing, so I was pretty sure that wasn't his deal. Still, I didn't know what he had hidden under the hood. I just had a bad feeling, so I said no. But damn, I wanted that car."

"What happened?"

"I stayed and watched as he hustled people. It was the next night that someone set up a race with him. It was a guy with a Porsche 911 Turbo. The Ford GT smoked it. He didn't say anything, just took the guy's pink slip and walked away. Later that night there was a party in Federal Way. Me and a couple of my friends were there and he pulls up in his Ford GT. He got to drinking and that's when he showed us his set-up."

I was curious as hell. "What had he done?"

"He popped up the trunk and unzipped a gym bag. There was a nitrous bottle inside the bag. He'd gotten some wood to mount the bottle brackets in the gym bag, then routed the nitrous lines underneath the carpet, through the AC tubes at the door, and then under the fenders."

"No way."

"It gets better." There was a twinkle in her eyes. She was obviously enjoying telling me this story. "He mounted the solenoids in the fender well and used shrink wrap to cover the nozzle line to the intake. Then he hid the switches in the center console. He rewired the cruise control to use them as the purge."

I grinned with admiration. "Genius."

"Did I tell you the guy wasn't a guy? He was a kid. He couldn't have been more than twenty. He's probably working in Silicon Valley now, making a gazillion dollars."

"Baby," I said.

"Yeah?"

"If you could explain that so well, it's time for another martini."

"Nah, I've had enough. I want to be awake for the dessert that they have here, and whatever dessert you might have planned when we get back to my house."

The look on her face was downright naughty.

"I like your thinking." I grinned. I saw our server and I motioned for her to come over. "Can we see the dessert menus?" I asked.

"Of course."

"You promised me something good," Lisa warned.

"I'm all about keeping my promises."

When the small menu was put in front of Lisa, her eyes got wide. "You weren't kidding. These choices are incredible. But the guy in the bar lied. There is no way that I can eat even one bite of any of these."

"Sure you can. There's carrot cake, pumpkin cheesecake, chocolate mousse, raspberry walnut torte and death by chocolate."

"I'd be like that guy from Monty Python, where they give him just one thin mint and he explodes," she laughed.

"Huh?"

"You haven't seen that?"

"No."

"Do you watch Monty Python?"

"No."

Her face changed. She got really serious. The frown lines were back and she picked up her napkin from her lap and put it on the table. "I'm sorry, Roan, but you're going to have to take me home."

"What? What are you talking about?"

"I can't date a man who doesn't appreciate the humor of the English comedy team of Monty Python. Let's get the bill."

I looked at her and saw that she was dead serious.

"Lisa?"

She started to giggle. "Gotcha."

I shouted with laughter.

Holy shit. For a second there she really had me going. Only my teammates had been able to pull shit like that over on me.

"You little wench. You really had me." I was still laughing.

"But seriously, Roan. You really need to watch Monty Python. They are the bomb. I have cable. We could watch it tonight."

"We'll be doing something else tonight, and you might be experiencing a little bit of retribution for that little stunt."

Her eyes gleamed. "Retribution, you say? Sounds interesting."

"So, what do you want for dessert?"

"Let's see if we can get it to go."

"But what do you want?"

"All of it," she laughed.

Lisa had been funny as fuck for the first half hour on the drive home, but she'd petered out by the time we passed Gatlinburg. The dress she'd worn for tonight's date had blown me away. When I said I loved it, she'd told me that two of the Avery sisters had picked it out for her, once again deflecting a compliment.

When I'd told her she was special the other night I'd thought I was going to be tossed out on my ear. But after hearing her story about that fucking cunt of a mother, I totally got where she was coming from. I didn't care how great her dad and granddad were, it would take an entire truck of cement to fill the gaping hole that jackal had left.

I loosened my grip on the steering wheel. This was, and was supposed to be, a fun night for her, and by God, I was going to make sure it stayed that way.

"We're almost home," Lisa commented as we hit the outskirts of Jasper Creek. "I'm always a little sad when I pass Millie's farm."

"Why?"

"She's always fine if I stop by for a cup of tea, or if I bring her some scones or a sandwich from Down Home. But when I invite her out, she always declines. I talked to Trenda and Maddie about it, and they say she's always been like that. Kind of a recluse."

"Huh. It sounds like the Avery sisters are the type of women who would try to coax someone out of their shell. I'm surprised they haven't with Millie."

Lisa had a great laugh. "You've read them right. Did you know them when you lived here?"

"No. They were after my time."

"How about their older brother Drake? Did you go to school with him?"

"I was probably a senior when he was in middle school

or a freshman, so I gotta tell you, I don't remember him. But Dad told me what the hell happened to him. My God, that was fucking horrible. To this day, I can't wrap my head around the fact that Drake had to save his little sister from his father."

"Yeah. Their father is still up at Pikeville. For the girl's sake, I hope he's never released again."

"What do you mean again?" I asked.

"Oh, they let him out. Then there was another show-down. This time the sheriff went down along with their dad… and their mom," she added softly.

"Their mom?" I asked just as softly.

"Yeah. Their parents were conspiring to get some land that belonged to the youngest Avery daughter, and they weren't above murdering her to get it."

"Jesus."

"Yeah. It makes my situation sound like a walk in the park."

"But they had one thing you didn't," I reminded her.

"And what's that?"

"They had each other."

I was heading down her street, then made the turn into her driveway when I noticed something on her porch.

"Looks like you have a package."

"That's odd."

"You mean you're not like most Americans who have a package dropped off at their front door every other day?" I teased.

"The last time I arranged for something to be delivered to my front door, I had to pay for it twice. No more deliveries for this girl. If I want something delivered it will be sent to the shop where I can sign for it."

I stopped my truck. Lisa opened her door.

"Let me help you down. It's a long drop, especially in those heels."

"To be precise it's a shorter drop in these heels, but I'll take all the help I can get. Because between the heels, the martinis, and the height differential, I'm thinking getting help will be the smart thing to do."

I laughed.

"You have a nice laugh."

"I was thinking the same thing about you, earlier."

She twisted in her seat and looked at me. "Really?"

"Really."

"That's nice. I don't like admitting it, but sometimes it's nice that you like things about me. But I still don't want to trust it, you know?"

I unbuckled my seatbelt and leaned over the console. I reached out to wrap my hand around the side of her neck, bringing her closer. She snuggled into my clasp.

"One day, Lisa, you're going to learn that I am a man you can trust."

"I want to believe that, but—"

"You'll just have to stick around and wait and see. Now wait for me to come around and help you out, okay?"

Her smile dazzled. "Yes, Roan."

When I got to her side of the truck, she slid into my arms, and I'd never held anything better. I didn't even care about the ache in my shoulder. I kissed her on her nose.

"Don't forget the desserts," she called out.

"I haven't. I'm holding my dessert."

She giggled. She was the slightest bit tipsy. It was cute.

I put her down, then reached behind her seat and picked up the rather large bag that contained the desserts.

"I'm going to have breakfast for a week," she cooed.

"That is not a good way to start the morning. You need brain food. Oatmeal and fruit would be a good start."

"Wasn't there crumbly bits on one of the fruit tarts? That was oatmeal, wasn't it?"

I rolled my eyes. "Let's go get your package and get you inside, out of the cold. Or better yet, let's get you into your coat."

"I don't need my coat. It's twenty feet to my front door. Come on, I'll race you."

"Hold up, Cowgirl. You're in heels. We'll walk sedately like adults."

Her dimple popped as she laughed. I had my hand at her back as I ushered her toward her front door. Right up until I got a good look at the thing sitting on her porch.

"Stop." I gripped her elbow tight, to keep her in place.

"What?"

"Get back in the truck."

"What are you talking about?"

I tried to turn her around so that she wasn't facing her front porch. But I wasn't holding onto her too tightly, because I didn't want to injure her. She wrenched away and walked four more steps and gasped.

"My God."

She sank down to her knees.

"Oh my God, no!" she cried out.

16

It wasn't until my stomach heaved that I was able to stop looking at what was in front of me. I turned and vomited into the dead bushes beside my stoop.

"Lisa, I need you to get back into my truck."

What is he talking about?

"Come on honey. Let's get you up."

I was trembling when Roan helped me up off my knees. I couldn't help but see the bloody human skull with the dagger lodged into its head.

I twisted away from Roan and bent over as I emptied my stomach again. This time he held my hair back from my face.

I leaned so hard against him as we made it back to his truck, he might as well have been carrying me.

"Am I hurting your shoulder?" I asked.

"You're fine, Baby. Let's get you inside."

He opened up the passenger side door and started to help me up, but I stopped him. "Wait, I think I might have vomit in my hair."

"Doesn't matter a bit. Now get in." He gave me a bit of a push, and my butt was in the soft leather seat.

He hauled ass to the driver's side, hopped in, then put my purse on my lap, threw the bag of desserts in the seat behind us, and started the car. "You're shivering, this should get you warmed up." He leaned across me and pressed the button to turn on my seat warmer.

Then he popped open his glove box. I was not surprised to see him pull out a gun. It was a much manlier gun than mine.

"Baby, give me the keys to your house, okay?"

I didn't even ask, I just did as I was told.

He backed the truck out of the driveway and got us out into the street. "Anybody ex-military on your block?"

"Uhm, Sheila Arnold, she's two houses down. She was an Army lieutenant, I think."

"Okay. We'll park you over there."

Before I even realized it, the car was stopped and Roan was getting out of the car, holding his gun.

"Wait! What are you doing?"

"I'm just going to make sure the house is clear before we go in."

"Shouldn't we call the sheriff?"

"Whoever did that might have got away by then."

"I thought you said you wanted to make sure the house was clear, not that you were hoping to find someone."

He came back into the truck, put his knee on the driver's seat and leaned into toward me. "Lisa, it's going to be all right."

"But—"

"I promise." He wrapped his hand around the side of my neck and pulled me close. Then he kissed me. It was short but potent. "Stay here. I'll be right back. Call 9-1-1. Got me?"

I nodded.

As soon as he left I dropped my chin to my chest.

I didn't know what to do. There was a dead person's skull on my porch. The back of my eyes started to itch. Why was there a dead person's skull on my porch?

I need to do something.

There was a dead person's head on my porch. A bloody skull. With a dagger. I couldn't not see it. It was there. Stuck in front of my eyes, like I was wearing glasses and the picture of the skull was pasted inside on the front of the glasses.

I closed my eyes, but it didn't help. I saw the head.

I need to do something.

Oh yeah.

I reached into my purse, pulled out my cell phone, and called 9-1-1.

The truck door opened.

"Did you call 9-1-1?" Roan asked.

A voice came over my phone. "What is the nature of your emergency?"

I held it in my outstretched hand toward Roan. He took it from me and hung up.

"We'll deal with that when I've got you inside."

"Okay."

He drove back to the house. We went in through the side door. I started trembling again, or had I ever actually stopped?

"Roan, wait a minute. We have to tell someone. The police. Fred. Someone."

"Who's Fred, Baby?" Roan coaxed me to my couch and guided me to sit down.

"He's the guy who's going to install my alarm. He's late."

"We're not going to call Fred. We're going to call the sheriff."

I huddled over and wrapped my arms around my stomach. I couldn't stop trembling. "Please don't make me talk to Deputy Wagoner again. He doesn't do anything but tell me to keep my gun close and get an alarm system."

"What?"

Roan sounded closer, but when I looked up, he was actually heading down my hallway. I hoped he would be back soon.

I looked up when I felt my comforter being wrapped around my shoulders. "Now tell me why Deputy Wagoner was suggesting that you keep your gun close by. What's been going on?"

He sounded mad.

"Are you mad?"

"Nope," he lied. At least I was pretty sure he was lying. "I'm concerned. But before we get into that. Let me call the sheriff."

"Okay."

He put his arm around my shoulder and pulled me tight. I mashed my face into the crook of his neck. I hardly listened as he spoke. But I did perk up when he called his father.

"Yeah. It's an emergency. Get over here right away. I want to take some pictures of the crime scene before the sheriff and his crew arrive, but I don't want to leave Lisa in here alone. And whatever you do, come in the side door."

I pulled back and looked up at him. "Why do you want to take pictures?"

"Because as soon as the sheriff gets here, they'll own the crime scene. We won't get a chance to see pictures of what they find on your stoop, it will all belong to them. I want to make sure that we have what we need."

I was too done-in to ask why. If he thought it was a good idea, then so be it. I just looked off into space and let Roan hold me until there was a knock on the door.

"Hold on, Lisa. It's Dad. I'll be right back, okay?"

I nodded.

Images of the skull kept flashing before my eyes. Logically, I knew it wasn't a severed head. Not exactly. Because the skull was old. It was bleached, like in a science lab, but there had definitely been blood coming out of the empty eye sockets. Then there was the ornate blade of the dagger that was showing from the top where someone had slid it into the cranium.

I leaned over, forcing myself to breathe deeply in through my nose, and slowly out my mouth. In and out.

I felt someone sit next to me. It wasn't Roan.

"That's it, darlin', just take your time. You've had a bit of a fright." He put his hand on my back and rubbed soothing circles around and around. His touch reminded me a little of Roan's. I was finally able to sit up.

"Where is Roan?"

"He's out front, waiting for the sheriff to arrive."

"Why would somebody do that? What have I ever done to anybody?"

"I'm going to kick Gene Hollister's ass from here to next week," Warren snarled.

I looked into gray eyes. They were so much like his son's. Warren was furious.

"This wasn't Gene. He would never do something like this. Get in my face? Yeah. Bad mouth me all over town? Yeah. Put something gross on my stoop to scare me? No way."

"Then who?"

"That's what I'd like to know."

My head turned from looking at Warren to the sheriff and Roan who had walked in from the side door. I hadn't even heard them come in.

"It was Gene Hollister," Warren said as he shot from the sofa. "Jimmy Manning told me all about what a prick he's been to Lisa. He's had it in for her for months."

I stood up and put my hand on Warren's forearm. "Hold up, Warren. Gene's gotten his revenge. He left us in a lurch by going over to the other shop in Gatlinburg without giving notice. I bet if we asked around, we'd hear how he's trying to crap all over my reputation, but what I saw out there for the brief moment I looked, is just too creative for Gene."

"You've got me there," Warren nodded.

"Deputy Wagoner said you had one other incident. You want to tell me about that?" the sheriff asked. He wasn't what I was expecting. He was someone you wouldn't even notice if you walked by him on the street. He was only a couple of inches taller than me, with a silver-haired buzzcut and blue eyes. I would've tagged him at about sixty years old.

"There was more than one incident, but I guess he just told you about the rat, right?"

The sheriff's gaze sharpened as Roan strode over to me. "What are you talking about? What incidents?"

"Last weekend, when Gene came over to talk to me. I found a rat stuck to the siding of my house."

"Stuck how?" Roan asked.

"Someone had used a thin knife, a stiletto, to stab the rat through the head into my house, right next to my sliding glass door out back. Deputy Wagoner was pretty sure it was done while the rat was alive, what with all the blood spray and smear."

I shuddered just thinking about it.

"For fuck's sake, and you're just telling me about this now?" Roan demanded to know.

"Why would I tell you? It was something for the sheriff's department to work on. That was the only incident that the deputy really seemed to care about. When I told him how someone had killed my plants, or how someone had turned on my water in my backyard and left it on all day while I was at work, he said I'd done both of those things. Then when somebody let out the air from all four of my tires when my Charger was beside my house one night, he said it was a teenage prank, and not to worry about it."

"How long has shit like this been going on?"

The sheriff came over to join us. "Miss Reynolds reported the first incident four months ago," he answered.

"And what has your department done about this?" Roan asked the man. He was pissed.

"He suggested she get an alarm system."

"He also told me to keep my gun handy," I said. "I'm sleeping with my gun beside me and I'm trying to get an alarm installed. They're just backed up and some of their employees are out with the flu. I'll be their first appointment as soon as they're fully staffed. Fred promised me."

Roan turned to look at me. "That's not good enough."

"What? I should have been taking them chicken soup?" I asked sarcastically.

"No, not you, Lisa. It's not good enough that all the sheriff's department had to offer was you getting a gun and installing an alarm. Did they ask you who might be doing this? Did they follow up on any leads?" He turned to glare at the sheriff.

"I called Deputy Wagoner while we were outside," the sheriff said. "He's the one who's been taking point with Miss Reynolds. No, he hasn't done anything with any of her complaints."

"What kind of shitshow are you running, Baxter?" Warren sounded exactly like his pissed-off son.

"Warren, I'm sorry. I'm supposed to get weekly copies of my deputy's incident logs, and Wagoner said he must have misplaced Miss Reynolds'."

"So, is he the culprit?" Warren asked. He turned to me. "Has Deputy Wagoner made a pass at you? Asked you out? Have you rebuffed him? Maybe he's harboring a grudge and wants to scare the bejesus out of you."

I started to laugh. Roan chuckled.

"Warren, I'm thinking you're watching too many of those TV whodunnits."

"I'm watching the true crime shows. These are *true*, Baxter. Stranger things have happened than it turning out to be a police officer who is the killer."

I gulped.

"Dad, would you think before you talk? Nobody is killing anyone. So far Lisa is just being harassed."

Warren turned to me, his eyes apologetic. "Sorry, darlin'. I wasn't thinking. We don't know that the deputy wants to kill you."

"Warren, stop it," the sheriff said. "I know Wagoner, he's a good man who's engaged to a woman he loves. He's just shit with paperwork," he ground out.

"He's shit with taking things seriously," Roan muttered. "Meanwhile, what are you going to do with the skull out on Lisa's porch?"

"I've got Kenny coming out. I woke him up as soon as you called. He's going to go over the crime scene. He's good. He graduated two years ago with a degree in criminal justice. Since then, he's taken additional courses. He'll handle things right."

"Then what?" Roan persisted.

"Well, right now I'd like to ask Miss Reynold's a few questions, as long as Warren won't accuse me of trying to kill her."

"Not funny, Baxter," Warren murmured.

"It kind of is." I smiled at Warren. "Do you mind if I make a pot of coffee? I'm cold and getting tired."

"I'd be obliged," Sheriff Baxter said.

"Let me," Roan insisted. "You sit back down and make yourself comfortable next to Dad. Sheriff, don't take too long. This hasn't been easy for her."

"For goodness sake, I'm not breakable," I admonished Roan. "Just make the coffee and I'll answer questions."

He held up his hands and gave me a partial smile. "Okay. But don't let him upset you."

"I'm right here, aren't I?" Warren spoke up. "You're going to be just in the next room. We've got her covered."

"Gentlemen, you're beginning to piss me off. I'm not going to browbeat the woman."

"Thank you, Sheriff Baxter. They are getting pretty overbearing."

"Come sit down, darlin," Warren coaxed. "We'll be good."

I sat back down.

"We'll be good, as long as the sheriff behaves," Roan said before he left for the kitchen.

17

"Miss Reynolds, according to Deputy Wagoner's notes, you've called him twice. Once when the spigot was left on all night and left your backyard basically a swamp, and then when the air was let out of all four of your tires. Is that correct?"

"Yes. But that first time when I talked to him, I told him how all of my newly planted flowers had all died within a week back in August. He blew that off, figuring I had a black thumb. And as for the water being on all day while I was at work, and all night when I was asleep, he figured I'd done that. I hadn't. I had no reason to turn the spigot on. He didn't believe me, I could tell. I knew that whatever he was writing down was going to go into the round file as soon as he got back to the station."

The sheriff wrote something down on a pad of paper. "What happened the next time you called him?"

"Ten days ago, I went out the side door to leave for work. When I saw my car, I realized that all of the tires were flat. When I looked closer, I saw all the air had been let out of each tire."

"And that's when you called our office?"

"No, first I called the shop so they could send someone over to pump up my tires. Then I called Deputy Wagoner since I still had his card. When he came out to my house, he seemed really cranky. It was almost like he thought I had let the air out of all my tires just to inconvenience him. He ended up saying he thought it was a teenage prank, and that was that."

The sheriff looked up from his notes. "Had you heard anything during the night?"

Roan came out and handed me and his father mugs of coffee, then disappeared back into the kitchen.

"If I'd heard something, I would have gone out and checked."

"You should have called 9-1-1," the sheriff said.

"I'm not going to call 9-1-1 if I hear a noise outside my house at night, when it's probably a racoon trying to get into my trash." I took a sip of coffee and smiled. Roan had made it with just the right amount of cream and sugar.

"Miss Reynolds—"

"Can we just talk about the skull? I'm tired and nauseous and I just want to go to bed."

"I won't take much more of your time."

There was a knock at the side door.

"Hold on, that must be Kenny," the sheriff said as he got up from one of my two lounge chairs.

Huh? Why did I have two lounge chairs when I never bothered to invite people over to my house? They looked nice.

Maybe I should invite Trenda, Maddie and Millie over some time. Maybe Millie would come since it was at my house.

I jumped when Roan touched my knee. Coffee almost sloshed out of my coffee mug. He was crouched in front of

181

me. He took the mug out of my hands and put it on the coffee table.

"How you holding up, Champ?"

"I'm fine," I assured him.

"She doesn't sound fine," Warren said.

"Why don't you go into your bedroom and pack a bag? You're going home with Dad and I tonight."

I shook my head, trying to shake out the cobwebs. "What are you talking about?"

"You can't stay here, honey," he said gently. "Not when bloody rats, and bloody skulls with daggers and stilettos are being left as offerings."

"I'm not going and staying with you guys."

"Yes, you are darlin'," Warren said. "Roan is right. You can't stay here."

"Fred said he'd get the alarm in soon, and I have my gun."

Roan shifted and sat down beside me. He put his arm around me and drew me in close.

"Lisa, you're not hearing me. You're not going to stay alone in this house tonight with your gun under your pillow."

"I sleep with it on the nightstand," I murmured.

"Lisa," he said sharply.

That got my attention. "Are you mad about something?"

"As a matter of fact, I am. I'm mad that someone is terrorizing you in a place that you should feel the safest."

"They're not terrorizing me, they're harassing me."

His gray eyes turned the color of molten steel. "I take that back—I'm not mad, I'm furious. Jesus, Lisa, you should have told me about this during our breakfast at Down Home. I would have been in Baxter's face right then. And you can be damn sure your alarm system would have been put in. I don't care if Fred had to get up out of a hospital bed to install it himself. You get me?"

"Roan, this has been a hard night, okay? My feet hurt. I need to brush my teeth. And there's a bloody skull on my porch. The last thing I need is for you to yell at me. You're supposed to be on my side."

I tried to keep my voice forceful, but dammit, I'd let him in a little bit. And I'm not just talking because we'd had sex. I mean because I was really starting to like the whole Roan Thatcher package. Didn't he know I was feeling vulnerable?

"Fuck. I'm sorry, Lisa, you're right. This whole thing has me spooked, I—"

"Don't mind me, I'm going to go introduce myself to Kenny," Warren said as he got up and headed toward the side door.

I chuckled and Roan joined in.

"Do you think he knows something is going on between the two of us?" I asked Roan.

"I'm afraid so." Roan answered.

I sighed. It was water under the bridge.

"I still don't want to go stay with the two of you. I just won't feel comfortable."

"Lisa—"

I held up my hand to stop him.

"I'm not done. Not that I want to run around the house naked or anything. But I was hoping you might end up in my bed again tonight. And at this rate with two sheriff's cars out front, and a bloody skull on my porch, Pearl will know all about it by the time her diner opens tomorrow. Right?"

"What does that have to do with you running around naked? I'm not following you."

"What I'm saying is, that everyone will know someone is harassing me, and if the big bad Marine is spending the night, they'll just assume you're protecting me, not that you're besmirching my virtue."

Roan snorted. "Besmirching your virtue? Do you mean playing fast and loose with the prettiest woman in JC?"

"Enough with the flirting until I've brushed my teeth. But are you getting what I'm saying?"

"Yeah, I am. But I'm not leaving you here while I pack a bag, even if it is with Dad and the sheriff. You're going to come with me while I pack up and grab some things out of the refrigerator."

"Oh, shit, the bag of desserts is still outside."

"I brought them in and put them in the fridge. They weren't part of the crime scene."

"I didn't barf on them, did I? Please tell me I didn't."

"I should tell you that you did. Sugar is not one of the four food groups."

"I'm aware of that. It is the glue between the other four that keeps them together. Without sugar, the world would be lost."

He kissed my forehead. "My girl is feeling better. Why don't you go brush your teeth and slip into something not *too* comfortable, because I don't want my dad to have a heart attack, and then we can go over to the house. Then we can come back here and go to bed."

"Are you saying I shouldn't put on the red lace underwear?"

"That's exactly what I'm saying."

Kenny and the sheriff were gone by the time we got back. It was well past midnight.

"Did you leave any groceries for me?" my old man griped when he saw the box of stuff I was loading into Lisa's fridge and pantry.

"I left the stuff I prepped for tomorrow's dinner. We'll figure out something for Monday so you won't starve."

Dad laughed. "I'm sure that Pearl and Lettie lost half their income when I moved to the Keys. I'll be fine, son."

I watched as he took Lisa into his arms and gave her a gentle hug. "Roan will take good care of you, but if he gets to be too overbearing, you call me. I'll come rescue you."

Lisa laughed.

"Take a few days off. When was the last time you took a couple of vacation days?" he asked.

"Last March," she answered.

"It's December. You're due. Take next week off, and I'll cover."

"Actually, Warren, I was going to work something out with Gene and Jimmy closer to Christmas because my dad and granddad are planning a trip out. But with Gene leaving, I knew I was stuck."

"Well, now you're not. Now that Roan's home, and since I don't have any bookings til mid-January, you can take all the days you want. Roan said Griff will be home on Friday?" He looked over at me, and I nodded in agreement. "Then there will be plenty of people to cover you at the shop."

"I don't want to impose."

My dad ignored her. God bless him. "When are your people due to be here?"

"I left it open-ended. I was really hoping to get all of

this nuisance business over with before they came out. I knew they would make too big of a deal out of it."

"That's because it *is* a big deal," I ground out.

She gave me a sharp look.

I held up my hands in surrender. "Hell, what do I know? I've never dealt with any bad guys. I just cook for a living." I turned back to putting things away on the shelves.

"He gets kind of testy when he doesn't get enough sleep, huh?" Lisa whispered to my dad.

"He was always like that as a kid. Something tells me you'll be able to handle him," Dad whispered back.

Lisa giggled.

"Well, you two, I need my beauty rest," my dad said. "It's time I got back home. Call me if you need me. Roan, why don't you walk me to my car."

"Sure."

We left out the side door. There wasn't any caution tape around the front porch, but I didn't want to use that door until I had thoroughly washed it off. When we were both standing in front of his rental, Dad turned to look at me.

"Did you grab my pistol like I told you to?"

I nodded.

"Good. Don't let anything happen to that girl. She's special."

I winced.

"What?"

"She doesn't like being called special," I told him.

"Found out about that, did you?"

I nodded.

He held my gaze for a minute. "Make sure you want to stay here in Jasper Creek before you work to convince her she's special. That girl's heart has been broken down to the core. Only step up if you know you're going to be around."

"I hear you," I murmured.

He bent to open the car door, then turned back to me. "The thing is, Roan, I didn't raise stupid boys. And since that's the case, you have to know Lisa is a once-in-a-life-time find. You'd be a fool to walk away from her."

I didn't say anything in return. What could I say? He was right.

And so was Blessing. Lisa was beyond special.

18

When I finally slipped into bed I'd figured Lisa would be asleep after the night we'd had, but I was wrong. She was awake. And she was no longer wearing her sleepshirt. She wasn't wearing anything at all.

"Lisa?"

"Will you make love to me?" Her voice was soft and shaky.

I pulled her close. I was wearing an old pair of pajama bottoms that I'd found in Dad's closet.

"Baby, I will do anything you want, whatever you want. But are you sure about this? Tonight was a lot."

With only the moonlight shining down upon us through the window, she kissed the edge of my jaw. "I'm sure," she whispered.

She'd showered earlier. The intoxicating smell of strawberries surrounded me as she curled even closer. She peppered kisses along my neck, until I couldn't stand it another minute. I wrapped my hand around the back of her neck and brought her in for the kiss that I so desperately needed.

"Yes," she hissed as our lips met.

I took control. Mindless, I plundered. I parted my lips, forcing hers open and felt her tremble, her nails biting into my back as her breasts plastered against my chest. I thrust my tongue into her mouth and I heard her whimper as she caressed it with her tongue. I felt like the top of my head might explode.

Slow it down, Thatcher.

I released my hold on her neck and cupped her cheeks, letting loose of her lips. I kissed each closed eyelid, then her nose, then gave her one languid kiss on her mouth.

I leaned up and pulled back the covers. I had learned a couple of things from the other night, and I intended to use every one of those new skills.

I thumbed the pink tips of her breasts and she moaned and pressed hard into my hands. She whimpered when I plucked and pinched her nipples.

"Roan, I love it when you do that."

I chuckled.

I dipped my head and sucked one of the succulent bits of flesh into my mouth and flicked it with my tongue, loving her whimpers and gasps. Lisa moved her hands and gripped my head, her nails now biting into my scalp.

I had to pull away, because there was no way I was done playing. I kissed my way down her body, kissing silken flesh along my way. Finally, I smelled cream and musk.

"No strawberries," I complained as I parted her legs even farther.

"Vanilla body wash," she panted.

I parted the lips of her sex and found pink wonder.

Divine.

I knew what she liked, and I intended to give it to her. I

licked and stroked. Using my fingers and tongue, I did everything I could to drive her wild.

"Fuck me, Roan. Please fuck me."

"Not until you scream."

"I'm screaming," she said softly.

"Not nearly good enough."

I kept at it. She tasted so good, and I was lost in giving pleasure to this woman. It took me long minutes to realize she was screaming my name.

I got up and grabbed a condom out of my duffel. Then I came back to her. I slowly entered her slick, tight depths. If this was what losing your mind felt like, I was all in. This was pure bliss. Her long legs curled around me as she pulled me closer.

"Please," she begged again.

I gave her everything, intent on having her come again. Soon I felt her catching the rhythm, her breathing quickened. She was squeezing me so tight, it felt like my dick was being strangled. I'd never felt anything half as good.

She whimpered as she got closer, and I felt a tingling at the base of my spine.

"Thank God," I groaned.

I began to move even faster and she met me stroke for stroke, as we hurled ever upwards. I wasn't going to last. In the moonlight, I saw her beautiful green eyes glow. I dipped in for another kiss that was like a punch to the gut.

"Lisa?" I was hanging on by my nails.

She thrust up against me. I felt her heels digging into my thighs. Her sheath tightened around me.

Then...

Then this *special* woman let out a blissful cry that was my name. She whispered and yelled and whispered my name again and again.

"Yes, Lisa. Yes."

I shot into a universe where just two of us lived.

A perfect paradise.

I was surprised to see that Roan was up before me. I was always the early bird, but I guessed it had something to do with his training. Then I smelled something heavenly, and it wasn't just coffee. I couldn't figure out what it was.

It smells really, really good.

Cookies?

Cake?

No, it didn't smell like a dessert. And he said he knew how to cook, so it wouldn't be a hot pocket, and anyway, this smelled much better than a hot pocket…

I got my happy ass up, found one of my nightshirts to put on, and found him in the kitchen. Unfortunately, he was dressed. All the way. Even in a shirt.

Bummer.

"Whatchya cooking?"

He pulled something out of the oven.

The smell wafted through the kitchen and almost knocked me over with its goodness.

"This, my dear, is a roasted red pepper, cheese, and spinach frittata."

"Spinach?"

"Spinach."

I watched as he put the pan on the stovetop. It smelled heavenly, but he'd said spinach. I walked over and put my arm around his waist and looked down at the pan. It looked really good. So much better than anything that had ever come out of my oven before. Come to think of it, this might have been the only time something *had* come out of my oven, since I only use my microwave.

I mean, cookie dough wasn't actually used for cooking cookies, Right? You ate that stuff right out of the plastic roll.

"I see the way you're eyeing this. It won't poison you," Roan teased.

I looked up and saw he was grinning down at me.

"Are you trying to get me to eat healthy?"

"Yes."

"Yes. Just yes. No subterfuge?"

"Yep. Jimmy told me how hard you work. Running on a crap diet must make that pretty hard. Just trying to help you out."

He got out a knife and started cutting the frittata.

"Did they teach you that in the Marines?"

"Yep."

I reached under his tee and pinched his waist. Not an inch of fat to be found. Nothing but muscle. "Guess healthy works for you."

He got down two plates and started serving up the food.

"Lisa, in case you haven't noticed, you turn me on. I think you're gorgeous, and I sure as hell don't want you to lose a single pound. As a matter of fact, I'm with Pearl; it wouldn't hurt for you to gain a little weight. I'm just thinking a vegetable here and there wouldn't hurt you."

"Now you're sounding like my dad."

"I can't wait to meet your dad."

I turned and did a faceplant into Roan's chest. "Oh, shit, you're going to meet my dad."

He tilted up my chin. "Is that going to be a problem? You've met mine."

"Yeah, but no guy I've slept with has ever met my dad."

Roan had the gall to laugh. "Then I'm honored. Come on, let's eat. We have a busy day."

I followed him into the dining room where I saw he had mugs of coffee and glasses of orange juice waiting.

Actually, this was not a bad way to wake up.

I sat down and took a bite of the eggs.

"This is delicious! You made this from scratch?"

Roan laughed again. "It wasn't that hard."

"But the kitchen was clean."

"Why wouldn't it be?"

"Because you made this from scratch, and it tastes amazing." I didn't wait for him to respond. I started digging into my food.

I was halfway done when I looked up and saw him staring at me.

"What?"

His lips curled up. "I'm thinking you're liking your vegetables."

"Hell yeah I am. This is great. I thought this kind of food was only available in restaurants."

"With all the different jobs you had, how did you not end up working in a restaurant?" Roan asked.

"Food never interested me, and the idea of serving the yammering masses never appealed."

"I guess I see your point."

"What about you? Do you regret staying in the Marines?"

"Nope. I can look back on a lot of different instances when I made a difference in people's lives. It was the right path for me."

I kept looking at him, I wasn't sure I wanted to go

there. But I was too damn into this man not to ask the question.

"But you were in for twenty years. Didn't you feel betrayed when you found out that some of the things our country asked you to do was based on bad intel?"

He put down his fork and took a sip of his coffee and then set down his mug. He looked me dead in the eye.

"Some people looked at it that way. I didn't. Bad intel or not, there was evil in the world. Real evil. I got to see up close and personal, the horror that some countries inflicted on their own people. I got to see what it was like when terrorists ran rampant. I know. I know, Lisa, that me and my team helped people. Saved people. I didn't sign up to look at things from a geo-political point of view. I signed up to protect and serve. I did that. I saved hundreds of Americans, and I made a positive difference in many, many non-American lives. That's a win in my book."

I shivered. I'd been deep in like with this man, but now? I was tipping over into love territory.

"Now eat up. Fred's going to be here soon. I don't want him to get an eyeful of you in that sleepshirt and a black thong."

"You can't possibly know I'm wearing my black thong," I protested.

"Sorry, Babe, but when you sat down, your shirt rode up. A guy notices these types of things."

I stared at him. "Really? You noticed that?"

"Damn right," he grinned as he picked up his fork.

"Wait a minute. Why is Fred coming over?"

"He's on the mend and he wants to see you protected."

"He's not sending one of his guys?" I asked.

"Nope." Roan looked at his wristwatch. "He should be here in twenty minutes. So, hurry up."

I hurried up.

19

Fred had been really apologetic when I called him to ask about Lisa's job. He'd been feeling better two days ago, but more of his crew had come down with the same bug, so he'd been out working on another job. When I told him what had happened, he'd dropped everything to come over and work on Lisa's alarm system.

While Lisa was doing laundry, I also had a chance to discuss with Fred the package that he would be installing. I was happy to hear that she was buying the top of the line.

"But if she's got some guy pulling this kind of shit, you and I both know a security system isn't what she needs. She needs someone to stop this fucker."

I nodded.

"I meant to give her Simon Clark's info, but things just got away from me. I brought his card."

Fred handed me a white card printed on heavy cardstock.

Simon Clark

Security

His telephone number and email were on the back of the card.

"Damn, Fred, I think my dad mentioned this guy, and I think I ran into him at the grocery store. Former SEAL, right?"

"He was a commander."

I whistled.

"Yeah. He's been out for a year and a half. I think he's worked on three jobs."

"Like what?"

"I have no idea. He's just taken three vacations without his wife and daughter. That tells me he's taken three cases."

"That makes sense," I nodded. "Let me talk to Lisa."

"I'm going to be at this for another six hours."

"Understood."

I wandered back to the laundry room and found Lisa wearing her yoga pants and a pink T-shirt that had the words, *Our Ink Tells Your Story*, floating out of a book.

"Did you come up with that design?" I asked.

"What? I didn't hear you come in."

"I asked if you came up with that design."

She looked down at her shirt. "Yeah, that's one of mine."

"I don't see any drawings or paintings around here."

"I have a couple of sketchbooks lying around here somewhere."

"I'd love to see them."

Her face lit up. "You would?"

"Absolutely. After all, you ate my food."

She giggled. "I'll let you look at my etchings and I'll do your laundry if you keep cooking."

"You have a deal."

She came over and put her arms around my waist and looked up at me. "How much longer is Fred going to be here?"

"He said six hours."

"Bummer."

"I concur. However, there's something else we can do. He gave me Simon Clark's card. He's a former Navy SEAL that Dad recommended I talk to. I'm pretty sure I saw him at the grocery store. His card says he does security."

Lisa's laugh caught me off-guard.

"Why are you laughing?"

She didn't stop. She grabbed me tighter and kept laughing.

"Baby, what is so damn funny?"

"Simon. Trenda. Husband."

She kept laughing.

"Lisa?"

Finally, her laughter quieted down to giggles. When the giggles stopped, she looked up at me. "My best friend here in town. I keep calling her Trenda Avery, cause it's easier. She's one of the Avery sisters. She's really Trenda Clark. She's married to Simon. This is hysterical. She told me that he was doing some private investigations, security, secret stuff that if she told me about it she'd have to kill me. No wonder Fred was recommending him."

"If Fred was recommending him, why didn't you call him?"

"He only said something about some guy."

"Well, let's call him. I have his number."

"Let me just call Trenda. I have *her* number on speed

dial. Plus, we can probably just go over to her house. That'll get us out of Fred's hair."

"Lisa, in case you haven't noticed, Fred doesn't have any hair."

"Ooooh. You're observant. Maybe you should be a private eye, too."

I couldn't get a handle on the man, but I liked his wife. His daughter was cute. She'd definitely made an impression from my time at the grocery store. The other woman, Maddie, who picked their daughter up to go to the park, she seemed nice as well.

"Why didn't you tell me about all of this?" Trenda asked.

"I mentioned the flooded backyard, remember?" Lisa said.

"Oh yeah. It was when Bella was in the school play and I was doing costumes. Now I remember. Whenever I thought about it, I remembered the part where you had that big septic bill. But you never told me you contacted the sheriff's department."

"I was too aggravated. Plus, I knew you'd go over there and raise hell, and I didn't want you to do that."

"Why not?"

I looked over at Lisa to see how she would respond.

"I don't know. I just didn't want to get any special treatment, I guess."

Trenda sighed. "I could see that."

"Are you going to be okay with us working on this for you, Lisa?" Simon asked.

Simon got it. Lisa had trouble taking any kind of help or being treated in any special way.

Lisa smiled at him. "Not if you're working for me. No, then that's fine."

Trenda returned her smile. "If you think my husband is going to charge you for finding some kind of crazy stalker who is putting bloody skulls on your porch and stabbing rats into the side of your house, you've got another think coming."

"Trenda, be reasonable—" Lisa started.

"She's right," Simon interrupted. "There doesn't seem to be a lot to go on. So, I'm not sure that I'm going to be putting in much time."

"And anyway," I said. "I can help, can't I?" I asked Simon.

"Roan, after spending a little time with my wife, I don't think it is going to come as too much of a surprise that she asked me to check you out on behalf of her friend, will it?"

"No," I said as I smiled.

Lisa moved even closer to me on the couch and put her hand over mine. "Roan. You have to believe me, I did not ask her to do that."

I looked down at her. "I know that."

"How could you know that?" Trenda asked.

Simon chuckled. "Honey, I gotta say, that was a pretty easy call for Roan to make."

"Are you saying it's obvious I'm a busybody?"

"I'm not going to answer on the grounds that it would definitely incriminate me."

Trenda threw back her head and laughed.

I liked that. I liked that a lot. For both of them. They were sitting together on the loveseat. His ankle was crossed over his knee, his arm was thrown over the back of the seat, and Trenda was snuggled up beside him. Add the cute little girl to the mix? Yep, I definitely liked what they had going on.

Simon cleared his throat. "Back to the matter at hand. I did a little digging. You definitely have some of the skills that I would want working with me. How much tech knowledge do you have?"

"Five years ago, I worked on something that was intense cyber-security. I wasn't point. Not by any means. But I worked on the project and I picked up a few things."

The right corner of his mouth curled up. "A few things, huh?"

"Yep." He was correctly reading between the lines. He realized I knew a hell of a lot.

"Did you stay up to date with the new technologies?"

"Not for the last year and a half," I admitted. "My team had gone dark, and we were working on something that wasn't cyber-related."

"Gotcha. I notice that you're favoring your right shoulder. How badly were you injured?"

"Nothing hit bone. But they operated on my bursa and tendons."

Simon nodded.

"I hear you were a commander. East or West?" I asked Simon.

"Did both. Ended on the East Coast."

"Did you work with Trenda's brother?"

"Drake Avery was hard to miss." Simon chuckled.

"So, you still kept your finger in the pie?"

He nodded. "I liked to feel useful from time to time."

Okay, now I had a bead on the man and I liked him. I could work with him.

"Now that you all spoke man-military-speak, how much do you charge?" Lisa asked Simon.

"I'm going to be working on this, Baby," I told Lisa. "Simon is going to be supervising me."

Simon nodded. "That's right. You're going to have to negotiate a fee with Roan without me present."

Trenda started laughing again.

"That doesn't sound right to me," Lisa protested.

"Lisa, let's drop it for now. We need to start working on this problem while the lead is fresh. Okay?"

She nodded at me. "Okay. But don't think I'm dropping this."

"I wouldn't dream of it. Now, last night you mentioned the spigot being on, the live rat being stabbed against the side of your house, your flowers being poisoned—"

"You believe me about the flowers?"

"Of course I do. You don't strike me as the type of woman who wouldn't figure out the right way to plant flowers before planting them. When did this happen?"

"August."

"So that was the first thing that happened?"

"Yeah. Then my groceries were stolen off my porch, the water spigot—"

""That's right, your groceries were stolen! I remember now." I recalled Trenda talking about it waiting in line at the grocery store.

Lisa looked at me. "Sure, I did. Or maybe I didn't. Last night was kind of a blur. Anyway, after the spigot, that happened in September, my groceries were stolen off my porch. It was a big order, about a hundred dollars' worth."

"Lisa, this is important, can you try to think of dates for me?" Simon asked.

She got up off the couch and grabbed her phone

from her purse on the kitchen counter. "Hold on. I should be able to. I should be able to look up receipts for the plant purchases, the septic services, and the groceries." We all waited, and then she gave us the dates.

"August twenty-ninth for the plants. September twenty-fifth for the spigot. November eleventh for the groceries. November twenty-eighth for the tires. December fourth for the rat and December ninth for the skull," she finished.

"Shit," Simon murmured.

"That about sums it up," I agreed.

"What?" Trenda asked.

"He's escalating, Honey."

I pulled Lisa in closer. I didn't like the sound of this. "Simon, Lisa sometimes works as a tattoo artist. She told me that I would be surprised how often she tattoos skulls onto people."

Simon leaned forward. "You don't say."

I looked down at Lisa. "Honey, have you ever tattooed someone with a skull that had a dagger going through its head?"

"Sure."

That took me by surprise.

"Ewww. That's gross. Why would someone want that?" Trenda wanted to know.

"Well, if it is just the skull itself, it's supposed to mean fragility and living life to the fullest. But a lot of people are getting it because it's on trend. Those people are going to regret it in a few years."

"But why a dagger?" I asked.

"Sometimes it just means death, don't get me wrong. But mostly it means bravery and protection. The most common meaning is to be ready to face anything without fear."

"I still vote against it," Trenda piped up.

"I agree with you," Simon smiled. "I don't want you to get a skull tattoo."

"But I could probably draw something up for you that you would like," Lisa teased.

I looked down at the teasing woman by my side and grinned in amazement. How could she find humor in all of this? She was something else.

No. She's special.

"Do you think this might be a representation of a tattoo you've done in the past?" Simon asked me.

I closed my eyes, trying to remember what I had seen last night. "I don't know. I didn't get a clear look at it. But I guess it could be possible."

"I have pictures of last night's skull. As long as you can handle looking at them," Roan said gently.

I tried to stop from shivering but it must not have worked, because Roan started to rub my arm, then he kissed the top of my head.

I held out my hand. "Give me your phone."

"Actually, why don't you email them to me? That way we can see it up on my computer screen."

"Wait til you see the setup he has in his man-cave," Trenda practically cooed. "It's almost as good as my monitor for graphics."

I watched as Roan took his phone out and sorted through his pictures and then emailed them.

"How'd you know his email address?" I whispered.

"It was on his business card. I put it into my contacts."
Definitely OCD.

"Sent," Roan said and offered his hand to help me up off the couch. I took it, then we followed Simon and Trenda out of their great room to a door that led to Simon's office. Trenda wasn't kidding. It looked like something NASA might have.

"Make yourself at home," Simon said as he sat down in front of three monitors.

"He had a friend of his, Gideon Smith, come and hook everything up for him," Trenda told us. "Then Gideon came and set up my computer and Bella's too. He does computers for his SEAL team."

"He does a little more than that," Simon muttered at his computer screen.

"I figured that out, Simon," Trenda said acerbically. "But you wouldn't let the poor man say practically anything. I thought you were going to have an aneurysm when he told me he worked with Renzo's brother, Jace."

"You were supposed to be over at Evie's that day," Simon said as he pulled up his email.

"If you hung out with Evie and Aiden, you'd be much more relaxed. He tells *her* things."

"He'd better not."

"It's okay. Not the mission-y stuff, only the problems that aren't mission-y."

"You mean the stuff I wasn't supposed to hear," he muttered again.

A bloody skull popped up on his screen, and I let out a squeak. Roan immediately moved his office chair close to me and grabbed my hand. I held on for dear life.

20

I really didn't want Lisa to be doing this. It'd scared the fuck out of me when she had shrieked, but she'd pulled it together almost immediately.

"Can you zoom in closer?" Lisa asked as she bent over Simon's shoulder.

"Is that a real skull?" Trenda asked.

"I'm almost one hundred percent sure it's not, but the sheriff's department will let us know in the next two or three days," Simon answered.

"It doesn't look like one," I agreed. "It's too white. Too perfect. No fractures. The teeth look too good. I'm guessing this is something that's been manufactured."

"Oh, that makes sense," Trenda nodded. "I'm sure these days, with 3-D printing and things, they're making them all the time."

"You'd be right, Honey." Simon nodded to his wife, then he turned to Lisa. "Is this where you wanted me to zoom in?"

"Closer to the eye socket. If the skull is fake, do you think the blood is fake?"

"Probably. It's probably something that you would buy at the Halloween store, right Simon?" Trenda asked her husband.

"Is this the spot?" Simon asked Lisa.

"Yes. Right there."

Simon hadn't answered Trenda's question about the blood. I'd already told him that it was real. I saw it and smelled it. You never mistake real blood for any other thing.

"What are you seeing?" I asked Lisa.

"Do you see that little bit of black under the blood around the eye socket? It peeks out on the left, then again underneath the socket. See?"

I nodded. "I see it," Simon said.

"It's barbed wire. And then there's the dagger. That dagger definitely looks like one I drew for a guy up in Elkton, Virginia. I was always doing ink for kids who went to James Madison University. Can you zoom in on that, Simon?"

He did. We all looked at it.

"Zoom in on the quillon."

"What's a quillon?" Trenda asked.

"It's this piece right here. It separates the blade from the handle of a sword or a dagger to protect your hand from getting hurt," Simon explained.

"Look at that. Do you see that big green gemstone in the middle?" Lisa asked as she pointed. "It's pasted onto the dagger. It's got to have come from some beading section of a craft store. I'm almost positive I know who I created this tattoo for."

"Just from this?" I asked Lisa. "How?"

"It was this really quiet guy. But he was sweet. One of the things he wanted was this jewel in the middle of the quillon, and he wanted it to be the same color as my eyes."

Trenda grimaced. "That wasn't sweet. It has creep factor written all over it."

"Not with him, Trenda. Seriously. He was this guy who was working on his PhD in philosophy. He wouldn't hurt a fly."

"You told me you had to leave Elkton. Something about itchy feet. But it was more than that, wasn't it?" I pressed. I watched her carefully. I saw her shift once. Twice. Yep. I was right.

"Lisa…" I coaxed.

"Okay, after working at the tattoo parlor for a month, the guy who owned it started to ask me out. He was chill about it at first, so I just declined and didn't think anything of it. But then he started making uncomfortable comments."

"Like what?" Trenda asked before I could.

"Little stuff. Things that I shouldn't have let bother me, but I did."

"Give me an example, Lisa," I asked softly.

She looked up at me and bit her bottom lip. "Okay. He suggested that I should learn how to do piercings because he wanted a Prince Albert."

I cringed. For so many reasons.

"What did you tell him?"

"I said I had a toolbox in my car with a Phillips screwdriver that might do the job."

Simon let out a laugh.

"He actually said that to you? He wanted you to pierce his penis?" Trenda asked.

"I think he really wanted her to play with his johnson," I corrected Trenda.

"Yeah, that was my take on it," Lisa nodded. Her frown lines were back.

"Anything else?" Simon asked.

"It went downhill from there. I lasted five months. I wouldn't have lasted that long, except his pregnant girlfriend, Raylene, worked a lot of the same hours I did. That put a crimp in Lonny's ability to be gross."

"Why stay at all?" I asked.

"Because it was spring and I was in the Shenandoah Valley. It was beautiful. I was pulling in good coin, and I could hike with a great group of women from James Madison University."

"Did he have a skull tattoo?" Trenda asked.

"Lonny? Nope, he was into tribal design tattoos. But while I was there, I bet I did over ten of them."

"But only one with a green gem in the quillon, right?" Simon clarified.

"That's right," I nodded. "And before you ask, no, I don't have his contact information. I wasn't impressed enough with the final product to put it up on my online portfolio, so I never had him sign a waiver. But Lonny over at the tattoo shop should have it. The shop is called Lonny's Tattoo Parlor. Real original, right? I should have taken that as a sign."

"I've got this. I'll go have a conversation with Lonny," I said to no one in particular.

"The shop isn't open on Sundays," Lisa told us.

"Do you have his phone number?" I asked.

"I might. I might have deleted it though after I blocked him."

"He continued to call you after you left?" Simon wanted to know.

"Yeah. He kept saying he would increase my pay. But

the thing was, I worked like someone in a salon. I rented my chair and space from him, then I collected all the money that my clients paid me."

"What about the tools?" Trenda asked.

"I have those, they were mine. I wouldn't work with someone else's tools. Most tattoo artists are really particular like that."

"Baby, check your phone," I urged.

She looked down at her phone and scrolled. "Oh, it's here. I guess that makes sense. My phone would have to know which number it was supposed to block." She rattled off the number for me and I called it.

A recorded voice said it was out of service.

When I explained that, Lisa was perplexed. "Lonny did half of his business from his cell phone. That's really weird."

"I'll talk to him face-to-face tomorrow when I drop in for a visit."

"Don't you think you should talk to him on the phone, first?" Lisa questioned.

"No," Simon said.

I knew I liked the man.

"Simon's right, Lisa. This is a conversation that needs to take place in person. I want to see if he has anything to hide. I won't be able to see that if we're just talking on the phone."

She nodded.

"I also need the name of the man who you gave that tattoo."

"I remember his name was Paul. I'm pretty sure his last name started with the letter 'M', but don't hold me to it. Like I said, Lonny will have all that paperwork. Besides getting his PhD, Paul was also working as a grad student over at the university. He was teaching classes of his own. That's what he was hoping to do when he graduated, teach at the university level."

"Okay, I'll also check him out at James Madison," I said. "I might be gone overnight. This time I really want you to stay at Dad's house."

"But I'll have the security system by then."

"It's either stay with Warren, or you're our houseguest," Simon told her.

Yep, he was definitely a guy I could work with.

When I pulled up to the address for Lonny's Tattoo Parlor, all I saw was a construction site. They were building something from the ground up. When I got out of my truck and got closer, I saw that the store to the right had recent repairs done to the right side of their building. I walked down the sidewalk the other way, and saw that on the left side of that building there were singe marks. I was not getting a good feeling.

"You thinking about buying?" A guy in jeans, T-shirt and a toolbelt asked as he left the building site and walked over to where I was standing. He held out his hand. "My name is Cy. I bought this property. I'm going to look to sell or lease when I've finished building it back up." I shook his hand.

"No. A friend of mine used to work here at Lonny's. She left about a year and a half ago. She told me if I was ever close to Elkton, I should definitely stop by and say 'hey.'"

"Oh, shit. So, your friend doesn't know about the fire and Lonny."

I shook my head.

"It was bad. The cops think that Lonny didn't die of smoke inhalation, but that he was burned alive. The investigation showed that he had boxes blocking the back door, so he couldn't get out."

"Damn. When did this happen?"

"About a year and a half ago."

Right after Lisa left town.

"My friend mentioned Lonny's girlfriend was pregnant. She worked there. She's all right, isn't she?"

"Hold on." He walked back to the front of the construction site. "Willy. Come over here, this guy wants to know some things about Lonny." I looked over to see some guy climbing off some scaffolding.

"He and Lonny used to smoke a lot of weed together. Willy's cleaned up his act after the fire. The fire chief ruled this as arson, but a lot of us think that Lonny was high and burned hisself up."

"Whatchya need, boss?"

Willy was a young, good-looking guy. Looked like a model for some clothing catalogue. I wondered if Lonny looked like that.

"This gentleman here. What was your name?"

"Roan Thatcher," I supplied.

"Roan here, he has a friend who knew Lonny. The friend didn't know about him dying in the fire. Now he's asking about Raylene."

"No offense, man. But who's your friend?" Willy asked suspiciously.

"Lisa Reynolds. She used to work here."

Willy whistled. "Well, shit. I know Lisa. She's prime. You doing her?"

I resisted the urge to punch him in the throat.

"Like I said, she's a friend," I ground out. "Anyway, I was on my way to the University to drop off some papers, and she said I should stop by and say 'hey' to Lonny. Then I see this. It's going to come as a real blow to her."

Willy paled. "It did to all of us. Lonny was chill."

"Lisa talked a lot about Raylene. She'd want me to check in on her. I'll call Lisa. I'm betting she'd want me to take Raylene some flowers. Hell, knowing Lisa, she'd want me to take a baby gift. What did she have, a girl or a boy?"

Willy's eyes got wet. "A girl. The sweetest little thing. She named her Londa. You're right, Lisa would do exactly what you're saying. Let me get you her information."

He pulled his phone out of his back pocket.

When I got back to my truck, my first call was to Simon.

21

Thank God for Bella. If it wasn't for her, I would have been a wreck. Roan didn't want to give me any details about the fire and Lonny's death. I know he was just trying to wait until he got back to town, but I didn't let him get away with it. I'd never had a panic attack in my life until I saw that head on my doorstep.

Okay, it was a skull.

But there I was at Trenda's house, having another one in front of Bella as soon as Roan said it was probably arson. That meant that Lonny was murdered.

"Honey, you need to put your head between your knees and breathe in through your nose, hold it, then slowly breathe out through your mouth."

"Why does she have to do that, Mama?" Bella asked.

"You do it too, Munchkin. It will help you relax. Hop up onto the couch beside Lisa and do what I say," she told Bella.

"I want you to slowly breathe in through your nose. Hold it. Then slowly release your breath through your mouth."

I was starting to feel better. It was like the twisty panic in my stomach was being released from my body every time I expelled a breath.

"Again, my girls."

"This feels good, Mama."

"Keep doing it, Bella. You too, Lisa."

I did it one more time, then lifted my head. I took a deep breath and sat up, then released the air through my mouth. "Okay, I'm good now," I told my friend.

"Of course you are," Trenda smiled.

"Me too. Can we do this every day?" Bella asked.

Trenda smiled at her daughter. "Maybe we can learn how to meditate together, how about that?"

"What's meditate?"

"I'll show you tomorrow. Let me talk to Lisa in private. Okay?"

"Okay," Bella chirped. "I'll go to my room and play on my iPad."

"How about you read a book instead," Trenda suggested.

"On my iPad," Bella rejoined with a twinkle in her eye.

"Yes, smarty-pants. On your iPad."

I watched Bella skip down the hallway, then turned to Trenda. "I need to call Roan back."

"Why?"

"He wants to go visit Lonny's girlfriend, but he wanted to talk to me first. After hearing about the fire, I couldn't talk anymore. I'm sure he's worried about me."

"I'm sure he is. But I bet he's on the phone with Simon right this very minute."

"Oh. I wouldn't want to interrupt."

"Haven't you figured it out? You're Roan's top priority. Call him."

"Where's my phone?"

Trenda and I both looked around, then I spotted it between the couch cushions. I called Roan, and he answered on the second ring.

"Baby, are you all right?"

"Yeah. It was just a mild panic attack. Trenda talked me through it. You wanted to talk about Raylene?"

"Yeah. Since Lonny's dead, she's the best lead we've got."

I whimpered at the phrase, 'Lonny's dead' and Roan paused.

"I'm really sorry. I know it's tough," he whispered.

"It's okay. I'll mourn later. Keep going."

"Lonny is no longer a stalker suspect. He wasn't alive when everything happened. I was really hoping that we could have found out about your grad student from Lonny's records, but he's not here to ask, and everything else was lost in the fire. I don't suppose he had a business partner or an office manager?"

"No, just Raylene."

"That's what I guessed. I found out where she's living. Right now, she's staying with her parents. She's our only hope of finding business records. I was hoping you could tell me the best way to approach her."

"I should do it. I'll drive up there."

"No. I'm here. If I can something from her, I'll go straight to the university. I thought that on your behalf I could bring belated flowers and a baby gift. Maybe while I'm there, you could get on the phone, sympathize with her a bit. Then we just lay it all out. You explain about the skull and everything, and we ask for the records. No need for subterfuge, right?"

"You're right."

"Okay, tell me how to get in the door."

"Raylene isn't the flowers type. She wouldn't want something that would die in a week. Take her a really bushy plant, or better yet, a bonsai. Did she have a girl or a boy?"

"She had a girl. She named her Londa."

I whimpered. "That is beautiful. Lonny would have loved that." I paused, trying to think. "There's a cute store in town called Treasure Chest. After you go to Arlene's Florist and pick up the bonsai, the clerk at Treasure Chest will have something waiting at the front."

I didn't know what, but I'd figure out something. Hopefully, Treasure Chest had a webpage.

"Thanks. I'll call you when I'm at her parent's house."

"Be safe."

"Honey, I'm going to visit a woman and her baby, nothing's going to happen to me."

"Yeah, but somebody burned Lonny alive. So be safe."

"I will, I promise."

I hung up the phone and looked at Trenda. "I think I'm going to have another panic attack. I need to get out of the house."

"I hate to admit it, but I'm on a deadline. I'm going to be a lousy hostess for the next five or six hours."

"Could I kidnap your daughter? That would take my mind off everything."

"She's sunshine in a bottle, that's for sure. Any idea where you would go?"

"You know who else needs sunshine in a bottle?" I asked.

Trenda shook her head.

"Millie Randolph."

"I don't know. The only person she's let over to her

house, besides repair people and the like, has been you. God knows my sisters and I have tried to get in there."

"I've got in, so I go over there every week now. She's really loosened up. I'm almost one hundred percent positive she will let me in with Bella in tow."

"Just so long as Bella's feelings don't get hurt."

"I promise I'll finesse it so she won't be hurt if Millie says no. But I know that won't happen."

"Okay."

"But first I need to go online shopping for a baby gift. Well, actually a toddler gift."

"Really?" Trenda's eyes lit up. "Can I help?"

"What about your deadline?"

"There's always time to shop."

After I talked to Lisa I went to pick up the plant, and then found Treasure Chest. When I got there, it was just the kind of shop I abhorred. Every nook and cranny was filled with so many knickknacks I could hardly breathe, let alone move.

I went to the register and opened my mouth to greet the woman behind the counter.

"Hi, you must be Roan Thatcher," she said.

"Lisa must have called you, but how did you know it was me?"

"I don't get many men who come into the shop in the middle of the day. Also, she explained how handsome you are," the woman said with a wicked smile.

"I think Lisa is a little bit prejudiced."

"I think she is spot on." The woman winked. She reminded me of Blessing from the USO.

"Anyway, here is the gift for Londa. Raylene has actually been in the shop and looked at this before, so I know this is what she wanted to buy." She held up the ugliest teddy bear I had ever seen. It was two feet high and made out of burlap. Its eyes were crossed, it was missing an arm, and it had on clown shoes.

"Are you sure?" I asked.

"I'm positive. One of the local artists makes these. She's a single mother and her daughter loves them. I kind of felt sorry for her, so I said I would sell them. I tucked them on the floor, out of sight, but little kids keep finding them and moms keep buying them. So yes. This is what Raylene wants."

I took out my wallet.

"Don't worry, Lisa already paid. I gave her a discount, so it was less than a hundred dollars."

I thought my eyes would bug out of my head. The woman saw my reaction and laughed. "Mr. Thatcher, you have to remember, these are homemade."

"Huh?" I still couldn't get over the price tag. I didn't care if it was made with diamonds, why someone would pay over a hundred dollars for something this ugly, was beyond me.

"Let me put a bow on him, and you'll be ready to go."

"Thank you."

I made my way over to Raylene's parents' house and found out the clerk at Treasure Chest knew her shit. The teddy bear was a hit, but the call between Raylene and Lisa was painful. They commiserated with one another a bit about Lonny's death, before Lisa started laying out the situation. When she did, the woman immediately wanted to help. But after that she hustled me out of the house. Even after all this time, I could tell she was still hurting pretty badly about Lonny. As soon as I got into my truck, I called Simon.

"We caught a break," I said to Simon after I left Raylene.

"Yeah?"

"Yeah. Raylene acted as Lonny's office manager. She had everything in QuickBooks. She was able to pull up all the clients that Lisa worked on. Three clients had tattoos with daggers through their skull. Only one was named Paul. His last name is Matushka. I intended to go over to the university, but then I figure with your setup, you can track him down for me, so there's no need for me to even bother getting a class schedule."

Simon laughed. "You've got that right. Go grab lunch or something. I'll have everything on this guy, including his blood type, as soon as you're done."

It felt really good to be working on this, and working with Simon.

I picked up some drive-thru and decided to eat in my car while calling Dad.

"Hi, son. What's going on?"

I filled him in on everything that had happened since he'd left Lisa's house late Saturday night.

"You sure don't let moss grow under your feet."

I laughed. "I try not to."

"Do you like Simon?"

"I really do."

"Think you might like to work with him?"

It took a moment for me to gather my thoughts. "First, there's no offer on the table. But yeah, he's definitely a man I would have wanted on my team, or leading it."

"And Lisa?"

"Dad, that's just too soon to tell. We've only gone on two official dates."

"Seems to me you've spent a lot of quality time with her." Dad emphasized the word quality.

"Don't get me wrong, I have. But this is still new."

He sighed. "I hear you. Just take care of my girl."

"Just because I said it was new, doesn't mean you can horn in on *my* girl."

Dad chuckled. "Are you coming home tonight?"

"Depends on when Simon gets me the information I need, and how soon I can track down this Paul Matushka guy."

"Drive safe, either way."

"I will."

It was two hours later when Simon called me. I was a quarter of the way through another Carl Hiaasen book.

"Whatchya got?" I asked as soon as I answered.

"I got nothing." Simon sounded frustrated as fuck.

"Nothing?"

"Nothing. After I came up empty, I called Gideon; he's one of the best cyber guys I know. His team isn't deployed at the moment. I had him do a search. There are plenty of Paul Matushkas out there, but nobody affiliated with James Madison University."

"So he was entirely made up?"

"Yep."

"All we have to go on is Lisa's tattoo?"

"We're going to need her to draw a sketch of him."

"Fuck," I sighed.

"That about sums it up," Simon agreed.

22

I was sitting in Simon's office and was feeling both pissed and dejected. I'd really had high hopes for the facial recognition play off of Lisa's sketch. So had Simon. It had been two weeks since we'd come up empty handed and I was on edge.

"There are two variables. The accuracy of the sketch and if the guy is in the system. From what you've told us, Lisa is a pretty good artist," Gideon Smith said. Simon and I were in front of his monitors. They were filled with seven people. Four SEALs, two wives of SEALs, and a fiancée of a SEAL. We'd been Skyping with them off and on for the last few days, and Simon and I had both been impressed.

"I knew they kept shit from me," Simon had groused one night when we were on his deck in front of a fire, having a beer. "I've always thought that we'd have women SEALs, and low and behold we do."

I laughed. He was right. Riley, Jada and Lydia were sharp. They caught things that their men didn't.

"Lisa isn't just a pretty good artist, she's excellent," I responded to Gideon. "Remember the drawing she did of

Riley after just seeing her on Skype the one time? She said she worked on this guy's tattoo in three sessions, totaling ten hours. I'm going to say her drawing was accurate."

I might have come off kind of strong. Especially the way Dex and Kane started laughing.

"We've got it," Gideon said. "It's not the drawing."

"So, we've scoured every official and non-official place where his face could have been caught on camera, and we came up empty. The guy's a ghost."

"I'm not going to believe we can't find him."

"It happens sometimes. You just have to wait for his next move," Dex said. "Trust me, I've been in your situation. My wife was targeted by a psycho."

Jada tilted her head. "You know..." Jada said really slowly.

"Spit it out," Kane commanded.

"Hey," Gideon said sharply. "You don't yell at my woman, and I won't yell at yours. How about that?"

"You were saying, Jada?" I prompted.

"We haven't done a search on his tattoo. Betchya he's pretty proud of that thing. There's a good chance he's posting photos on social media. What's more, we don't have to depend on a sketch by Lisa, she took a picture of the final product."

I watched as all seven faces on the screen started to grin, and I mean *grin*.

"Not only will I never yell at your wife again, I will be sending her flowers," Kane told Gideon.

"Me too," Riley chimed in.

"Me three," Dex shouted.

"If anyone is sending Jada anything it will be me," I interrupted all of the talking.

"Everybody just take it down a notch," Jada said. The

only one I want rewarding me is my man. And trust me, it won't be flowers," Jada purred.

There were some pained expressions, but also some hoots and hollers and laughter.

These are good people.

"Let's reconvene after Christmas," Simon spoke up.

"Unless we find something," Kane pointed out.

"Of course," Simon agreed.

"Yeah, I've got a lot of cooking to do," I said. "I'll talk to you after the holidays. And let's make our next meeting after the new year. Lisa's dad and granddad are due in tonight."

"Sounds good," Gideon said.

We all wished one another Merry Christmas and Happy New Year, then Simon shut off the feed.

"I like your team," I told Simon.

"I hate using them. But this is too important not to. They all volunteer their time. This is the first time all seven of them were available at the same time. So, you're meeting her family, huh? Big step." Simon looked over at me, his expression curious.

"She told me I was the first guy she slept with who's met her dad."

"Then it's a really big step."

"She's skittish. I get the feeling she runs when things get too deep."

"Trenda's mentioned that," Simon nodded.

I picked up my mug of coffee from the desk. "I'm just lucky that she's entrenched in Thatcher's."

"What about you? Are you going to run?"

The question caught me by surprise, but it shouldn't have. "My dream has always been to move back to Jasper Creek and work with Dad at the shop. But he and I have talked. I think that was a dream that I had as a teenager, that's not who I am today."

"Who are you today?"

"A protector."

Simon set down his mug. "Yep. That's how I see it."

"How do you know it isn't just because I'm protecting Lisa?"

"I know because you're a lot like me. Protecting people is in your blood."

I chuckled. "There's worse things in the world than being like you."

Simon shrugged. "I feel good about where we're going now on the investigation. I think we'll come up with something."

"Your voice to God's ear."

I pulled my Charger up to Millie's front door. I looked over at Bella. "You ready?"

"I'm ready. Do you think she'll like my present?"

"I'm positive she will."

"What about the cookies we baked?"

"Lovebug, I didn't help much. It was really more you and Roan."

"But you put on the frosting, and they're really pretty now. Even the ones you burned."

"I threw those away," I told her.

"But those were good. I like things that are black and crispy."

"I knew I liked you, kid." She was so cute, but she was going to turn into a beauty. *I wonder how Simon's going to handle it when she starts to date.*

Millie's front door opened. She was wearing a poofy jacket and was waving at us to come in.

"Stay in your seat, and I'll help you carry everything in, okay?" I told Bella. She had everything in her lap. She'd insisted on holding everything on the drive over.

As soon as we climbed the stairs, Bella started talking.

"We brought you presents. I made some of the presents. I had to start over on one of them. Can we have hot chocolate? Lisa brought some in case you didn't have any, so don't worry. Can I see your greenhouse today? I like looking at all your baby plants. Do you have a Christmas tree? Do you want to come over to Lisa's house for Christmas? Her dad and granddad are going to be there, and don't worry, she's not going to cook, Roan is."

Millie was giggling, which was so nice to see.

When Bella took a breath, Millie said. "Hold on, let me answer some of your questions, but only when you're both inside."

We followed Millie into her house. It had all hardwood floors, and the walls were painted a very soft shade of blue that made her leafy-green-patterned sofa and chairs pop. She might've been a recluse, but she had made her nest a gorgeous place to hang out in.

"Give her the presents, Lisa. Give her the presents." Bella was jumping up and down.

I knew Trenda wouldn't like her behavior, so...

"Let's calm down a bit, okay, Bella?"

"All right."

I thought back to what Trenda would say next.

"How were you behaving?"

I watched her tilt her head and consider my question.

"It was rude that I was bossing you around. I'm sorry."

"That's okay. But let's follow Millie and have a nice visit

and do things nice and slow and savor our time with one another."

"Savor?"

"It means relax and enjoy."

"And have hot chocolate," Millie said.

"Well hell to the yes!" I agreed.

"You owe me a dollar," Bella put out her hand and I sighed.

"How much money do you have in your savings account now?" I asked as I pulled my wallet out of my purse and pulled out a dollar for swearing.

"Mama says for an in-state college, I have enough to pay for my freshman year. But I want to go to Stanford."

"California? Why? That's so far away." Millie looked horrified.

"I want to be near the Pacific Ocean and scuba dive."

"Okay," Millie shrugged.

"Oh yeah, and I also want to work my way up in Silicon Valley until I'm the richest woman in the world and then I can give all my money away and nobody ever has to go hungry again."

"Why limit yourself to being the richest woman?" I asked. "Why not go for being the richest person in the world?"

Bella tilted her head to the side and put her finger to her chin. "You're right. I want to be the richest person in the world. Now can we savor our hot chocolate?"

"Sure thing, lovebug."

The scary thing was, I could see her living her dream.

"Are you sure your dad won't mind letting my dad stay at his house?" I asked for like the fiftieth time.

"I'm absolutely positive." Roan was driving Jimmy Maddox's SUV to pick up my dad and grandad from the airport. I figured that should give us enough room for their luggage and for my relatives to sit comfortably.

"And it won't bother you to have Granddad in the kitchen helping you cook?"

"Not at all."

"He can be kind of bossy," I warned.

"Seriously, Lisa, it's all going to be fine."

His long arm crossed over the counsel and grabbed my hand. It felt good.

"Do you need to put your head between your legs?" he teased.

"Smartass," Lisa chuckled. "Okay, it'll be fine."

We were waiting at the bottom of the down escalator when my dad and granddad got through the secure area. I was practically jumping up and down. When my dad pulled me in for a huge hug, I felt like I was home.

"How about me? Am I chopped liver?" Granddad asked.

"Granddad!" I cried.

He pulled me in even tighter than dad had. When he let me go, I stepped back and put my arm around Roan's waist. "This is Roan Thatcher. He's the man I've been telling you about."

Both Dad and Granddad gave us genuine smiles. "We've heard a lot of great things about you," Dad said as he held out his hand. "What's even better is how happy my daughter sounds when she talks about you."

I love my dad!

"The same goes for me," Granddad said. "The only

difference is, she writes me letters. But her happiness does come shining through."

"Well, let's get your bags before someone takes them by mistake. This place is a madhouse."

"Well, you didn't want us to come too early. So that's why you have to endure picking us up the day before Christmas," my granddad admonished.

He was right. As usual.

23

Except for one big hairy monster, things were coming up aces. I couldn't believe how many people I was putting on my 'A' list. First there was Simon and his SEAL buddies, then there were the Avery sisters, and now Lisa's dad and granddad. I might be giving up my dream of Thatcher's, but it looked like I might be starting another dream.

Everybody had loved Christmas dinner the day before, and now we were all over at Trenda and Simon's house. Lisa told me she wanted to show me off to the rest of the Avery sisters. It was bad enough she said that. It was worse that she actually meant it.

My dad and Lisa's dad were getting along like a house on fire, and her granddad had mingling down to an art form. There wasn't one woman in the great room who he hadn't managed to charm. Right now, he was sitting on one of the loveseats with Bella sitting on his knee. He had even made her a Shirley Temple.

I saw Griff and Lesley near the fireplace. They were sipping hot toddies and people-watching. It was nice to know what had delayed Griff.

Lesley.

And she was definitely worth the delay.

She also had a big ole diamond ring on her finger. Talk about no moss growing under one's feet. Griff had just met her four months ago. I went over to talk to them. Griff saw me coming and gave me a wide smile.

"Hey, Roan. This is a great party. I'd never met Simon while I lived here, and I only knew Trenda enough to say 'Hey.' Seems like you've gotten embedded into the community pretty fast."

I smiled. "Guess so."

Lesley spoke up. "I love your dad. Are you two going to miss him when he flies back to Florida?" Lesley asked.

I nodded. "But he's got to do what he wants. From everything he's told me, he's built a great life for himself."

"This life wasn't agreeing with him," Griff said softly. "I was really happy when Cousin Marty showed up."

"I'd like to go down and visit Dad sometime and meet Marty."

"Are you going to take Lisa?" Lesley asked.

"Of course."

Where did that come from? I'm already planning vacations with her?

Get a grip, Thatcher, and pull your head out of your ass. Of course, you're planning a future with this woman. You love her.

"I'm sorry, what did you say?" I asked Griff.

He grinned at me. "Never mind. Your mind wandered. I think I see Lisa over there, looking for you."

"Did she get a chance to talk to you about taking over the restoration arm of the shop?" I asked, trying to cover up me blanking out.

"We're discussing things, and so are Lesley and I. You'll know when we know." Griff dipped his chin and pointed it behind me. "Lisa is at your six. Better go get her."

"Good talking to you." I turned and was gifted with a gorgeous smile.

"Hello, Beautiful," I said as I took her into my arms. "What do you say we blow this show and go home early? We can get in some loud action before your granddad comes home."

"Normally I'd be all for it, but Trenda said that Simon wants to see you in his office. Are you really going to start working for him?"

"We're talking it over, but it's looking good."

Her smile wobbled. Then she bit her bottom lip. Yep, this would be the time she'd normally do a runner.

"Lisa, I want you to know, I'm looking for a house. I don't intend to be living with you forever, because if I did, I'd be contributing a lot more than just groceries. Right now, I'm here because of that fanatic who's after you. Once he's neutralized, I'll need somewhere to live. Dad says that his next booking is January fifteenth, and he's kicking my butt out."

And just by telling her all of that, she relaxed.

Dammit.

I was somehow going to have to sneak my way past all her barriers when it came to a long-term relationship.

I knocked on Simon's door and opened it when he called for me to come in. There weren't any people up on the screen, just a bunch of documents. I pulled up a seat beside him so I could see what he was looking at.

"This is our guy. Rod Nevins." Simon pressed his

mouse, and on the right-side screen a picture came up. It looked just like Lisa's sketch.

"He uses the name Anthony Carlyle online," Simon continued. "We found him by a post he made on a site known for harboring homegrown terrorists. He was showing off his tattoo. We tracked him to where he lives because he was using his mother's credit cards online. Other than that, he's damn near a ghost. He was born twenty-six years ago to Wilma Nevins, no father listed. He has no social security number, no nothing. Wilma inherited the house where the two of them are living from her grandparents."

"Let me guess," I jumped in. "A gamer."

"You got it in one. When he first started his account, he didn't post at all. But when Lisa moved to Elkton, he started going head-to-head with the misogynists, telling them they were wrong about women. He got a lot of hate thrown his way."

"And when she left?" I asked.

"He first started asking for people who knew ways to track someone. He was ignored. But then someone spoke up, and they agreed to meet in a private chat room. Wanna guess when this was?"

"August," I said as I cricked my neck.

"Bingo."

"So he came up here to kill her plants? That makes no sense."

"Most of these numb-nuts never do."

"I'm leaving first thing in the morning. I'd leave now, but the roads are icy and I want to be rested."

"Good. I agree." Simon gave me a long look. "Are you going to tell Lisa?"

"Yeah. She tries to mask it, but this has been looming large."

"I understand."

"But I'm not telling her tonight."

I loved seeing the passion in Roan's eyes as we made it to the bedroom. I loved my granddad, but having him here was playing hell on my sex life.

"We wouldn't have a problem if you weren't so loud," Roan teased.

"I am not loud," I protested.

"Yes, you are, and I love every moment of it."

"I am not."

"Baby, you are. Especially when my face is between your legs, and I'm licking up all your cream."

My eyes went wide. "Did you just say that? Out loud?"

He laughed. "You can handle me doing it, but not saying it?" He tugged at the sweater dress I was wearing, and in one quick pull it was over my head and lying on the floor. "I love the color blue," he said as he stared down at my blue satin panties.

"Tonight, we're going to try something different. I want you on top."

I felt my eyes widen and my lips curl up. "I could go for that. But we have a problem."

"What's that?"

"You're overdressed again."

He started unbuttoning his shirt. "Aren't you going to help me?"

"That would just waste time. Come on boy, hurry up. I

don't want to lose my place in line for this ride." I was positively giddy.

He hurried up, and as I got out of my bra and panties, I saw him take a condom out of his pocket and throw it on the bed. Normally he nudged me onto the bed, and I'd get to cuddle up to all of his heat. Not tonight. Tonight, I pushed against his chest, hard. He tumbled onto the bed and I straddled him before he had a chance to change his mind on tonight's festivities.

His hands came up to cup the back of my head and he started tugging me downwards.

"Oh no you don't. I'm in charge."

"You're not going fast enough."

"Hands above your head, and you'll like what I do."

I watched him reluctantly put his hands above his head, touching my headboard. Mr. Protector didn't like giving up control. No big surprise there. But I liked it. I needed to reward him. I bent down and smashed my breasts to his chest, then kissed him long, wet and hard. He groaned.

Loudly.

"Please let me touch your breasts."

"Not yet."

I'd never sucked on his nipples before. Were they as sensitive as mine? I kissed my way down his furred chest and sucked on one brown nipple. He bucked up beneath me.

"You like that," I purred.

"Fuck yeah, I like that. Baby, I have to touch you."

"Them's not the rules."

I sucked one nipple and tweaked his other with my fingernail. Not satisfied with this, I headed further down until I found my prize. I stroked his hard, thick cock. It felt luscious to the touch. Up and down. Down and up.

"Baby, if you don't climb on board in less than three seconds, I'm taking over."

I reached over to where he had thrown the condom, picked it up, and ripped it open with my teeth. I soon had him sheathed. When I started to lower myself on all that male strength, I let out a long moan of pleasure.

"See. I told you; you're loud." He teased me through gritted teeth.

I threw back my head and concentrated on getting the rhythm just right. Up and down with a little swirl. Again, and again. I wasn't surprised when Roan's hands gripped my hips. He helped me and I needed it. I needed to go faster, him to go deeper.

I couldn't keep track of who was moaning and who was groaning.

"Get there, Baby. Please. Get there."

"I'm so close."

He moved his right hand, and soon his thumb was rubbing my clit. "Look at your clit, all swollen and needy."

"Yeah. Roan. Do it some more."

"Like this?"

I was past the point of words, but he must have known my answer was yes. He continued to stroke up and swirl hard.

"Yes," I screamed my release.

Roan bucked up into me, his hands holding me tight as he throbbed inside me.

It was glorious.

I couldn't help it. I fell over, my hands landing on his chest. My hair enclosed us in our own little island.

I stared into his gray eyes and they spoke volumes. I could get lost in their depths, and it scared the hell out of me.

24

My truck made mincemeat out of the icy roads. Gotta love American-made vehicles. This time I wasn't going to need to stop by the florist or the Treasure Chest shop. Nope, this time I was pissed as hell, and I wanted to unleash.

I took a deep breath and called Forrest. Talking to him would calm me down.

"How's life? Dad says you're in love."

"I'm thinking he might be right," I admitted.

Forrest let out a big laugh. "How fast was that? Three weeks?"

"Something like that," I muttered.

Forrest started laughing again. "So you and Griff are going to be old married men, just like me. Soon you'll be having kids."

"I didn't plan to talk about this. I was really going to talk about something else, but since you brought it up, maybe I should talk about things with Lisa."

"You know, I'm capable of listening to more than one thing. Maybe even two. After all, I have two ears."

"Smartass."

"At your service."

"Okay, Lisa is wonderful."

"I know, I've met her. I'm the one who told you she was wonderful, remember?"

"Yeah, yeah, yeah. Well, I pulled my finger out of my ass soon after you hit me upside the head. We're in a relationship, but God forbid I should use that word where Lisa could hear it, she just might leave Jasper Creek."

"No she wouldn't," Forrest scoffed.

"No, for real. I haven't had a chance to talk to her dad or granddad about this. What's more, I don't know if they know about this, because she's been on the road since she left Oregon at eighteen. She told me that I'm the only lover that they've ever met."

"Okay, so you're special."

"We'll get to the word special. Hold on."

"Her mom was a cunt."

"Shit, did you just say that?" Forrest sounded appalled.

"Yes I did. She told her six-year-old daughter that she was going on a permanent vacation, packed her bags in front of her, told her to quit crying and left her alone in the house."

"Okay, the word was justified. I just can't use it, because I know Mom will kick my ass all the way from heaven."

"Gotcha. Anyway, that did serious damage to Lisa. My guess is she bails on people before they can bail on her. My idea is to just stick around and be here until she realizes I will be here for her."

"You're living with her, right?"

"Did Dad explain about the stalker stuff?"

"All Dad said is that she was having some problems."

I snorted. "I'll say. We've tracked down a guy who's left

some pretty gruesome stuff at Lisa's door. Simon and I think he's escalated."

"Who's Simon?"

"I'll get into that some other time," I promised.

"Okay."

"It took a lot of digging, but Simon and his cyber team were finally able to track this guy to a house next to James Madison University. He had Lisa give him a tattoo, and he fixated on her. That's all we can guess. I'm driving up there to confront him. I want to scare the hell out of him so he doesn't do anything ever again because the sheriff is saying the best they can do is have her get a restraining order."

"Fuck."

"My thoughts exactly."

"Call me back after you've had your conversation with the sicko."

"You got it."

I sighed after I disconnected. I felt better after talking to my brother.

I went in soft because I didn't know what I was going to find at the Nevins' house. It was a good thing. What I found was a middle-aged woman who looked like she was dressed to go to church.

"Hello," she smiled at me. "Merry Christmas."

"Hi, I'm here to see Rod."

"Rod? My Rod? Are you sure?"

This was odd. "Yes, ma'am. I'm sure."

"What a surprise. Rod has never had any visitors since the third grade. Come in, come in."

I was invited into the house and ushered into a living

room that actually had plastic covering the furniture. Who does that?

"Can I get you a glass of water? Some sweet tea?" she asked.

"No, ma'am. I just wanted to have a few words with Rod."

"Sweet tea will be good. I'll be right back."

What the hell?

I waited for ten minutes on the hardest sofa I'd ever sat on, until Mrs. Nevins came out with a tray.

"Ma'am I didn't get a chance to introduce myself. I'm Roan Thatcher. I really appreciate the tea and all, but I really, really need to talk to your son."

And just like that, her face crumpled and she began to cry.

She rushed across the room and pulled tissues from a tissue box.

"It's all right, Mrs. Nevins. I'm sorry I've upset you. But it's very important I talk to your son."

She said something, but I couldn't understand her.

"I beg your pardon?"

She whirled around and shouted. "He ran away from home. He took my car and he left me. I don't know why. I don't know what I could have done wrong. But last summer he ran away from home."

Ran away from home? Was she for real?

"What kind of car did you have?"

"It was a blue Impala."

"Mrs. Nevins, it's very important I get ahold of him. Did he take anything besides the car? Anything of value that would help him stay hidden?"

"He probably took the money from his mattress."

"From his mattress?"

"When he was a teenager, I paid him fifty dollars a week in cash to do chores. After he turned eighteen I paid him one-hundred dollars a week. Since he never left the basement, I don't think he ever spent the money. After he ran away, I searched his room extensively. There was no money."

"Does your son play video games?"

"He does, all the time. He's very good and very popular. He told me that in the game he has many trophies. He's printed some of them out and I've posted them on the fridge."

Jesus.

"Did he mention any friends of his in particular that you remember?"

"Oh, no. I didn't like those names they used. They were disgusting. One boy called himself Bloodsucker. Disgusting. Rod assured me that he would never do that. He said his name was LambofGod. All one word. I really think one of those disgusting boys put him up to this."

"Thank you Mrs. Nevins. You've been very helpful."

Once again I called Simon as soon as I got back to my truck.

"That is really high on the creepy scale."

"You got that right. I'm thinking he's holed up somewhere in Jasper Creek." I fucking hated that idea. But that's what I thought.

"Now that you explained about all of the cash, I'd have to agree."

"I'm thinking this is just a matter of knocking on doors."

"Yeah. But if he's squatting in one of the empty cabins up on mountain, we're never going to find him."

"Simon, I can't imagine some slug who's lived in his Mommy's warm basement is going to go live in a cabin in the middle of winter."

"People have been known to go to outrageous lengths for love."

I sighed. "There is that."

25

"Little Girl, I hate leaving you like this. Are you sure you won't come home with us until Simon and Roan find this bastard?"

My dad and my granddad were on either side of me, each with an arm around my waist. "I'm going to stay. I know that they will handle it. I'm going to be just fine. What's more, my job is here."

"No, your company is here," Roan's dad interrupted. "Remember, you bought in. The rules are, you buy it, you babysit it."

I laughed. It was true. The decision scared the hell out of me. But I loved Jasper Creek and I had made such good friends. I didn't want to leave. Then there was whatever Roan and I had. I knew it wasn't going to last, but I still wanted to play it out to the end.

"You're right, Warren. My company. Or half my company," I grinned. "Do you realize that with Hollister gone, our restoration work has gone up? Apparently, his personality was turning off potential customers."

"Well, Griff won't be doing that, that's for damn sure," Warren grinned.

"I expect calls from you, Roan," my dad said.

"Me too," my granddad piped up.

"We don't want to be left in the dark."

I watched as Roan stretched his neck. Ever since he found out that Rod had 'run away,' he'd been eating antacids like he owned stock in the company. He said it was because real estate hunting was getting to him, but I knew he was full of shit. He was hardly looking, instead he was knocking on doors from Pigeon Forge to Gatlinburg up to the Jasper Creek mountains. He was worn out. Simon was doing the same thing.

Luckily the shop was keeping me busy, otherwise this waiting would be on my last nerve.

"Well, we're packed up. Better get moving. Don't want to miss our flight," Granddad said.

"You know, you definitely have time to stay for lunch," I said for the fourth time. "Your flight isn't for five hours, and it's only an hour's drive to the airport."

"You never know what traffic is going to be like. Gotta get there early," Granddad insisted.

I peeked over at Roan and I could tell he was chuckling on the inside. I hoped I wasn't like that when I got to be their age.

When we got home that afternoon, Simon called Roan. He had a small job up in Knoxville. It needed two people, and he asked Roan to join him.

"What do you think, Lisa? Are you okay if I'm gone for a couple of days? The timing couldn't suck any more than it does, what with your dad and granddad leaving today, and my dad fixing to leave tomorrow morning. But you could go stay with Trenda."

"Roan, I'm done."

"What?" he said sharply. "What do you mean done? Us?"

"Of course not," I said really fast. "I meant, I'm done waiting for this asshole to make a move. I'm going to live my life the way it's meant to be lived. You got it?"

"And that includes me, right?"

"That didn't sound like a question, it sounded like a statement."

"That's because it was."

"Absolutely it includes you." I didn't say for however long he was going to want me. Because I knew eventually things would end.

"Okay, I'll call Simon."

And so began our life together.

"Lisa, are you listening to me?" Griff asked.

"Nah, she's gone. She went into 'Roan Land.' He came over and brought her lunch. I saw the kiss he laid on her. She still hasn't come out of her fog." Jimmy laughed.

"Damn, wish that'd happen to Lesley."

"It does. I've seen it. It used to happen with my wife, but raising four boys makes those times few and far between."

"I'm listening to Jimmy gossiping and you talking about kissing," I told him. "This is the fifth weekly staff meeting in a row that turns to nonsense. We end up shooting the shit and being silly instead of reviewing the weeks wins and losses, and how we want to prep for the following week." When I pointed that out, Jimmy laughed.

"That's because going over our fuckups in the past is stupid," Griff groused. "We know where we screwed up, and we've put new processes in place to fix it. End of discussion."

"And as for prepping for the following week, we already have our list of cars coming in, with what needs to be done on 'em," Jimmy said. "On Monday I assign people to get 'em done, and they get 'em done."

Griff grinned. "Yeah, what he says."

I nod. "Y'all have a point."

"Did she just say y'all?" Jimmy asked Griff.

"She did. I don't think that's allowed. She's a Yankee."

"I am not. I own a home and a business here. Well part of a business. So, I'm now a Southerner."

Jimmy shook his head. "That's not how it works. After fifty years you can become a Southerner. That's it."

"That's not fair," I protested.

"Wait a minute, Jimmy. There's another way."

Jimmy leaned back in his chair and put his clasped his hands over his belly. "You're right. There is a way, but I'm not sure she's up to it."

"Tell me."

"You can marry into a Southern family."

I waited. Nope, I didn't start trembling. No shakes. *Hmm.*

"There has to be another way."

"Nope," Jimmy declared. "Hell, if you don't live in the South for fifty years or marry into a Southern family, then I don't think they'll even let you be buried here."

"You two are full of hooey."

"That's another term you can't use." Griff laughed.

"Gentlemen, on that note, I'm calling it a day. You two lock up, would you?"

"Sure thing," Jimmy winked at me.

As soon as I got into the car, I checked my texts. I told Roan that I would do the grocery shopping on the way home, as long as he texted me a list. He said he could do the shopping, but I insisted. His job was just as important as mine was. Right now, he was working on something that he couldn't talk about and when he left the desk in the guest room, he was usually pretty cranky when he came out.

It'd usually take me a half hour of telling funny stories about the shop before I could coax him out of the cranky mood. He let it slip once that he was working a missing person case that had led him to a sex trafficking ring. That was more than enough info for me.

If I couldn't think of funny stories for him, I always made sure to have his dad or my dad on call to lift his spirits.

Who knew I was working with a crimefighting cyber nerd?

Besides that first time he left to go to Knoxville, there was only one other trip. He and Simon went up to Minneapolis. That trip lasted for a week. He never said anything about what went on, and I didn't ask.

There was quite a list on my phone, and that actually made me smile. Come to think of it, a lot of things made me smile these days.

I was still smiling when I hit the checkout stand next to Pearl.

"Lisa, what's happened? I haven't seen you hardly at all. When I was talking to Lettie during our monthly poker game, she said you haven't been showing up at her place either. I was worried that you might be trying some new-fangled diet, but instead you're filling out them there jeans just fine."

I grinned and stood a little straighter. "Check out my cart."

Pearl leaned over and took a look. "My God, when did you learn to cook?"

I leaned over and whispered in her ear. "I have a deal with Roan. If I heat things up in the bedroom, he cooks things up in the kitchen."

Pearl's loud laughter had everybody's head turning to see what was going on.

"You go girl. You go girl."

We were both still chuckling when it was my turn to be checked out. Of course, it was Amanda working, but no matter how slow she was, she wasn't going to burst my bubble today. Today I was smiling.

Roan wasn't home when I got home, which was odd. I checked my phone to see if I had missed any calls or texts, but nothing. Didn't matter, I knew he'd check in soon. He was good like that. He never left me worrying. Out of the two of us, I was the one who didn't tell him where I was going.

I was definitely working on trying to get better at that. It was a process. I'd say I was now at eighty percent, not twenty percent. Despite that, most of this living together rocked. And I never would have guessed that. Hell, I would have bet that little 401k I had tucked away that I would hate living with someone, but nope, it definitely rocked.

It was great having somebody to come home to and

shoot the shit with. Even better because Roan knew all about the business. And while Roan might not be able to tell me specifics of the case he was working on, he was able to tell me about some of the other computer experts he interacted with. I was surprised to hear that some of the SEAL techies had wives who were as good as they were.

My phone rang as I put away the last bit of feta cheese.

"Hello?" I answered before looking at who was calling.

Nobody said anything. I looked down at the display and it was Roan calling.

"Hello, Roan? I can't hear you. Speak up."

Still nothing.

"—Baby? A little late because—" then I couldn't hear anything again. "Call— for me."

"Roan, you're cutting in and out."

"—mountains—later—" Then the line went dead.

Maybe I would get him a satellite phone for his birthday.

I opened the freezer door and plucked out the chocolate chip cookie dough and considered eating it like an ice pop, but decided to be a grown up. I cut it open and spooned some into a bowl, then went over to the couch with my eReader and started to re-read *M*A*S*H* by Richard Hooker. It always made me laugh out loud.

I was halfway through my bowl of cookie dough when Roan came in. He was looking pretty pleased with himself. He got out of his wet coat, walked over to me, and gave me a quick kiss, one that soon turned into a nice long kiss.

"You taste good."

I motioned to the cookie dough on the coffee table. Roan sat down and had me put my legs over his thighs, then picked the bowl up and tried a bite. His eyes widened.

"This is good." He took another bite.

"Why were you in the mountains? Didn't you say that you and Simon were done looking for Rod up there?"

"Yeah, we are." He scooped up another portion of dough and I motioned for him to give it to me. He lifted his eyebrows but acquiesced. He fed me the spoonful and I sucked it down slowly.

"You little temptress."

"Gotta have my fun where I can get it. Now why were you on the mountain?"

"I was getting some supplies to some of the folks up there. It's something that normally Simon does, but he asked me to do it. It was easy enough after having been up there last month."

"What kinds of supplies?"

"Anything they request. Bernie Faulkes gets a list from them and brings it down. You know Bernie."

"Yeah. I've replaced his clutch once, and at the rate he's going, I'm going to have to replace it again. I know it's good business for the shop, but somebody needs to tell him to get an automatic truck next time."

Roan chuckled. "Anyway, I just wanted Simon to tell Trenda that the twins wanted her to come visit real soon. That was all. Since they said that, I thought it would be nice to hear your voice."

I sucked in a deep breath, and Roan's eyes narrowed. "You doing okay there, Chief?"

I did a couple of those deep breathing exercises that Trenda taught me, then I could talk. "I'm fine."

"Wanna tell me why you wigged out when I said I called for no other reason than to hear your voice?" His tone was soft, but it felt like a whip flaying my flesh.

I shook my head.

"Please, Lisa. You know the answer. It's in there. You can tell me."

I couldn't respond. I felt the back of my eyes start to sting.

"Come on, Baby, answer the question."

"Because I love it when you say things like that. I want you to say them to me forever." I whispered so softly I didn't think he would be able to hear me. But he did.

He set the dish down and pulled me onto his lap and hugged me close. "I want to say them to you forever."

"There's no such thing as forever." I bit my lip so hard I tasted blood.

"You're right. Nobody makes it out of here alive," Roan teased.

My laugh didn't sound right, then I realized it was kind of a sob. "I want forever with you, and you're going to leave me."

He tilted up my chin so I was staring up into his eyes. He was blurry because of my tears. "I'm not going to leave you, Lisa. I love you."

I shuddered. He didn't mean it. I must have said that out loud.

"I do mean it."

"Roan. It won't work. You *will* end up leaving."

He did a little hug and shake and tilted my chin up again. "Lisa, is that your gut or your head talking? And think before you answer."

I thought. I really tried to figure out what was going on.

"It's my gut," I admitted.

"What does your head say?"

I snorted. "It says you wouldn't be cooking for me and reminding me to wear socks to bed so my feet don't get cold unless you loved me."

He smiled. It was beautiful.

"And your gut?"

"I'm scared to death," I admitted.

"How about your heart?" he whispered his question.

I swallowed. "My heart is going to love you for forever and ever, and that's why my gut is so scared."

Then I burst into tears.

I don't know how long he rocked me in his arms. He kept saying he loved me, and he would stay with me. I think I fell asleep. When I woke up there were warm cookies and milk waiting for me.

I loved this man, and I really hoped we could have a future together.

26

I braced. From everything I heard, this many Averys in one place could be a madhouse. But Lisa was as excited as hell, so I was going. Not everyone could make it to their youngest sister's graduation in San Diego, so they were having a surprise party for her at Aiden and Evie's house here in Jasper Creek. I'd been there once, when it was calm, and I'd really enjoyed myself. I was hoping I would today, as well.

"I can't wait," Lisa said again.

I looked over at her. She held a big present in her lap, wrapped in silver paper.

"What did you get her?"

"*We* got her a comforter. Evie was all over everything. She had an entire list of what we could buy. Piper has been living with them while she'd been going to school out there in San Diego, but she got into medical school at UCLA. Evie found her a cute little apartment close to school. After she gets settled and meets some people, there's enough room for a roommate. Drake didn't want her to just get into a roommate situation until he vetted her."

I couldn't help but laugh. "He sounds a little intense."

"I would be too. You've got to remember, twice her dad's tried to kill her. I'm surprised he hasn't wrapped Piper in bubble wrap."

All of a sudden, my fingers hurt. Yep, I was trying to crush my steering wheel. The whole story made me nauseous. "But she's all right now?"

"According to Trenda, she's amazing. She had to go into counseling while she was living with Drake and Karen, but she's definitely come out the other side."

"Karen?"

"That's Drake's wife. They have two little boys. Andrew and Rex. Andrew is four and Rex is two. Add in Aiden and Evie's son, Holden, and it's mayhem."

"I can imagine." I smiled. "Do you like kids?" I asked in what I hoped was a nonchalant tone.

"Oh yeah. You know I adore Bella. And she's really helped Millie come out of her shell more. I really wish Millie was coming. She would love all the kids."

"Do you ever wish you had kids of your own?"

Lisa was quiet. I glanced over and saw her playing with the bow on the package. I didn't say anything, hoping she'd be forced to fill the silence. Praying she wouldn't deflect.

"I never saw kids in my future. But sometimes I would think about what it would be like to have a little person to nurture and care for. I'd think how every single day I would ensure they'd know they were loved."

A rock that had been sitting in my gut for months, dissolved. I silently sighed.

"You're smiling," she noted. "I take it you want kids too, right?"

"Yeah, I do."

"So, you're thinking about futures again, aren't you?" I

could barely hear her. I couldn't tell if she was freaked or happy.

"I'm thinking of our future. Ours," I admitted.

"You sure do work fast."

"Baby, it's March. We met in November. I wouldn't call that fast. My brother had a ring on Lesley's hand in less than four months."

"Well, we met in November," she quickly corrected me. "Can we talk about something else?"

"I'll give you that play. But we'll eventually circle back to it. Just so you know, I want a little girl who has blonde hair and green eyes."

"You do?" I could hear the surprise in her voice.

"I do."

"Huh. I want a little boy with sandy brown hair and gray eyes."

"Anything's possible."

I pulled into a big circular drive with at least a dozen vehicles, most of them trucks. Yep, this was going to be mayhem.

"Did you see how I babysitted my cousins at the party?" Bella asked me. She had been chattering non-stop about her cousins since I picked her up to go to Millie's.

"Babysat," I corrected. "You babysat."

"Babysat," she repeated. "Andrew is my favorite cause he can do more things. He helped the most to make the fort. Did you see how big it was?"

I laughed. Bella always made me laugh. "I did, lovebug. You were such a good big cousin."

"I was. Excepting when Holden started yelling because

he wanted to get cushions from the couch and I said no. I couldn't make him stop yelling, so Uncle Aiden had to make him."

"Yeah, well, if Uncle Aiden told me to stop doing something, I would too," I laughed.

"Do you think Millie will let us help her pick some lavender today?"

I smiled. Bella had been asking that same question the last three times we'd come for a visit. "I don't know. But I bet Millie will let us go see the plants and do a sniff test."

Bella clapped her hands. "Then we can make sachets."

"You're right, then we can make sachets," I said as we pulled up to Millie's house.

It was a beautiful spring afternoon. I'd picked us up some sandwiches from Down Home, as well as desserts. I was getting that while Bella was getting out of the car and running up the steps to knock on the door.

By the time I got to the bottom of the stairs, Bella was already inside.

"I hope you have sweet tea," I hollered. "I have brisket sandwiches on fresh-baked bread." I used my shoulder to push open door and look for Bella and Millie.

"Millie, I have lots of different desserts for you to choose from. Except you don't get the snickerdoodle cookie. Bella called dibs on that."

"What happens if I want the snickerdoodle cookie?" a familiar man's voice asked.

I spun around and saw Millie slumped against the dining room wall, her long dark hair covering her face. The bags of food and my purse dropped from my nerveless fingers. Bella was sitting beside her, her eyes wide and scared. Rod was standing over them, a long dagger in his hand, a gun stuffed in the front of his pants.

"What are you doing?" I asked softly. "Why do you have a knife?"

"Lisa, it's not a knife. It's a dagger." Rod smiled. "Look. I had it specially made. It has a green stone in the quillon."

Bella whimpered when he lifted the dagger up into the light.

What could I say?

"That's amazing," I whispered.

I glanced away from Rod and saw Millie struggling to push away from the wall. Her hair parted and that's when I saw the bruises on her face.

"What did you do to Millie?" I prayed he hadn't raped her.

"Don't look at me like that, Lisa. You know I'm not that type of man." He sounded hurt. "I would never hurt a woman in that way."

"Then why does she have bruises?"

"Yesterday, she tried to get to her phone and fought me. I had no choice. She gave me no choice." It was then I realized that her hands and feet were tied.

"How long have you been here?"

"Since the day before yesterday. You're late. You usually come on Saturday. Why are you late? Is it because of that man?"

"Millie, are you okay?" I asked.

"Water," she pushed out the word. "Please, water."

I turned on Rod. "Have you even been giving her water?" I demanded to know.

"Don't listen to her," he roared. He pounded across the floor and stopped right in front of me. I could smell his foul breath. "You pay attention to *me*!"

I heard Bella start to cry.

"I'm listening."

"You better be. Because you sure weren't when I tried to get you to leave this town and come home to Elkton." His face was red with anger. The dagger was clutched in his right hand and he lifted it above his head.

"Rod, I'm sorry, I never meant to not listen to you," I said soothingly. I so badly wanted to yell at this fucker, but I couldn't. I couldn't do anything that might endanger Bella. And Millie. But especially Bella.

"You didn't pay attention. Couldn't you see you weren't wanted here?"

I frowned. What was he talking about?

"I can't think with you holding that knife over my head."

"Dagger," he yelled. "You know it's a dagger. I had it made special. It means something. It's our special thing. Don't call it a knife again."

"I'm sorry. You're right. It's beautiful. Can I see it closer?"

"I'm not stupid, Lisa. You'll try to take it from me."

"If you think that, then what do you want from me? Why are you here? What is your plan?"

"We're going to stay here awhile. We had a connection. I felt it. You felt it. You'll forget all about that Thatcher man. We'll go somewhere and make a life together."

"I can't do that. I need to take Bella home."

"I thought about that. You're going to call the brat's mother. You're going to say she wants to sleep over for a couple of days. It's going to be some kind of woman's night party."

"A girl's night?"

"That's right. Then we'll have time to get to know one another."

He was definitely more than a few cents short of a dollar. I was getting ready to tell him that, when I realized I definitely wanted to talk to Trenda. It would be my chance to get us rescued.

I licked my lips. "Okay." I made sure my voice was wavering.

He lowered the dagger.

"Go shut the kid up and tie her up."

"I can't do that."

"If you don't want something bad to happen to her, you will definitely tie her up." Rod's menacing voice made me shiver.

"Tie her up with what?"

"I found some twine in a drawer. It's on the counter. Use that."

"I can't use twine," I protested. "That'll cut off her circulation. Did you use that on Millie?"

"So what? Do what I said." He shoved me toward the kitchen, then shoved the dagger into its sheath on his belt and pulled out his gun. "I'm watching you."

I went over to Millie to check her bindings and Bella hurled herself at me. Suddenly I had little girl arms around my neck and legs around my waist.

"Don't tie me up," she wailed. "I want to go home to my Mama."

I plopped my ass down next to Millie and started to rock Bella in my arms.

"Get up," Rod yelled.

"You told me to get Bella to calm down. That's what I'm doing," I ground out.

I could see that he was getting agitated. Well, more agitated than before.

"Rod, I'm doing the best that I can. I need to calm her down. Please be patient."

I saw his shoulders relax.

Good.

I started to whisper in Bella's ear. "Lovebug. I need you to be really, really brave. You know that your daddy will come and save you. You know that, don't you?"

She moved her face from the crook of my neck.

"Really?" she said.

"Shhh, whispers only." I murmured back in the little girl's ear.

"Really?" she whispered in my ear.

"Really," I whispered back.

"And Uncle Drake and Uncle Aiden?" I could barely hear her, which was wonderful.

"Yes." I promised her. "I'm going to need you to be brave," I said in a louder voice.

My brave little Bella caught on to the fact that we needed to put on a show for Rod. "Okay," she said loudly.

"Can you let go of me, and sit next to Millie while I get things to tie you up?"

It killed me to see a fresh set of tears roll down her face. "Okay, Lisa."

"Good girl."

I put Bella aside, then got up and went to the kitchen. I found scissors, some dish towels, and twine.

Rod came over holding his gun casually hanging down in his right hand. "What are you doing?"

"I'm going to tie her hands and feet over the dish towels so that the twine doesn't cut into her skin and stop her circulation. I'm also going to check Millie's bindings."

"No, you're—"

I jerked back my head and glared at him. "Yes, I am. Now you either convince me you're the kind and patient man I met at Elkton, or I'll have to believe you're some kind of monster who hurts women and children."

That stopped him. I could see the contrition on his face. "Of course, I wouldn't want the kid to be hurt. And if I hurt Millie, please fix it."

I gave him the best smile I could muster. "I knew that's the type of man you were." I took all of the supplies over to Millie and Bella and got to work. I was relieved to see that Millie's hands weren't purple, but she'd been trying to get loose, so her wrists were bloody.

When I cut the twine off Millie's wrists, she looked up at me. Her gaze was clear. "You're going to make that call, right?" she whispered. Obviously, she had been tracking my conversation with Rod the entire time.

I nodded.

"There is a third way into the house. I have a door in my bedroom, on the east side." That made sense. I knew that one of Millie's biggest fears was being trapped in a burning house with no way to get out. It was also the reason she had two fire extinguishers prominently displayed.

"I'll try to let Trenda know about the other door," I told Millie.

Rod came and stood over where I was working on Millie. "Aren't you done yet?"

"Almost."

"Good, I'm hungry. Those sandwiches sound good."

"We need to let Millie and Bella eat too."

"They can eat tonight. It won't hurt them to wait. I'm hungry now. After we eat, you can call the girl's mother.

Then we can start talking. I've missed you so much." He stroked my cheek with the tips of his fingers. I struggled not to shudder.

"That sounds real good." I agreed softly.

27

I knew if I took a bite of the sandwich, I would throw up.

"Why aren't you eating?"

"I'm not hungry."

We were sitting on Millie's pretty couch, right under one of her fire extinguishers.

Rod put his hand on my thigh and squeezed it. It was something that Roan would do and it made me even sicker.

"You need to eat, Baby."

"Don't call me that!" I yelled.

He squeezed my thigh so hard I knew it would leave bruises.

"Don't you dare yell at me. I'll call you any fucking thing I want! I'll call you a bitch if I want. You hear that, Bitch?"

"You know, Rod, you're not winning many points in the boyfriend stakes," I said sarcastically.

I bounced against the back of the couch, then fell onto the floor. I saw stars as pain exploded throughout my head, my cheek, my eye.

I started to shake my head to clear it, and I moaned as

flames shot through my face. I heard myself moaning, but the sound was coming from far away.

"Get your ass back up on the couch and eat a cookie." Rod yanked my arm so hard I thought he would rip it out of the socket. I landed on the couch and rolled against his body. I jerked away, causing more hurt. It didn't matter.

He shoved a cookie at my parted lips. I spit it out.

"Don't make me punish you again."

I heard Bella crying and Millie trying to comfort her. I picked up the cookie and started eating it.

"There's my good girl. Now I need you to make that phone call. Here's your phone."

I didn't know when he'd grabbed it from my purse, but he pulled the cookie from my hand and exchanged it for the phone.

"Don't try anything funny. I'll know if you do."

I nodded, and immediately regretted it.

Trenda answered on the third ring. "Hi, Lisa. What's up? Are you and Bella going to make another stop before coming home?"

"Probably. Millie is itching to go to the mall."

"Millie?" Trenda's voice was incredulous.

"Then maybe we're going to take in a movie. Millie's picked out a doozy. Then she wants the three of us to go out to dinner."

"You're kidding, right?"

"After that, she invited us to spend a couple of days here to have a girl's night or two. Maybe do facials and stuff. Millie's going to show me how to do my make-up."

"Lisa, what's going on?"

"No, you and Simon don't need to come over here and drop off anything for Bella. We're going to buy her things to wear at the mall."

There was a long pause, and I could hear Trenda thinking.

"You want Simon and I to come over, don't you?" She said the words slowly. Yeah, she was catching on.

"Oh, you don't need to have Simon come over with Bella's teddy bear. And her uncles don't need to come over to say goodbye. She'll call them when we get back. Millie wants to spoil her because of all the times Bella has come over and kept her company."

"Her uncles. I get it," Trenda whispered.

"Thanks, Trenda, I knew you'd understand. We're going to have a blast." I emphasized the last word.

I hung up. I looked up at Rod. "Satisfied?"

"Yes. Now, let's get some ice on your face. You really shouldn't make me punish you."

"What the fuck?"

I raced to my truck. I was closer to Millie's farm than Simon, and I wanted to go over there, guns blazing. Simon must have known that because he was still speaking.

"I need you thinking like a Raider, not as a lover. He has my daughter, I get where you're coming from. We need to have a plan. Get over to Aiden's house. He's the closest to Millie's farm, and he practically has an armory there."

I took a deep breath as I climbed into my truck.

"I'll be there in fifteen." I hung up and threw my phone on the passenger seat. It was normally a thirty-minute drive to Evie and Aiden's but I *would* make it in fifteen.

When I got to their house, Evie answered the door with Holden on her hip.

"I'll walk you back to the armory."

"That's for real?"

"Yep. It's really just a large gun safe. After I show you where they're at, I'm going to put Holden down."

She led me through the great room, and then turned a sharp corner to a door that I would have assumed was just a closet. Instead, it opened up to an eight-by-eight room. Drake, Simon and Aiden were all in it. There was a long shelf and an open gun safe that was mostly empty. On the shelf were all sorts of weapons. It was like being back at base. I didn't ask how or why.

"Good, now that you're here, we can start strategizing," Simon said.

I stood where I was and the others spread out, leaning against walls and shelves so that we were all looking at one another.

"Trenda took the call, and Lisa made it clear that she's at Millie's and Rod's holding her, Millie, and Bella." There was no rage in Simon's voice or on his face. He looked like ice. It was four times worse than rage.

"Lisa made it clear that 'Simon,'" Simon used air quotes around his name, "wasn't supposed to bring either clothes or her teddy bear for Bella. She also made it clear that they had a day out planned and they wouldn't be back until after dark. We know that isn't true, but if we use that as an excuse, we can go in on a full frontal, and I can show up after dark with a bag for Bella with her teddy bear."

"Yeah, that sounds plausible," I said. "But he won't come out onto the porch to greet you. He'll send Millie or Lisa."

"But I'll insist I want to give my daughter a hug. It will only be natural."

Aiden piped in. "I have comm systems for all of us. Do you think he'll notice if you're wearing one?" he asked Simon.

"I'll wear a windbreaker. As soon as I have Bella I'll give the word, then you all hit the back and take him down." Simon gave each one of us a look.

Each one of us nodded.

———

I couldn't believe the made-up world that Rod had in his mind. I didn't realize that one day when he'd left his house to go to the post office to sign for something, I'd been there too. Apparently, I had opened the door for him, and smiled at him as he was trying to take a big box out the door. That's when my life changed.

"I knew then that we were destined to be together."

He gently took the ice pack away from my face to look at the bruise. He pressed at my cheek and I whimpered.

"I hope I didn't break anything." He leaned over and kissed my cheek. I knew better than to flinch. He carefully put the icepack back on. "Keep this on, Princess."

I looked over to where Bella and Millie were and was grateful to see that Bella was leaning against Millie and she was asleep. Millie's hair was covering her face, but I could see the glitter of her brown eyes, watching everything. I had not tied her hands or feet very tightly. I wanted her to be able to help Bella and run when the men came to rescue us.

Yes, I was that sure they would rescue us.

"Do you remember how we worked together to get the drawing for my tattoo just right? Lonny was a prick. He kept saying I was taking up too much of your time, but not you. You liked having me come over. I knew this."

I remembered. I just figured that was the way it was with Philosophy grads; they had their heads up in the clouds, and they were into details, so I went along with it. At the time I thought he was a really nice guy.

"Do you remember, Lisa?"

"I remember."

"I saw Lonny brush up against you. He acted like there wasn't enough room, and he had to turn sideways and brush against you with his crotch. I could see he had a hard-on. He did that multiple times. He was disgusting."

Rod was not wrong.

"He was the reason you left Elkton, wasn't he?"

I nodded.

"I'm glad I killed him."

I knew this was coming but why did it hit me so hard? I started to gag.

"What's wrong, Princess? Do you need some water? A cookie? Some lemonade?"

"You killed Lonny? You burned him alive?"

"Of course, I did. He deserved it for the way he treated you."

I swallowed down vomit and closed my eyes.

When I could talk again, I asked him a question. "It was you who killed all of my plants, wasn't it?"

"Yes."

"And you turned on my water, so my backyard would turn into a lake."

"Yes, that was me too. I also stole your groceries and let the air out of your tires."

"Why?"

"I wanted you to leave this place. I wanted you to see how bad it was and come home to Elkton."

"And the rat?"

"You had that man at your house! I needed to do something that warned you not to have other men in your house. Why did you have that man at your house!"

Who is he talking about? Then I remembered.

"That was Gene Hollister. He was an employee who was quitting. He was no one."

"You were giving him tea."

"You were watching me?"

"I was always watching you. At least until you got that security system. Then I had to think of something else."

I dropped my head. This was all my fault. I'd led him to Millie.

"Look at me," he demanded.

I couldn't. I was too tired. Just because I was polite to a stranger. I did this. I got Lonny killed.

"Don't you want to know about the skull?"

"Sure," I said, looking down at my lap.

He grabbed my chin and jerked my head up so I was looking at him. "I finally realized you weren't going to leave. Not for nuisances. So, I needed you to remember me. You spent so much time marking me. You spent hours and hours inking my skin. You did each mark with love. You wouldn't have done that if you didn't love me. I knew if I showed you the skull, then you would come to me."

I shook my head. "I wouldn't have."

"That's because Thatcher turned you into his whore. But I'm going to fix you. I have money. A lot of money. We're going to go away together. You'll see. We'll have a perfect life together. We love one another."

I closed my eyes in defeat. How could I have brought this man into the lives of the people I love?

Rod kept talking to me. I kept answering him. I had no idea what he said. But apparently my answers satisfied him, because he didn't hit me again.

When the sun set, he put his arm around me.

"Look at that sky, Lisa. Isn't it beautiful?" He kissed my forehead.

With that last gross move, the cobwebs cleared and I woke up.

I'd told Trenda that we wouldn't be back to Millie's til after dark. My man would be coming. But how could I ensure Bella and Millie would get out of this alive?

The entire time he'd held me, he had his dagger in its sheath, and his gun on the couch cushion beside him, far away from me. After that hit, I knew he was too fast for me. I didn't want to risk going for it and failing. I knew he would end up taking it out on Millie and Bella.

"You promised me we could feed Bella and Millie," I whispered.

He stopped stroking my back and sighed.

"I did. Let's go see what's in the refrigerator."

He shoved me up to my feet and picked up his gun. When we got to the kitchen, I found yogurt cups and bottles of water. That would do. I got spoons and scissors.

"What are you doing?" he asked when he saw the scissors. "You're not going to untie them," Rod growled.

I picked up the twine. "Don't worry, I'm going to tie them back up as soon as they're done."

He hesitated, then nodded.

I walked over to Millie and Bella. I gently shook Bella awake.

"What happened to your face?" she demanded to know.

"I fell down," I lied.

"I don't believe you. He hit you, didn't he?"

I nodded. I put down the yogurts and the waters, then cut their wrist bindings.

"I'm scared," Bella whimpered.

"It's going to be fine. I promise." I handed her a yogurt.

"I want water first," she said.

I handed her and Millie the water bottles. They both drank half and then asked for the yogurt. When they were done, I tied them back up even looser.

I was crouching down next to them, picking up the empty containers, when I heard the sound of a truck pulling up. I knew it was a truck because of the big engine.

"What the fuck?" Rod said. He sounded angry. "I thought this bitch didn't get any visitors."

There was knock on the door.

"Hey, Millie, it's me, Simon. Bella's dad."

"It's my daddy," Bella cried out. "It's my daddy."

"Ah fuck." Rod shook his head. I could tell he didn't know what to do.

28

"Get out there," Rod shoved me toward the door. "Whatever you do, make him go away."

"He's going to want to see Bella. You can be damn sure of that," I hissed.

"I don't care. That's not going to happen. You get rid of him, or I'm going to slit her throat."

I heard Bella let out a high whimper.

He stalked over to Bella and pulled out his knife. "You shut up. If you make any noise, I'm going to kill you, you got that?"

"This isn't going to work, Rod. You've got to let me untie her, and at least let her hug her dad. It's the only way he'll go away."

"She's a kid, she'll give it all away."

"No, she won't. She's too smart for that."

"Millie? Lisa? Open the door." Simon knocked louder.

"Okay, do it." He bent over until his nose was practically touching Bella's. "Do you see this knife? When you're out on the porch with Lisa, you hug your dad and make him go away, otherwise I will stick this dagger in Millie's eye. Do you understand me, little girl?"

I ran over to Rod and shoved him away from Bella. "Scaring her won't help. She'll start crying and then she won't be able to fool her dad."

He looked at me, then pushed his finger into my cheek and I gasped. "It's probably better that she answers the door anyway. You look like shit, and it will make him suspicious."

Simon knocked again.

Rod bent down and used his dagger to cut Bella out of her bindings. I helped her to stand up.

"My feet don't work," she whispered to me.

"You've got to try. I know you've been sitting too long. But lovebug, you've got to try." I walked with her really quick. When her legs seemed to be working okay I sent her toward the door.

When she started to open it, I sighed in relief. Bella would be safe now. So, I practically ran back to Rod and Millie.

"Hi, Daddy," Bella said.

"Hi, Sweetheart," he replied.

Rod was pointing the dagger at Millie. I shoved his arm and he teetered backward.

Rod righted himself and looked at me. "Bitch!" His expression was maniacal. He lifted the dagger.

Blood erupted.

It spurted.

It exploded.

I went blind as I was covered with a fine red mist, then I was knocked over by a headless and armless Rod Nevins.

I started screaming.

"Get him off me! Get him off me! Get him off me!"

In seconds Rod's body was lifted off me, and Roan was kneeling beside me, shirtless, wiping blood off my face and neck with his soft green tee.

He had to wash away my tears. Lots and lots of tears.

"Bella?" I asked when I could get my mouth to work again.

"She's fine, Baby."

"Millie?"

He looked over his shoulder. "Aiden's looking her over."

He bent down and whispered in my ear. "And most important? The crazy brave, special woman I'm in love with is fine."

EPILOGUE

I jerked awake.

It was the same nightmare. It was always the same nightmare. Instead of having a dagger, Rod had a can of gasoline and a match. All three of us were tied up and he poured the gasoline all over the couch and lit it on fire. That's when Millie would scream and I would wake up.

"Babe," Roan whispered as he pulled me close. "Same dream?"

I nodded as I nuzzled into his neck.

"I really think you should see someone."

I shook my head.

Roan sighed. "You know, if you did, I really think that Millie might see someone too."

"Pulling out the big guns, huh?"

He kissed my forehead. "I just hate seeing you so tangled up. Trenda and Simon had Bella see someone for a couple of months. You've seen her, she's right as rain. Still bossing her cousins around and demanding money."

I smiled.

"What's the real reason you don't want to go?"

I didn't answer his question.

He stroked my naked back for long minutes.

"Do you want to know why I think you don't want to go?"

I shook my head.

"I think it's because you're afraid of what's going to come up regarding your mom. But do you want to know what else I think?"

"I think you're going to tell me whether I want to know or not."

Roan chuckled. "You'd be right." He tilted my chin up and kissed me slow.

Languid.

Soft.

With love.

"So, tell me."

"I don't think your mom leaving you is hurting you as much anymore. That's what I think. I think if you talk to your heart, you're going to find out that hurt has disappeared, and that hole has been filled up."

I closed my eyes and moved my head so I could listen to Roan's heartbeat. "That's what I've been thinking lately too," I whispered. "You've helped me."

"You know how special you are, don't you?"

"Sometimes, yeah."

Roan started to laugh, then he pulled me up for another kiss. "Yep, I'd say when it comes to the mom stuff, you're good, my special lady."

I frowned.

"You used to run away when I told you that you were special, do you remember that? I think your exact sentiment was, if you started to believe you were special because I called you that, you might believe it, and then I'd leave, and then you'd have nothing."

I frowned harder. "Did I say that?"

He gave me a quick kiss and patted my bare ass. "Yes, you did."

"Huh."

"Now you have to get rid of those nightmares."

"You're right, I really do."

"What do you think? Will you call somebody and make an appointment?"

"Yeah."

I knocked on Millie's door and a very good-looking man opened it.

"Hello?" I said before he had a chance to say anything, "who are you?"

"I'm Renzo Drakos. Who are you?"

"Lisa Reynolds. I brought lunch for Millie." I held up the bag from Down Home.

The door opened wider and Millie appeared. "Hi, Lisa, I wasn't expecting you today. You usually come on Tuesdays."

"It looks like I've been missing out, not coming on Fridays."

Millie blushed. "I'm sorry that you came all this way and brought lunch. Can we do this some other time?"

I winced.

"Millie, I hate to be a problem, but we just had someone trying to pull a fast one by trying to force Bella to say something at the door to get rid of Simon. I don't feel comfortable leaving this guy here with you."

Renzo started to laugh. He had a really good laugh. "I like you. I'd invite you in, but you're right to be cautious. Why don't you and Millie go out to your sweet ride and give Simon Clark a call? He can vouch for me. Will that do it for you?"

I immediately nodded. I knew I was going to end up feeling like an ass, but I wanted to be sure.

Millie followed me down her steps to my Dodge Charger. We got inside and I called Simon.

"Hi, Simon."

"Hello, Lisa."

"Can you vouch for a guy named Renzo Drakos, and also describe him to me?"

"That's an odd request. What's going on?"

"I found him at Millie's house. She's here in my car with me. You're on speaker."

"Hi, Simon," she said quietly.

"Hi, Millie." His tone was gentle. "Renzo is almost six feet tall. He has dark skin because he's Peruvian. His brother used to work for me, as one of my Navy SEALs. Renzo manages construction projects all over the world, and he helped to rebuild our rec center. So, to sum it up, he's an all-around good guy. I trust him."

I sighed. "I knew I was going to end up feeling foolish."

"Absolutely not. You were being really smart, and I'm impressed."

That made me feel good, so I was smiling when I hung up.

"Are you okay now?" Millie asked.

"About Renzo? Yes. About you and Renzo? I'm curious. What's up with that?"

"I haven't the slightest idea. Nothing makes sense."

"Oh. Yeah, I've been there."

Millie grimaced. "No, it's not like you and Roan. This is platonic. I have no idea why he wants to be my friend and insists on hanging around. Like I said, nothing about him makes any kind of sense."

"I always have two ears to listen, Millie."

"Thank you."

She got out of my car and went up the steps where Renzo was still waiting with the door open. He tilted his chin to me, then closed the door with a smile on his face.

"Honey, you just got home from a week in Kansas. We should have gone out, not have you cooking."

I looked at Lisa and smiled. These days she glowed with happiness and I rarely saw those frown lines. It had been three months since she started counseling and two months since she'd had a bad dream. I put that in the win category.

"I like cooking for you, Baby."

"But you didn't leave anything for me to clean up."

"Tell you what. I'll make all sorts of a mess in the bedroom, and you can clean that up, what do you think?"

Her dimple popped out, right before I was gifted with a sexy smile. "I think that is a fabulous deal."

"I also whipped up a dessert that you are sure to love."

"Oh, it's a sure thing, huh?"

"Yep."

I went into the kitchen and pulled out two bowls from the fridge. I also grabbed the small square box out of the upper shelf that I'd been hiding for three weeks. I knew

Lisa wouldn't find it. One, it was the cupboard with the spices. Two, it was too high for her.

I'd really wanted to propose as soon as I'd bought it, but I had to talk to her dad and granddad first. When I flew out there after my Kansas trip, they knew what was up. Her granddad tried to pull one over me and say I didn't have his permission. For just a second, I bought into it, but then I remembered how often Lisa pulled that crap and started laughing. Then he and her dad did too. They got out a good bottle of scotch and said a toast, welcoming me to the family. As for getting Lisa's permission, I figured some cookie dough would help things along.

I was grinning as I brought the bowls out and placed them on the table. Lisa burst out laughing.

"Cookie dough!"

"Yep, and it's going to be better than the stuff from the tube, cause this stuff is fresh."

"Ooooh."

I watched as she started to suck cookie dough off her spoon. The minx knew what she was doing to me.

"That was fantastic. Homemade is the way to go."

"Have I got you in a good mood?"

She licked her lips. "Oh yeah. You're so getting to slide into home base."

"Home plate, Baby."

"Whatever, you're getting to slide home."

I chuckled. "Since I've got you all happy, I want to ask you something," I said casually.

"Shoot."

I took the box out of my pocket, opened it, then set it down on the table in front of her. I watched her closely as her eyes started to glisten.

"We're doing this?" she whispered. "For real Roan, we're doing this?"

"Yes. We're doing forever. Together. A family with babies and ups and downs, laughter and tears, and through it all we'll be holding on to each other. Taking care of one another. Loving one another. So yes, we're doing this."

She held out her trembling left hand. "Put it on me...please?"

I plucked out the platinum band with the emerald-cut diamond with two emeralds on either side to match her eyes.

I reached out and grasped her delicate, capable hand and slid the ring in place.

She pushed the bowls out of the way and knocked over her beer bottle. She grabbed me around the neck and gave me a salty flavored kiss.

She pulled back.

"You came as such a surprise in my life, Roan. I never, ever expected I'd get so lucky. But now that you're here, I want it all. I want it all, because of you, Roan. Only because of you."

I shivered as I remembered Blessing's words to me.

Just remember that surprises often turn out to be beyond special.

Wasn't that the truth.

My special lady was finally home.

Did you enjoy your trip down the Long Road Home?
Make Sure you read all the books in this years' series:

Make sure to check out Renzo and Millie's Story in Her Hidden Smile (Book 2). Coming out in February.

ABOUT THE AUTHOR

Caitlyn O'Leary is a USA Bestselling Author, #1 Amazon Bestselling Author and a Golden Quill Recipient from Book Viral in 2015. Hampered with a mild form of dyslexia she began memorizing books at an early age until her grandmother, the English teacher, took the time to teach her to read -- then she never stopped. She began re-writing alternate endings for her Trixie Belden books into happily-ever-afters with Trixie's platonic friend Jim. When she was home with pneumonia at twelve, she read the entire set of World Book Encyclopedias -- a little more challenging to end those happily.

Caitlyn loves writing about Alpha males with strong heroines who keep the men on their toes. There is plenty of action, suspense and humor in her books. She is never shy about tackling some of today's tough and relevant issues.

In addition to being an award-winning author of romantic suspense novels, she is a devoted aunt, an avid reader, a former corporate executive for a Fortune 100 company, and totally in love with her husband of soon-to-be twenty years.

She recently moved back home to the Pacific Northwest from Southern California. She is so happy to see the seasons again; rain, rain and more rain. She has a large fan group on Facebook and through her e-mail list. Caitlyn is known for telling her "Caitlyn Factors", where she relates her little and big life's screw-ups. The list is long. She loves hearing and connecting with her fans on a daily basis.

Keep up with Caitlyn O'Leary:

Website: www.caitlynoleary.com
FB Reader Group: http://bit.ly/2NUZVjF
Email: caitlyn@caitlynoleary.com
Newsletter: http://bit.ly/1WIhRup

facebook.com/Caitlyn-OLeary-Author-638771522866740
x.com/CaitlynOLearyNA
instagram.com/caitlynoleary_author
amazon.com/author/caitlynoleary
bookbub.com/authors/caitlyn-o-leary
goodreads.com/CaitlynOLeary
pinterest.com/caitlynoleary35

ALSO BY CAITLYN O'LEARY

Protecting Olivia

Isabella's Submission

Claiming Kara

Cherishing Brianna

SILVER **SEAL**s

Seal At Sunrise

SHADOWS **A**LLIANCE **S**ERIES

Declan

Made in the USA
Las Vegas, NV
15 December 2023

82799122R00164